THE NIGHT ITSELF

"...panese mythology meets urban awesomeness (and ...on-worthy romance!). *The Night Itself* captivated me."

L. A. Weatherly, author of the Angel Trilogy

"...o is a wonderful heroine who reminded me of some ...favourite superhero characters, and her connection w... Shinobu is touching and believable. The Japanese ...ology was refreshing, and I absolutely cannot wait for the next book in the series!"

Karen Mahoney, author of the Iron Witch Trilogy and Falling to Ash

"...A beautiful, awe-inspiring ride through an iconic L...nd... landscape harbouring extremely dangerous secrets. T... N...ght Itself is a fantastic blend of Japanese folk tale and t...en...-first-century thriller, populated by characters you will be rooting for at every breathless step."

Katy Moran, author of Hidden Among Us

"...I fell in love with sassy, courageous, w...se...rack...ng Mio from page o...e."

Ruth Warburton, author of the Winter Trilogy

Books by the same author

The Name of the Blade Book 1
The Night Itself

The Swan Kingdom
Daughter of the Flames
Shadows on the Moon
FrostFire

THE NAME OF THE BLADE
BOOK 2

DARKNESS HIDDEN

ZOË MARRIOTT

**WALKER
BOOKS**

First published 2014 by Walker Books Ltd
87 Vauxhall Walk, London SE11 5HJ

2 4 6 8 10 9 7 5 3 1

Text © 2014 Zoë Marriott
Cover illustration © 2014 Larry Rostant

This book has been typeset in Berkeley

Printed and bound in Great Britain by Clays Ltd, St Ives plc

British Library Cataloguing in Publication Data:
a catalogue record for this book is available from the British Library

ISBN 978-1-4063-4239-0

www.walker.co.uk

In loving memory of David Marriott.
You were always there for me.
I know you'll always be with me.

In search of the perfect costume for the fancy-dress party she's attending with best friend Jack, Mio Yamato steals a priceless antique katana from her family's attic. This turns out to be a big mistake. Paranoia and monstrous visions descend on her, causing her to run into traffic. While unconscious, she dreams of a beautiful warrior boy fighting a nine-tailed cat-demon – a Nekomata. An explosion of power from the sword heals Mio, but she is spooked and tries to put the katana back in its box in the attic. She can't. Trying to walk away from the sword makes her physically ill.

When the Nekomata from Mio's dream appears and tries to take the katana, only the arrival of the dream warrior boy saves her and Jack from the monster's claws. After they escape, they learn that their mysterious saviour, Shinobu, has been trapped in the katana for five hundred years.

Foiled, the Nekomata kidnaps Rachel, Jack's older sister. Shinobu calls for help from the Kitsune, immortal spirit foxes who owe him a favour. Mio, Jack and Shinobu travel to the spirit realm with a friendly fox guide – Hikaru – and meet with the powerful Kitsune King. Mio convinces the fox spirits to fight the Nekomata with her, but in the process realizes the danger of the katana's incredible powers.

At the monster's lair in the mortal realm, they enter into a desperate battle. Shinobu sacrifices himself to save Rachel, and Mio gives into rage, bonding with the sword to destroy the Nekomata. Once the cat-demon is dead, Shinobu's wounds miraculously disappear, and he wakes up. Mio and her friends leave the site of the battle triumphant, but knowing their fight for control of the katana has only just begun…

CHAPTER 1

FAREWELLS

The Kitsune were celebrating.

Their court – a massive natural amphitheatre, hidden deep underground – echoed with wild music and giddy laughter. Immortal fox spirits in both human and animal form wandered up and down the grassy terraces and danced around the huge golden trees that ringed the steep earthen bowl. They had been eating, drinking and making merry for hours. Some of them were making so merry that it was kind of hard to know where to look.

"They are relieved," the king said. His young-sounding voice drifted down to where I stood with Shinobu and Hikaru at the bottom of the Kitsune throne, a low green hill at the centre of the amphitheatre. Despite his grave tone, I thought I saw a hint of pearly fangs – a foxy grin just twitching his whiskers – as he looked at his subjects acting like kids on the first day of the summer holidays.

9

"It has been a long time since any of our people marched into battle. Some feared that victory over the Nekomata could only be bought with our sorrow."

I met his acid-green eyes for a fraction of a second. The sheer weight of ancient power there made my spine go loose and jelly-like. In its new, finely crafted leather harness on my back, the katana gave a sullen buzz. *You shut up,* I ordered it. The last thing I needed right now was the sword interfering again. I transferred my gaze to the king's paws and stared at them determinedly.

A faint sensation of warmth in the pit of my stomach told me that Shinobu, who stood a little way off to my left, was staring at me with the same concentration I was giving to the king's feet. A part of me needed to meet that look – yearned to, the way that you yearn to rest when you're tired or eat when you're hungry. But I couldn't. When we arrived back in the Kitsune Kingdom we were separated almost straight away, and by the time we saw each other again all the old awkwardness – and some new, extra awkwardness for good measure – had somehow sprung up between us.

What was supposed to happen next?

Were we going out now?

Did people even go out with each other five hundred years ago?

He hadn't exactly asked or anything. But he had kissed me, so maybe that counted...

And why did any of that matter to me when he made me feel the way he did? He'd fought for me, died for me, and I'd thought he was lost forever – but then he came back, just like a miracle. I flinched from the memory of the scaffolding pole breaking through his chest, the blood gushing up around it like a red flower...

The green blade flashes down in the red light—

I flinched.

Hikaru cleared his throat conspicuously at my elbow. I'd let the silence drag on too long. The king was waiting. I rubbed at burning eyes with the palm of one hand and tried to force my sleep-deprived brain to whirr into gear. *Inter-dimensional diplomacy now. Freak-out later.*

"The Kitsune Kingdom should be proud, Your Majesty," I said, finally. "Your people marched right up to the gateway of Yomi with us. If it weren't for them, we'd never have made it in there. They were incredible. Especially Hikaru."

Hikaru shuffled in place, his face slowly flushing dull red.

A tiny sizzle of blue-white lightning passed between two of the king's nine tails. The fan-like spread, one for each of the hundred years that he had lived up to the age of one thousand, marked him as the most ancient of the immortals here. "But even with my best warriors at your disposal, it was you who slew the Nekomata, sword-bearer. Alone. Though its powers were beyond anything

11

my Araki-san had seen in all her long life."

He was making it sound like I was a hero, which was laughably far from true. Hikaru, Araki, Shinobu, Hiro and Jack had done ... amazing things. I had messed up – again – and let the sword take me over. Let it take my human anger and twist it into an inhuman desire to kill and destroy. The battle with the Nekomata had been over very quickly after that. And if I hadn't managed to kill it so quickly, I wasn't sure what would have happened to me. Just a few minutes longer, and I might not have been able to resist the sword's beguiling voice in my mind when it offered me power in return for its "freedom", even though every instinct I had told me that the sword's idea of being free was most definitely not a good thing for me or the world.

But this wasn't the time to kick my own butt over that. Or the place, either. I had to keep it together and get us home.

"Well, it wasn't exactly like that," I mumbled. "But ... thanks."

There was a pause. It felt significant. I tried to figure out what else I should have said.

"Sword-bearer." The king's voice rang like the toll of a warning bell. "You have not yet asked for the favour that was promised you."

"Oh." I blinked a couple of times in my bewilderment and ended up looking the king in the face again by accident – *damn* – before I managed to glue my gaze to his ear.

After we'd left the abandoned power station at Battersea, the fox spirits had hustled us straight back through a rupture in the veil between the mortal realm and the spirit world. We'd washed in steaming, opal-green hot-springs under the trees while the Kitsune brought us delicious food and ministered to us with strange potions and ointments that magically numbed the pain of our various injuries. I'd taken the brunt of the Nekomata's attack last night, and after our little disagreement on who was going to be wielding whom, the sword had shown no signs of being willing to heal me the way it had when I had the car accident, so I'd really appreciated those potions. Once we were fed and fixed up, the Kitsune gave us clean clothes to replace the shredded, blood-covered ones we'd fought in. I had new leather boots that fitted me as if they'd been hand-tailored for my feet, and a new back harness for the katana. The plain wakizashi and katana that Shinobu had borrowed for the battle were taken away and replaced by a much finer pair with silver wrappings and a saya inlaid with mother of pearl.

The Kitsune had lavished particular care on Rachel, and by extension Jack, since Jack wouldn't leave her sister's side even if Rachel had been willing to let go of Jack's hand. Being kidnapped and held captive by a psychotic cat-demon had already pushed her to the limit. Jack's and my mostly unedited confession of just what had been going on before and during her ordeal – swords of mass destruction, trapped warrior spirits, immortal armies and all – had been too much. Rachel was almost catatonic with shock by the time Hikaru had carried her into the spirit realm. But the last time I'd checked, Jack and Rachel were tucked under a tree listening to soothing music and drinking warm drinks, with Rachel just nodding off on Jack's shoulder. They'd both looked much better.

The spirit foxes had treated us like treasured members of their own family who had returned from some legendary quest. And since no one had mentioned the favour that the king had promised me again, I'd sort of assumed this treatment was their way of paying us back for taking the Nekomata out while managing to bring Hikaru and all the other soldiers back alive.

You should never assume anything when dealing with supernatural creatures. I ought to have learned that by now.

"I'm sorry, Your Majesty. I hadn't forgotten, but I thought…" I gestured at myself and then at Shinobu. "I thought that your kind attention to us was payment enough for any service that we – um – might have performed for you."

There was another growling silence. Hikaru rolled his eyes at me. His blush had faded to leave him tense and pale.

Crap. What did I say? What didn't *I say?*

Shinobu took a step closer, his large frame unmistakably shielding mine. My hand brushed against his sleeve, and suddenly, regardless of everything else that was happening, I *had* to look at him.

Those endlessly dark eyes were waiting to meet mine. Our gazes connected with an almost physical shock, and the strange connection between us leapt up, alive and dangerous, like the arcs of electricity that danced between the king's fanned tails. I stopped breathing as I heard Shinobu's sharp intake of breath.

There you are, the yearning part of me whispered, deep inside. *I've got you. I won't let go.*

One of Shinobu's eyebrows quirked expectantly. *You can do this. Go on.*

I made myself start breathing again and reluctantly turned my attention back to the immortal ruler stewing in front of me. *All right, he's right. I* can *do this. Focus.*

"If the offer of a favour from Your Majesty still stands," I began, "would it be possible for me to hold it in reserve for now? I wouldn't want to waste such a – a precious thing by failing to consider it properly."

Hikaru let out a little sigh, and his tail drooped in what looked like relief. The king inclined his head regally. "A very wise request, Yamato-dono. The Kitsune shall stand ready to serve you."

Thank God.

"Now that all matters of business have been discussed, I thought you would wish to return home. We shall summon your other companions from their rest, and a new rupture from my throne to your place of residence in the mortal realm will be readied."

In other words: *Get lost, humans.* Fine by me.

"Your Majesty is very thoughtful," I said. "Thank you again."

The king inclined his head once, stood, and was gone. I blinked. Either he was very, very fast, or he'd just gone invisible. Something to bear in mind for the future...

Then I saw Jack and Rachel heading down the green terraces towards us – and Rachel was walking under her own power, without hanging onto Jack. Long, damp hair fell around her face in thick curls that the world never usually got to see. There was a faint flush in her golden-brown cheeks, and the blank stare from earlier was gone. She looked better than Jack even, since Jack still had a black eye. Relief brought a huge grin to my face. The fox spirits' medicine and music had done an amazing job.

"Hiya, She-Ra!" Jack called cheerily, dodging around a couple of giggling Kitsune.

"Hey!" I ran to meet them. "How are you—"

The words choked off as the sight of Rachel's neck hit me like a hammer to the gut.

The Kitsune had given her some dark trousers and a clean white shirt. The last time I saw her, the shirt had

16

been buttoned up to her throat – but Rachel had undone some of the buttons now, and the open collar revealed a horrifying wound on her neck. A ragged circle of deep puncture marks and torn, puffy skin. It was the size of a dinner plate.

A bite.

A Nekomata bite.

Nekomata were blood drinkers – that was how they stole people's shapes and memories. The monster had Rachel all to itself in its lair for hours before we finally turned up to rescue her. It had used her like a cat toy in its sick game.

"What?" Rachel's tentative smile disappeared and she grabbed the collar of her shirt, clutching it together. *"What?"*

Jack aimed a glare at me over her sister's shoulder. *This is not about you, Mio. Get it together!*

"No – um – nothing," I said, stumbling over the words. "Sorry, practically asleep on my feet. How are you both doing?"

Rachel started buttoning her shirt up again with jerky movements. "I'll be better when we can get out of here and go home. I don't know why we even had to come to weirdsville in the first place. It's not like we don't have clean clothes and antiseptic in the flat."

"We could all probably use some real sleep," Jack said, a shade too loudly. She gave Hikaru an apologetic look.

He shrugged, flashing his fey smile at her. "No biggie. They're readying a way back to the mortal realm for you now. It shouldn't be long." He hesitated, his tail swishing through the air in a wide circle. "So – um – maybe I could – you know, after you're settled back in, I could come and visit … check in, just to see how things are going?"

"Yeah. Right." Jack nodded. "Yeah. We … we need to talk, don't we?"

"Oh, for God's sake," Rachel muttered.

She turned away in apparent disgust, but the vulnerable shape of her back as she hunched over her folded arms sent a sharp stab of guilt and sadness through me. I stepped towards her – not sure if I could repair the damage I'd already caused, but determined to try – and bumped into Shinobu.

"Sorry, I didn't—"

He backed away hastily. "It was my fault, Mio-dono."

We both stared awkwardly at the space between us.

This kept happening. It was like we'd forgotten how to be easy with each other. Every time I thought we'd got that sense of – of *rightness* back, it vanished and left me closing my hands on smoke.

Before I could reach out to either Rachel or Shinobu, or just fall on the floor and have a screaming tantrum – which was pretty tempting at that point – a familiar voice said my name. It was Araki, the king's archer and personal servant. She stood beckoning to us at the base of the king's throne in her human form. The king himself was still nowhere to be seen.

"I think that's our cue," I said to the others with my best attempt at lightness. "Ready to blow this popsicle stand?"

"I was ready an hour ago," Rachel said as she stomped forward.

Jack moved past me with Hikaru. They weren't looking at each other, and Hikaru's expression was forlorn. Shinobu and I followed, walking side by side but with a careful distance between us.

We're all pathetic.

I could see the rift into the mortal realm taking shape on the grassy side of the little hill. Long streamers of blue lightning blew out of the earth, dancing in the air and then catching hold of others as they emerged, entwining to form a glowing wreath. When the ring of electricity was complete, the grass it encircled faded out of existence, leaving a gaping black hole in the slope.

Rachel walked right into the rift, leaving the bright light of the spirit realm for the darkness of Between without a backward glance.

Jack bit her lip. "This never gets any easier. I wish I could make my own fox lights."

"You're not the only one," Hikaru whispered, so low that I thought only I heard him.

Did he mean that he wished Jack was a fox spirit,

like him? Or just that he wished he were older and more powerful, able to control his lightning the way the others did? I had no way of knowing, and somehow I didn't think he'd appreciate being asked.

Jack nodded a respectful goodbye to Araki, squared her shoulders, and stepped after Rachel. I moved forward, hyper-conscious of Shinobu silently shadowing me. My instincts were begging me to sneak a quick look at his expression, but the rest of me shied away in sheer embarrassment. I couldn't understand why this was so hard.

"Farewell, sword-bearer," the king said, appearing again – OK, that was getting freaky – on the crown of the hill overhead. "I wish you good fortune, and offer a piece of advice. Keep a close eye on your friend's sister. She may have trying times ahead of her."

Before I could ask what he was getting at, the king's head snapped up. A deep shudder worked through his body, making his vast fan of tails lash the air; their white tips blazed into jagged blue cones of lightning. Araki took a step back, one hand flying up to cover her mouth.

"Grandfather?" Hikaru began uncertainly.

My katana shrilled – a fierce, high-pitched tone that vibrated along my vertebrae. Without thinking, I reached back to grab the hilt, ready to draw the blade. My blood tingled and my heartbeat surged as my palm made contact with the silk wrappings. Then I froze. *What am I doing?* I whipped my hand away and stared at it for a moment as I flexed my fingers to confirm that they were under my control.

The ground jumped under my feet. Beyond Araki, the other side of the throne erupted with electricity. A new rupture. A small crowd of Kitsune – four of them, none older than a two-tails – stumbled out. They were ashen-faced and covered in dirt; one of them, splattered with blood, was clutching at her arm. She collapsed face-first into the grass and lay there, gasping for air and shaking with what looked like agony. The others hastily drew away from her.

Araki darted forward, falling to her knees beside the Kitsune girl. I saw with horror that the girl's twin tails were withering, the lush reddish fur turning powdery grey and shredding off before our eyes. Horror turned to disbelief when the dignified Araki threw back her head and let out a terrible wail.

The Kitsune who had come through the rupture with the injured fox spirit picked up the note, their voices joining into a low, wavering keen of sorrow. The noise spread through the amphitheatre, celebrations dying away as the whole assembly of fox spirits fell still in the aching song of grief.

"What's happening to her?" I cried out over the wailing. "Can't someone help her?"

Hikaru didn't even look at me. He lifted his face to the canopy of trees above and howled.

I felt Shinobu's hand grasping mine, trying to pull me towards the rift. I shook my head, yanking free. I couldn't leave. They needed help!

The king's tails flicked in my direction. It was as if a massive hand had scooped me up and tossed me straight at the waiting blackness of the open rupture. I tumbled inside. Shinobu landed half on top of me with an "*Oof*".

"Wait!" I shouted, struggling to get up.

It was too late. The light had vanished and the rupture closed.

The Kitsune Kingdom was gone.

Klara Wozniak pulled the little cloth cap off her head in a puff of flour and stuffed it into her locker with one hand, swiftly undoing her tight French plait with the other. Long, curling strands of dark hair fell around her face, and she shook them out, sighing with relief.

"You think you're in a shampoo advert or something?" Sharon, the other baker's assistant, sneered as she walked into the back room.

Sharon's blonde hair was about three inches long, ragged-looking, and tipped with orange after an ill-fated home-dyeing attempt. Klara knew Sharon was just jealous – and in a bad mood because she had been scolded for messing up the iced buns – so she didn't bother to reply. *No time for bad thoughts today,* she reminded herself, changing out of the white baker's overalls and back into her usual uniform of jeans, T-shirt and jacket.

Her boyfriend had managed to get a couple of days off from his job at the warehouse, and Klara had the next two days free too. She wanted to enjoy the time to the fullest. If she knew Stephen, he'd be making her breakfast in their tiny flat right now. She could feel the silly smile on her own face as she remembered her twenty-first birthday, when he'd presented her with scrambled eggs, toast and a pink rose in a jam-jar.

She wrapped her scarf – a present her baba had sent from Poland for that same birthday – around her neck. She fingered the ends of the brightly coloured scarf for a moment, remembering the letter she had got from her grandmother the day before. The old lady was getting eccentric. Baba claimed to be having bad dreams about Klara, and actually begged her to come home, as if she really thought Klara was going to up and leave her whole life just because of one of Baba's silly premonitions! Baba was famous in Klara's village for her so-called sixth sense, but Klara and her father had never set any store by it. Especially since Baba claimed Klara had a little of the gift too. That always made her laugh. She'd never had a vision or seen a spirit in her life.

Still smiling, Klara slammed her locker shut and scooted out of the bakery's rear door into the small back street the business shared with a book/coffee shop and a pub. It was frosty cold, but the sky Klara could see between the roofs was primrose yellow, tinged with baby blue. It was going to be a beautiful day. Even the strong smell of burning and rot in the air – probably from the skip – couldn't ruin her mood.

"Hey, Klara!" Sharon shouted, shoving the door open just as Klara was about to slip past the skip and out onto the main road. "You didn't wipe down – it's your turn."

"No, it is not." Klara turned back reluctantly. "It is yours. I did it yesterday."

"You're always skiving off," Sharon whined – without, Klara noted, bothering to deny it.

"You would get your own work done faster if you spent less time worrying about mine," Klara said firmly. She was already reaching into her pocket for her mobile. Stephen would be waiting.

Sharon muttered something nasty about immigrants under her breath. Klara hesitated just for a second, the urge to respond rising up like bile in the back of her throat. She bit it back. *She's not worth it. She's not worth it…*

The alley went dark, as if a cloud had passed over the sun. A sudden gust of that awful rot-and-burning scent stirred Klara's hair, filling her ears with the eerie sound of dead leaves scattering over concrete. But there were no leaves on the ground. Instinctively, she glanced up.

A great misshapen *thing* was crouched on the roof above her, talons digging into the wall of the bakery. Its monstrous wings blocked out the sky.

Klara's knees gave way and she hit the ground next to

the skip, hard. The mobile flew from her hand as she flung her arms up over her head.

No. It was impossible. It couldn't be real. There was no such thing as monsters. No such thing.

"What are you doing, freakshow?" Sharon demanded. "*Euw* – what's that smell?"

Klara realized that the other woman hadn't seen *it*. She was coming closer. *Idiota!*

"Shut up!" Klara managed to choke out. The rising stench of death, singed hair and decaying flesh made her gag. "Get down! Get inside!"

It was already too late. Darkness and dry chittering filled the alley as the thing swooped. Sharon let out a shrill, terrified scream – then went silent.

Klara didn't have the chance to scream at all.

CHAPTER 2

BROAD DAYLIGHT

"**W**e have to go back," I said. I reached the living-room wall, spun around and paced back to the fireplace. "We have to. Something's horribly wrong there."

"The king sent us through the rift himself. I do not think they want our help," Shinobu said, very gently, from his place in the corner by the bookshelf.

"Maybe not, but they're our friends, and you don't just ... leave your friends to die."

"Come on, Mimi," Jack piped up from the sofa. "They're Kitsune. They're not that easy to kill."

"Something was really wrong," I insisted, hitting the fireplace with the flat of my hand and then pacing away again. "You didn't see that girl just lying there. You didn't hear the *noise* they were making—"

"No, but I've been listening to you rant about it for the past ten minutes," she interrupted. "Look, don't you think that I want to know what's going on too? I care about them as much as you do. But they're not answering. The only way to get back is if they open a rupture on their side and they're not answering us. So what's your plan? Start digging under the mulberry bush and hope you hit the spirit realm before you get to the earth's core?"

I stopped pacing and stared down blankly at the carpet. "There has to be something we can do."

There was a snort of muffled laughter from the window seat. I turned round to see Rachel slumped with folded arms in the glow of weak, wintery sunlight. One of her hands was playing with the end of the woolly scarf she'd wrapped around her neck.

"This isn't funny," I told her.

"No, but you are."

"I'm sorry, what?"

"Here's a newsflash: This isn't Gotham City, and you are not Batman. You're a fifteen-year-old girl with some kind of dangerous energy weapon that you have no idea how to control – and everywhere you go, you leave a trail of destruction behind you. Gee, what a shocker that your foxy pals don't want you around."

We all stared at her in shock. I sank slowly down onto the arm of the sofa. Jack knelt to put her hand on my shoulder.

"That was harsh, Rach," she said sternly.

Rachel sighed. "Sorry, OK? But this situation is nuts."

"I know that," I muttered.

"I don't think you do," Rachel said. "I – I can't even believe we're having this discussion."

"Yeah, we get it," Jack said. "Monsters, magic, mega-swords. It's freaky."

"No, I mean I can't believe we're having *this* discussion." Rachel sat up, swinging her feet down to the carpet. "This one. Why aren't we having a discussion about us and what's going to happen to us next? Mio, that nightmare – the Nekomata – threatened us with its 'Mistress' coming after the sword. She could be coming right now. So *why do you still have the sword*? Why isn't it on the bottom of the Thames?"

"She already tried that," Jack said. "We told you. It doesn't work."

"Mio-dono is compelled to protect the sword. She cannot be parted from it without unbearable suffering," Shinobu said, his voice deadly serious.

"Oh, really?" Rachel snapped. "Unbearable suffering like, say, being strung up on the wall of an abandoned warehouse and tortured by a monster that wants to eat you alive?"

Jack recoiled, speechless. Shinobu bowed his head, his face very grave.

I swallowed hard, all too conscious of the weight of the faintly buzzing sword on my back. *Is it listening?*

I tried to ignore the insistent pulse of energy, but

when I spoke, my voice didn't come out strong and calm like I wanted. I sounded … defensive. "If I could get rid of the katana somehow, believe me, I would do it. But I can't let it fall into the wrong hands. It's too dangerous for that. Nuclear-bomb dangerous. I don't really know what it could do if its powers were unleashed. The Nekomata seemed to be able to smell it, or sense its energy somehow, so even if I could hide it, more creatures might come after it – us – anyway, and without the sword in my hand I couldn't even fight them off to protect us. We have no choice but to keep hold of it."

Rachel glared at me for a long moment. Then she stood up. "That's it. I've had enough of this crap. I'm calling your parents."

The room seemed to tremble around me; my voice came out in a sort of roar. "*WHAT?*"

Shinobu was out of his corner in a flash, his hands closing over my shoulders. I realized that I'd launched myself off the sofa at Rachel. He was holding me back by both arms. Jack was on her feet too, hovering, like she wasn't sure who to protect from whom.

Rachel didn't flinch. She lifted her chin and stared me straight in the face. "I said I'm calling Mr and Mrs Yamato. This mess is not my and my sister's responsibility. It's not even yours. The sword belongs to your family and that means it's up to them to figure something out. They need to get back here and deal with this."

"*Deal* with it? Deal with it *how*?" I demanded. "What, you think my dad can turn up and slay demons for us? Just because they're adults that doesn't mean they can handle *this*. They won't believe us, they won't know what to do, and they might get killed!"

"So might we! And you just want to put your hands over your ears, close your eyes and sing 'La la la, I'm not listening'!"

"Oooookay," Jack said, sliding between me and Rachel and making calming motions in the air. "Can we dial this down a notch?"

The sight of Jack playing peacemaker was enough to freeze both me and Rachel for a second. Jack took advantage of the pause. "Let's not turn on each other now. When friends fight, the monsters win, right?"

"Jack, tell her that we can't bring my parents into this."

Rachel bristled. "Don't try and get my sister on your side!"

"She's got the right to her own opinion even if she is your sister!"

"Her own opinion? That's rich! Did she get a vote before you dragged her into this mess?"

Shinobu let out a little grunt of effort. I realized that I was straining forward against his hands – and with my still unfamiliar new strength, he was actually struggling to hold me.

Jack was hanging onto Rachel's arm with both of hers. "Stop it!" she shouted. "Just stop it! This isn't helping. Mio, don't shout at Rachel – she's been through enough, it's not fair."

I shut my mouth with a snap. Rachel grinned. The expression congealed as Jack turned on her. "And you, don't start bossing people around and giving orders. You are not in charge here. It's Mio's sword, and she saved your life with it. She gets to make the decisions."

"Wrong. The parents left *me* in charge," Rachel snarled. "Which means *I* get to make the decisions about what goes on in this house."

"I said stop it!" Jack grabbed a handful of her own hair and tugged. "This isn't getting us anywhere."

"Fine!" Rachel screeched, her voice hitting a pitch that raked up every fine hair on the back of my neck. "*Take* her side then. Whatever!"

She marched to the door into the hall and threw it open, turning back at the last moment to stab me with a vicious look. Her narrowed eyes glinted in the sunlight. She was so furious that they looked almost yellow. Then the door slammed behind her.

Jack grabbed me into a crushing hug. I hugged her back, feeling her shoulders jerk just a little, exactly like mine were. "It'll be OK. I'll talk to her. I got your back, Maverick," she whispered.

"Oh my *God*," I managed to mumble. "Seriously? *Top*

Gun quotes are *never* going to be cool, Jack."

"Sez you, She-Ra."

My choked laugh was nearly a sob. Jack let go of me, knuckling her eyes, and disappeared out of the room after her sister, leaving me alone … with Shinobu.

I stood very still. He was just as still behind me. Right behind me. So close that I imagined I could feel his breath disturbing my hair and the warmth of his large body sheltering mine. I wanted to turn around into his arms and just sink into him. But I couldn't even bring myself to look at him. I just *couldn't*.

"Mio…"

"Sorry," I blurted, tearing free of the magnetic pull of his presence. I fled, taking the stairs to my bedroom two at a time and then slamming the door shut behind me.

The iPod dock said it was ten-thirty in the morning. This time yesterday the most terrifying thing in my whole world was the Nekomata. I would have promised anyone anything if they could just tell me that we would be able to get away from it, to survive it.

And we had. It was gone. I had cut its head off myself. Yet somehow the world was a more terrifying place than ever. Rachel was clearly not OK. Jack was struggling to cope with a sister and a best friend who were both melting down in different ways. I was half-sick with feelings for a boy who was – let's face it – a complete stranger.

And Rachel was right: None of us knew what might

be coming after the sword next.

Who was this great "Mistress" that the Nekomata had been willing to die for? It had feared her and threatened us with her arrival right to the end. Shinobu had argued that the cat-demon could be the servant of any number of powerful supernatural beings from Yomi, the Japanese Underworld ... but that had been before Battersea. Before we had found ourselves fighting beneath the moon of Yomi, had seen the mortal realm warped and twisted and made into a tiny piece of hell on earth, just for us.

I couldn't escape the fear that there was only one being in Yomi powerful enough to do that. Izanami. The Mistress of Yomi.

The Goddess of Death.

Slowly, with clumsy fingers that felt too long and thick, I took off the sword harness and dropped it on the floor. The sheathed katana gleamed in my hands, black and gold. *Beautiful.* I could feel its power humming through my palms, singing with the same strange note that seemed to run in my own veins now.

"How am I supposed to protect you? Why me? Why us?"

It didn't react. Its power kept on humming and my blood kept singing. I didn't know whether to be relieved or disappointed that it wasn't speaking to me – that it still couldn't communicate while it was sheathed. The memory of the sword's inhuman, metallic voice in my mind made me shudder with revulsion. It had been inside my brain, inside *me*. But even as I shuddered, a part of me was overwhelmingly tempted to remove the saya now, to reveal the crescent moon silver of the cutting edge and feel the white-hot flood of the katana's power engulf my body.

A part of me? Was it really a part of *me* that felt this way? What if this urge to unsheathe the blade was really a part of the sword? Its intelligence, its will, its voice, still inside me. How could I ever know?

"I hate you," I whispered. My voice was so quiet I could barely hear it over the heavy percussion of my heartbeat. *"I hate you."*

The sword was responsible for every bit of pain and suffering and fear I had known in the past two days. It had put Jack, Rachel and the Kitsune in danger. It had caused the deaths of those innocent men and women who had been caught and eaten by the Nekomata. I hated the fact that the sword's powers had already *altered* me, that my body was no longer solely mine. For years I had prayed for some long-delayed growth spurt to come along; now I wished that I was back in that old, familiar frame, even if it was smaller and weaker. At least it had been mine. By changing me, the sword had taken possession of me. My newly long, newly strong legs and arms were the property of the katana.

What did that make me?

I didn't even know yet how much influence – or control – it had over my mind. In the horror and blood of the battle at Battersea, when my body had seemed to move on pure instinct and I never had a split second to stop and think, had I really been making all my own decisions, or had the katana moved me, thought for me? In that moment when Rachel's life was at stake and I'd had to make my choice between her and the sword – when I had hesitated – had the hesitation been mine, or the sword's?

Which was worse?

And with all that … with all that … *I still loved it.* That love glowed like a fistful of embers beneath my ribs, and couldn't be ignored or denied.

That was why I couldn't do what Rachel wanted and just toss the sword away. Why I wouldn't try. Beneath my desire to keep the sword from the dark forces that hunted it, and protect those I cared for, there was love. *Need.* The katana was mine, and I would fight to keep it, no matter what. I would fight anyone or anything who tried to take it from me. Even myself.

Love and loathing clawed inside me, fighting each other until I felt sick and dizzy. I just wanted everything to go away.

I crawled up onto the pale pink duvet of my bed and lay down, pushing the sword as far away as I could stand – not even halfway across the mattress – but keeping one hand firmly wrapped around the silk-covered hilt. Then I buried my face in my pillow and cried.

When I dragged myself out of the bedroom half an hour later, puffy-eyed and exhausted, and with the sword in its harness on my back, Shinobu was sitting patiently on the floor outside. He leaned against the wall, long legs folded up. One of my dad's coffee-table books, full of pictures of London's landmarks, was balanced on his knee.

His eyes zeroed in on mine like lasers, stopping me short. Every inch of my skin flushed with feverish heat, and I looked away hastily. I didn't feel strong enough to deal with Shinobu, or my own heart, at that moment. It was touch and go whether I would back into my room and close the door again.

As I hesitated, he closed the book carefully and put it down. He rose in an economical, fluid movement. Without my permission, my eyes traced that movement, lingering on the crisp lines of muscle flexing in his thighs. My hands tightened on the doorframe, fingernails biting into the painted wood, as I resisted the sudden, intense urge to touch him.

The conflicting needs – stay, go, reach out, back away – reminded me of my feelings for the katana. At least the saya seemed to protect me from the sword a little. Nothing could protect me from Shinobu or the way he made me feel.

Why couldn't this be simple? I'd liked boys before. I'd had hopeless crushes that set me doodling love hearts and initials all over my school exercise books. I'd gone out with Dylan Brentwood for nearly a year, and cried for a week after he and his family moved to America. I thought I knew how all this was supposed to feel. But Shinobu was different, and he made me different. I didn't know where to look, what to say, how to be.

Is this love?

"I heard you crying."

My gaze flew up to his. It was like walking into an electrified fence. *Zap.* Everything lit up.

The scaffolding pole broke through his chest, blood gushing up like a red flower…

The green blade flashes down in the red light—

I winced involuntarily from the visions that flashed before my eyes. Shinobu's jaw clenched. He made a small, jerky gesture with one hand, telegraphing helplessness and frustration. "Have I done something wrong?"

Guilt squeezed my insides. I shook my head wordlessly.

"This is the first time you have looked at me for more than an instant since we arrived in the spirit realm. You flinch when I move towards you, turn away if you think I will touch you. If you have…" He stopped short and took a deep breath. "If I have done something that has hurt you, please know that it was the last thing in the world I ever wanted."

"Shinobu, you haven't done *anything*," I said wearily.

"I'm just … overwhelmed. Confused. Can you understand that? My whole world has changed. Everything is upside down. I don't know what to do. Falling in love must be pretty scary even at the best of times. In the middle of everything else it's…" My voice trailed off as I saw a flash of emotion transform his solemn face, lighting his eyes.

"Falling in love?" he repeated a little hoarsely.

I pressed my lips together, but it was too late. *Me and my big mouth.*

He took a slow, purposeful step towards me. The corridor wasn't wide. Even with me hovering in the doorway of my room, he was now close enough for me to smell the sweet, spicy fragrance of the Kitsune's soap, mixed with Shinobu's own distinctive smoke-and-pines smell. He was close enough to reach out, his hand trembling a little, and lift a flyaway strand of hair from my forehead. As he tucked it behind my ear, the almost imperceptible brush of his fingertip against my skin made something inside me melt.

"Falling in love?" he said again.

We were slowly leaning into each other's space, moving closer, closer, with each breath. Shinobu's fingers were still touching my hair, not quite cupping my jaw. My hand had crept out to curl into a fold of fabric at his waist.

"Yes." The word slipped out of me on a long sigh.

The corners of his lips tilted up in that heartbreaking, half-shy, half-cocky smile. He bent his head and I lifted mine. My body prickled with nerves and excitement as our lips touched—

The katana jumped against my back, sending out a painful buzz of energy. "Ow!"

Shinobu jerked back. He looked dazed. "What happened?"

"The sword!" I said crossly. "What was *that*, you – you stupid hunk of metal?"

The katana responded with another harsh buzz, even stronger than before. It seemed to shudder against my spine. I frowned. That didn't feel like a laugh. It felt like … like the way it had buzzed last night in the Nekomata's lair. *A warning.* "Something's wrong."

I ran for the stairs and bolted down them, with Shinobu right behind me. My feet hit the chequerboard tiles in the hall with a slap and I flung open the door to the sitting room. Rachel was on the window seat again. She started as we burst in. By the time she opened her mouth, my eyes had already done a lightning-fast scan of the room and ascertained one vital fact: My best friend wasn't there.

"Where's Jack?"

"Listen, I was just—"

"Rachel, *where is Jack*?"

Rachel huffed. "She went to try calling those fox

39

people again. She's worried about that guy."

"She went outside on her own?" Shinobu asked urgently.

"I just said that." Her eyes widened as she took in our expressions. "It's broad daylight!"

Shinobu was already across the room, swiping up his new katana and wakizashi from the sofa as he passed. He had the sliding doors to the kitchen open before I got halfway there.

But not before we heard Jack scream.

CHAPTER 3

FOUL WOMEN

Splinters of the kitchen table and crockery that the Nekomata had destroyed scattered around my feet as I darted towards the garden door. But somehow Rachel managed to get there before either me or Shinobu. She wrenched the door open with so much force that the hinges shrieked. Shinobu was only a second slower. I was the last one into the garden.

Jack lay prone on the dead grass. A huge, dark *something* hovered over her. I let out a hoarse yell of anger and fear. Without stopping to think, I ripped the sheathed katana from its harness on my back, readying to free the blade.

The thing reared back, unfolding with a dry chattering noise that made me think of pulled teeth rattling in a box. An overpowering stench of burning hair and decay blasted my nose as the creature took off into the air. The

41

sun was high and bright, directly above us, making my eyes blur with water as I tried to track the creature with my gaze. All I could make out was a jagged black shape growing smaller against the sky.

"What was that?" I breathed. "How did it—?"

"Jack!" Rachel fell to her knees beside her sister.

My stomach lurched as I saw the empty look on Jack's face. Her eyes passed over us like she didn't know who we were. She rolled away from Rachel's hands and curled up into the foetal position.

A cold wind seemed to blow around my neck. I heard the rattling noise again – getting closer. My head snapped up in time to see the thing plummeting down at us.

I ducked instinctively, folding down over my knees with the katana clutched to my chest. Rachel threw herself across Jack, shielding her sister with her body in exactly the same way that Jack had tried to shield her last night. Shinobu spun, drew his short wakizashi blade, and then threw it.

The sword whistled through the air, burning a golden streak across my vision as it caught the light. The blade struck home with a wet thud.

The creature let out a high-pitched, seagull cry that made my teeth ache. Wings thrashed, filling the garden with that eerie rustling rattle and spreading so wide that they blocked out the sun. In their shadow I could finally see the creature clearly.

It was a nightmare vision of a woman, at least eight feet tall, with a ragged mane of silver-black hair and greyish lizard scales covering a muscular, naked body. Her legs bent the wrong way, like a dog's, and ended not in feet but massive paws, tipped with yellowing talons. The creature's lower jaw looked as if it had been designed to crush through bone.

It had no eyes. Only empty black sockets.

The monster keened, clawing at its own shoulder as it tried to rip Shinobu's blade from its flesh. Yellowish liquid bubbled up around the wound as the talons gained traction. The creature wrenched the sword out – and flung it straight back at Shinobu. He dodged. The blade sank hilt-deep into the hard soil where he had stood only a second before.

The creature's wings kept thrashing, nearly deafening me with their rattle. They were grey, dry and dead-looking, marked with a pattern of yellow rings and dots. No. Not dots. *Eyes.* Dozens of them, yellow and gleaming amid the dull grey feathers.

Eyes that were now fixed on me. On the katana in my hand. The thing surged upwards and then dived again.

"Mio-dono!"

I was already moving before Shinobu's shout of alarm reached my ears. I fell flat onto the grass, the impact rattling my bones. The monster's swoop carried it just above my head. It screamed with what sounded like frustration as it missed, its claws raising long white scratches on the concrete patio ahead of me. At the last moment, the thing shot back up, narrowly avoiding a collision with next door's brick wall.

Breath sawing painfully, I flipped to my feet. Then I shoved the katana firmly away into the harness on my back.

"What are you *doing*?" Rachel demanded.

"My job. Protecting the sword," I snapped.

I couldn't risk fighting with the katana, not like this. If I'd ducked a second later, the creature, whatever it was, would have seized the blade from my hand and flown away with it. This monster was already injured, thanks to Shinobu; there was no need to risk unsheathing the blade and unleashing its power here.

Shadows and blood...

"Are you crazy?" Rachel shouted as the monster wheeled around in the air above the garden and came in for another attack. "Do something!"

I ignored Rachel and the sword's angry-hornet buzz against my back as I looked around for something else to use as a weapon. Anything! Even a rake would do. As I hesitated, Shinobu hurdled Jack and placed himself squarely in the monster's path. He raised his sword defiantly. My heart turned to rock in my chest.

"No! Shinobu, get down!"

He acted as if he hadn't heard me, the muscles in his

back and shoulders tensing as he prepared to face the thing alone. *Stupid, fearless boy!*

My eyes lit on the big terracotta planter by the back doorstep. My dad used it to grow mint and other cooking plants. Two feet long, half a foot wide and filled to the brim with soil, it probably weighed more than I did.

Time to find out how strong I really am.

I lurched forward, grabbed the edges of the planter and then *heaved*. As the heavy pottery scraped across the patio tiles, amazement and elation mingled inside me. It was moving. It was really moving. Dragging it sideways and up, whipping my body around to build momentum, shoulders and back screaming, I lifted the planter, higher, higher, above knee height, above waist height, above shoulder height—

The winged monster stooped over us.

Now!

I let the planter go.

The pot smashed into the monster's face and chest with enough force to flip it over in midair. I leapt back as Shinobu ducked, both of us barely avoiding the swipe of deadly claws as the creature cartwheeled. Frozen clumps of soil and chunks of terracotta rained down, and the monster crashed to the ground with a sound like a helicopter falling.

Shinobu leapt onto the thing's massive chest and sank his katana deep into its heart.

The grey wings jerked, beating at the air spasmodically. Gusts of stinking air tore at my skin and clothes. Rachel choked; I thought she might be sick. Shinobu swayed back from the force of the wind. He pulled his sword free and jumped off, ready to deal another blow if necessary.

The dry chittering sound faded away like a sigh as the grey wings fell still. Among the feathers, the gleaming yellow eyes closed.

Rachel took her hand away from her mouth, her gaze flicking from the smashed wreckage of the planter and the dead monster to me. I could see the thoughts scrolling through her head as clearly as I could read the banner at the bottom of a daily news programme:

How could she pick that up?

How could she possibly throw it?

What is she?

There was fear in her face.

The air seemed to have turned to ice, trapping us all in that beat of time, hurt, afraid, disbelieving. We might have stood there for hours.

Jack made a strange gurgling noise. Rachel and I broke eye contact as I skidded forward, almost collapsing onto the grass as I reached them. Jack was still curled into a ball, painful shivers working through her body.

"It's OK, Jack, it's OK. It's gone." I was babbling. My hands shook uselessly in the air above her back. I didn't know how to deal with this. I thought I knew every mood Jack ever had, from fury to terror, but I'd never seen her react to anything this way. Rachel grabbed her sister's arms and dragged her roughly over onto her back.

I cried out in protest. "Don't—"

"She's convulsing. She could bite her tongue."

Jack's eyes had rolled back in their sockets. Her limbs, stretched out, were stiff and twitching uncontrollably. Her face was contorted. But there wasn't a mark on her, apart from the pink pressure marks on her left cheek from lying on the grass. She hadn't been bitten, or clawed. The only sign that the thing had even touched her was one of those dull moth-grey feathers clinging to her short hair. "Oh my God. Oh my God…" I whispered.

"We must get her inside," Shinobu said urgently.

"Shut up." Rachel didn't look away from her sister. Her hands clutched desperately at Jack's face as she tried to hold her still.

"It is not safe out here."

"He's right." Pathetically grateful that there was something I could do, I caught hold of Jack's legs. They kicked against me. I bit my lip, using the pain to force back useless tears.

"You get away from her!" Rachel snarled. She let go of Jack to shove me away. My knees skidded across the grass. Shinobu caught me before I toppled over.

Rachel scooped her arms under Jack's body and lifted her in one smooth movement. I gaped. Jack was three inches taller than Rachel, and she was pure muscle. Rachel shouldn't even be able to win an arm-wrestling match with her, let alone lift her like that. *Adrenaline rush?* The grey feather spiralled out of Jack's hair into the wind. The sun sparked yellow in Rachel's eyes as she turned away from us and marched into the house.

I swiped tears off my face, scrambled to my feet and followed Rachel with Shinobu at my heels. Rachel carried Jack into the living room and laid her down on the big sofa, then knelt next to it, clasping her hands together as if she was praying.

For a moment I thought those prayers had worked. The dreadful shuddering in Jack's body stopped. Her arms and legs unstiffened. Her eyes slowly rolled back down, the irises sliding into their proper places just before her lids eased closed. She expelled a deep sigh that sounded like relief.

Then Rachel gasped. The marks on Jack's left cheek were getting darker, deepening like a new purple bruise against Jack's golden skin. Those weren't pressure marks from the grass. It was some kind of rash. The marks spread as I watched, blooming across Jack's face and down her neck to make a pattern of rings and dots. Rings and dots.

Exactly like the eye pattern on the monster's wings.

"What is this?" Rachel sobbed. "Oh Jesus, what's happening?"

I snatched up the phone and dialled 999.

"Jacqueline Juliette Luci?"

The raspy voice brought me, Shinobu and Rachel to our feet. The world tilted oddly under my boots; Shinobu's hand on my shoulder kept me upright until the dizziness had passed. Behind me, the *beep-beep-beep* of Jack's heart monitor carried on unaffected, reassuring and infuriating at the same time.

A middle-aged male doctor stood in the gap in the floral-patterned curtains around Jack's bed. Jack's eyelids – a dark, bruised purple in her chalky-pale face – moved. But her eyes didn't open.

"That's her," Rachel said, her voice wavering.

"Is she asleep?" the doctor whispered as he began to back out of the little enclosure around the bed, clearly relieved to have an excuse to escape.

"M'wake," Jack mumbled. Her eyelids flickered open for a second, but squeezed shut without giving me more than a glimpse of her eyes.

"She has a headache. The light hurts," I said.

My voice didn't tremble like Rachel's. It came out flat and emotionless. Rachel sent me a resentful glare. I couldn't explain that the only way I was keeping it together was to shut everything down. If I let a single emotion out, I would break. Messily. That was the last thing Jack needed.

"I'm Doctor Singh. How are we feeling, Jacqueline?"

"Bad," Jack said faintly. "Everything hurts."

"Well, that's only to be expected. You've had quite a scare today, hmmm?"

Rachel and I exchanged a look across the bed, united for an instant in dislike of the baby-talk, before she looked down at Jack again. She tugged on the ends of her scarf. "Can you please tell me what's wrong with her?"

The doctor shuffled slowly around the bed. He peered at the monitors, peered at Jack, made a notation on the clipboard and then offered us an apologetic shrug. "We're still waiting for the test results to come back. Until then it's hard to pinpoint the cause of her reaction."

He's stalling. He doesn't want to tell us.

"Some form of ... of meningitis?" Rachel asked. One of her hands reached out to touch the lump in the blue hospital covers that was Jack's feet.

The doctor was peering at his clipboard again, as if the information on it might have changed since the last time he looked. "Hmm? Oh, the rash. No, the symptoms don't point to any kind of infection. Our current theory is that this is a severe systemic anaphylaxis."

I could feel my face crumpling with confusion. Rachel frowned. "Like ... an allergic reaction? To what? Jack doesn't have any allergies."

Jack's head moved in a pained twitch that might have been a nod of agreement.

"I take it you youngsters don't watch the news?" the doctor said, still not looking at us. "There are … several similar cases at this hospital, all admitted since this morning. We're not sure yet what is causing the reaction."

Next to me, Shinobu shifted his weight. The movement caught the doctor's eye, and he jumped, gazing at Shinobu in surprise and consternation. But then his eyes slid away from the space Shinobu occupied. He frowned, shook his head slightly, and shrugged. It seemed Shinobu was still mostly imperceptible to normal humans – ones who'd been lucky enough to avoid direct contact with the monsters and magic that the katana had set free.

"Ah – Jacqueline is a minor. Where are her parents?" Dr Singh asked.

Rachel squared her shoulders. "Our mother is not available. I'm taking care of Jack."

Something relaxed inside me. That was the end of that argument. *No parents.*

"Ah. I see. Well, we'll let you know when the test results are in." He nodded vaguely, then walked back out of the little cave formed by the curtains without another word.

Rachel flopped into the moulded plastic chair by the bed; the legs squealed on the lino floor. Jack flinched.

"Allergies my arse. That thing did this," Rachel hissed. She didn't look at me, but her resentment was like a wall between us. I couldn't even blame her.

"So stupid," Jack whispered. "Walked into it—"

"Hush," Shinobu said firmly. Jack's eyes peeled open into a surprised squint. "We all relaxed our guard this morning," he told her. "The fault is shared equally. And you have been the one to suffer by it."

A pair of nurses passed by the gap in the curtains, pushing a trolley. I caught a fleeting glimpse of the patient and stared as I saw that the pale cheek was marked with a vivid purple rash, just like Jack's. The ward's air of quiet frenzy was explained now. When the doctor had said "several" cases, he hadn't meant three or four, had he? It was much more – much worse – than that. I'd vaguely noticed that in the time we'd been here at least half a dozen new patients had been squeezed into the ward, many of them on trolleys. They must be suffering with the same thing as Jack. Probably if the nurses weren't desperately trying to keep up with the influx of patients, we'd have been kicked out by now.

Shinobu pushed at me gently, and I realized he wanted me to sit down again. I eased onto the rickety plastic chair next to Rachel's, tucking my feet under so that my leg didn't brush against hers.

"I don't understand why all these new cases are still coming in," I said softly. "The thing is dead. We killed it after it got Jack. So how can it still be … infecting people?"

Shinobu dropped his hands onto the backs of our chairs and leaned in so that his broad shoulders seemed to shelter us from the rest of the ward. He hesitated, clearly debating whether to speak, then finally said, "There may be more than one."

"Of those monsters?" I said, appalled.

"I could be wrong. But I think the creature that attacked Jack-san today is one I have heard described before in stories and myths."

"Spill," Jack said weakly. She had rolled her head towards us, and I could hear the faint crackle of her breathing over the heart monitor.

"I think it was a Shikome. A Foul Woman. They are denizens of Yomi." His jaw clenched. "They are also known as Izanami's Handmaidens."

Jack said, "Shit."

Izanami. Her name just kept cropping up, over and over. The Nekomata had been a denizen of Yomi too – and it had never shut up about its "Mistress". A Mistress so powerful that when the Nekomata called on her power, it had created a portal into the underworld. And now more creatures from Yomi had found me and hurt my friend.

Could that possibly be a coincidence?

"Yomi is hell, right? And this Iza-person is the god that

lives there," Rachel said, clearly running back over the rushed account of events we had given her this morning.

"Izanami is the queen of the Underworld. The Goddess of Death," Shinobu told her grimly.

She was more than that. Izanami and Izanagi were the mother and father of Japanese gods – a matched pair, created for each other – identical in their perfection. They had loved each other passionately. But Izanagi had a weakness. He was obsessed with beauty, and repulsed by anything ugly or imperfect. So strongly repulsed that when he was unsatisfied with his first two children, he tried to fling them into the sea to drown, and only gentle Izanami's intervention had saved them. After his wife died, he followed her down into the Underworld, and told her that he loved her and wouldn't leave without her. He persuaded her to follow him back into the light. But when he saw the change that death had wrought in her and the decay and rot of her once perfect form, he fled from her in disgust, and blocked the entrance to Yomi so that she could never follow him.

Broken-hearted Izanami had sworn vengeance. Sworn that she would kill and kill and kill until he returned to her.

Shinobu met my eyes. I could see him making the same connections in his head as I had.

This is bad. Very bad.

"So you really think this god is after the sword? Mio's

sword? That's ... I mean, how powerful would a weapon have to be for a god to want it?" Rachel's eyes strayed to my left shoulder, where the katana's hilt protruded from the leather harness on my back. Both sword and harness were hidden under a baggy sweatshirt – one of my dad's – that I had shrugged on over the rest of my clothes before we ran out of the house, but a slight bulge was just visible. The sword's energy throbbed against my back, as if it could feel Rachel's gaze. I shrugged restlessly.

Shinobu reclaimed our attention. "Izanami's Handmaidens, the Foul Women ... the stories say that they spread a plague wherever they go. Their feathers are diseased, and a single touch of one of those feathers marks the victim with foulness. They are mindless monsters, as stupid as animals, but they love destruction. And when enough of them gather, they will swarm like locusts, ruining everything in their path."

"So if we've seen one...?" Rachel began.

He finished, "Then others may already be here."

CHAPTER 4

TREACHEROUS REFLECTIONS

The hospital was packed now. Every bed in Jack's ward was occupied, and most of the gaps between had trolleys jammed into them. There were a lot of anxious relatives wandering around. Near the doors, an old man lay in his bed all alone, curled up on his side with one hand over his face. The skin of his hand and lower arm were marked with the swirling patterns of the rash, so dark they looked almost black. His shoulders jerked as if he was silently crying. I averted my eyes and moved past.

Out in the corridor, more rash-marked patients on trolleys lined the walls. Through the Perspex windows, I could see into other wards. They seemed crammed full, too. A handful of harried-looking nurses and auxiliaries scurried here and there. They must be stretched to breaking point.

A low, agonized moaning noise came from behind

one of the walls. The sound clawed at my nerves.

God, I hate hospitals. To me, they were places that people – people you loved, like my ojiichan – went to die. The moment you went through the doors, control was wrenched away from you, whether you were the patient or someone who cared about them. Hospitals wrapped the ill up in layers of medical-talk, wires, tubes, and hospital gowns until you could barely see them any more, and before you knew it, they had slipped away from you – stopped being a person and become a list of symptoms and drugs, a piece of paperwork just waiting to be stamped and filed and forgotten about.

I won't let that happen to Jack.

The visitors' toilets were past another couple of full wards, at a T-section in the corridor. They were empty, and predictably disgusting. One of the sinks, blocked up with wads of paper towels, was almost overflowing with cloudy water, and two of the three fluorescents overhead were flickering, making that odd buzzing noise.

I was alone.

Shudders scurried down my back like a handful of millipedes. I hurriedly picked a stall and shut myself in, plonking down on the wobbly toilet seat and drawing my knees up to my chin. With my arms wrapped around my legs, I took a couple of deep breaths, struggling to think past the terrible weight of panic and worry. Of responsibility.

If Shinobu was right – and I had no reason to doubt him, even if I wished I could – then Jack and everyone else in her ward was sick right now with some … supernatural disease. A plague that baffled medical science. And it came from the Foul Women.

The Shikome had to be here to steal the katana, like the Nekomata. There was no other explanation for their presence in this realm. But this time Izanami – if it was really the Goddess of Death behind this – hadn't sent just one monster to do the job. There could be any number of them out there, dropping infected feathers everywhere while they combed the city for the scent of power that the katana exuded. The plague that they spread and their "mindless" love of destruction had all been set loose on London because of the katana. Because their Mistress wanted them to hunt me down. Which meant every single infected person in this hospital was, in some way, my responsibility.

My fault.

Realizing that was like lying under a giant rock, a rock so big I couldn't see the edges. Like being slowly crushed alive even while I was desperately fighting to hold it up. I found myself clinging to the katana's hilt, where it rose above my shoulder. The blade's energy hummed against my palm, and I hated the craven, senseless part of myself that found the hum comforting. I hated myself for cowering in the toilet when my friends needed me to be strong.

I had to stop melting down like this. I had to start thinking like the person that Jack and Shinobu and Hikaru thought I was. Like the sword-bearer.

If I removed the blade from its saya, would it speak to me again? Would it tell me what to do? How to defeat this terrible new threat?

I had thought that I could handle the blade. I had fought with the katana several times without losing myself. But when I summoned the sword's power in the spirit realm by calling its true name, it had seemed to ... invite it to do more, somehow. Change my body. Take hold of my emotions. I worried that it had come dangerously close to actually controlling my actions.

It was a terrible, slippery slope. Every time I spoke to it, every time I fought with it, its hold on me seemed to become stronger. But it wasn't human and I couldn't trust it. I might not understand all of the katana's powers or what it was capable of, but I did understand that.

I had to work this out for myself.

I quickly used the toilet and exited the stall. At the row of sinks, I shoved my sleeves up to my elbows to wash my trembling hands, then held them under the cold water tap and splashed my face. Maybe the chill would shock my brain into alertness. My reflection stared back at me through the gaps in my fingers. The yellowish, flickering light made my skin seem alarmingly grey, and my eyes were too dark, too full of secrets and screams. I had *that* look. The look you see in photos on the front of newspapers. An expression that belongs to war refugees, kidnap victims and, sometimes, kids who are already dead by the time anyone cares enough to start looking for them.

The Kitsune had told me that people like us, people who were born with magic or stumbled on to it, walked with a foot in two worlds, never fully a part of either. But to me it felt like since this whole thing started, the other realms – the spirit realm, the Underworld, and whatever place nightmares came from – were constantly reaching up and grabbing at my feet, trying to catch hold and drag me under. I was hanging onto the real world by my fingernails.

What happens if I let go?

I closed my eyes and rubbed my face with my damp, chilly hands. What I needed was for Jack to slap some sense into me. But this was not the time to go and snivel on her shoulder. It was my turn to be strong for her now. In the meantime, I had to stop looking in mirrors. These days it was just never a pleasant experience.

Sighing, I opened my eyes – and stared.

The reflection in the mirror didn't show a row of dingy grey stalls. It didn't show flickering fluorescent lights. It didn't show a pasty-faced, wide-eyed teenager.

Soft golden light radiated from the smooth surface. Where it fell on my skin, I could feel its warmth just as if I was standing in front of a sunny window. A bent tree, its twisted, spreading branches heavy with autumn leaves, was silhouetted against the sun. The leaves spiralled gently downwards into the tall, waving fronds of ripe yellow grass below. Beyond the tree, not far away, there were low green hills and a shape that I was sure was the roof of a house – a steeply pitched, thatched roof, with the suggestion of a curl of grey smoke rising from some unseen chimney.

My throat ached with inexplicable, irresistible longing. It was the same feeling that Shinobu gave me at times, as if I was looking at something too beautiful to be real, too wonderful to last. Somewhere deep inside me something recognized this scene. It felt like … *home*.

A gleaming copper leaf drifted towards me, passing through the mirror with no more than a tiny ripple on the glass surface. The leaf landed in the water of the hand basin to float in the cup of white porcelain like a glowing jewel.

One of my hands lifted involuntarily, reaching out for the golden warmth beyond the mirror. Distantly I was aware of the sword snapping and fizzing a warning against my back, but I didn't care. I couldn't help myself. I had to touch.

My fingers found the glass … and passed through.

She lies back in the long grass, pillowing her cheek on Shinobu's knees. His legs – along with the rest of him – have grown as quickly as the grass itself this past year, and the girl feels more as if she is curling up on a pair of solid logs than on human flesh. The wind stirs the grass into a soft murmur around them, making dancing patterns of light and shade on the insides of her closed eyelids. A sleepy smile tilts her lips.

"Are you laughing at me?" he asks, his voice a low rumble. "What makes you smile?"

A blunt, callused finger brushes the stray wisps of hair gently behind her ear. Her smile creeps wider as the girl remembers all the times that finger has played with her hair just so. Even the very first day she met him – as mere strangers, mere children – he had been unable to resist those rebellious, untidy strands of hair.

The girl praises her ancestors a dozen times a day for granting her the blessing of hair that he loves so well.

"Tell me," he commands, his voice tickling her ear as his shadow falls over her like an embrace. Laughter trembles the edges of his words. "You know you cannot keep secrets from me."

She opens her mouth to frame some careless, teasing phrase – and freezes as another voice, a terrible voice that does not belong here in the living world, falls upon her ears.

Sunlight, *it hissed.* Oh, the sun. I had forgotten how it felt...

I cried out as the light disappeared, snuffed like a candle doused with water.

Blackness. Without shape, without shade, without end. It flooded my eyes and ears, poured into my mouth like smoke.

Trying to see anything was like ... like trying to outstare the vacuum of space.

Something dripped near by. Thick, slow drips that landed in more liquid. The sound echoed, giving me a sensation of space, vast empty space all around me, like standing on the top board at the swimming pool.

Drip. Drip. Drip.

Someone was watching me. I could feel their gaze on my face, like fingers grazing my skin. They could see me. I couldn't see anything but they could see me. Was I blind? Was this what being blind was like? I didn't dare move. Not even an inch. I knew – somehow I knew – that if I moved, I would fall.

Drip. Drip. Drip.

Cold breath, scented with rust, ghosted against my cheek.

Yamato Mio…

I bit a scream in half. I wanted to flinch, to back away – but I couldn't move. I had to be still. I had to stay still. My fingers curled and uncurled.

You are frightened again. *The blood-scented whisper caressed my ear.* Always so afraid, little mortal. I can hear your poor heart, pitter-patter. A tiny bird, trapped in an ivory cage. Poor thing. Poor birdie. Little wings, so fragile. Snap. Crunch. All broken.

I knew that singsong, child-like voice. I knew it from a dream.

Was that a dream?

Was this?

63

"I can't see you." The words came out as a harsh croak.

I know, *she said, pleased as if I'd praised her.* You did not like seeing me before. It distressed you.

I remembered. The mirrors all around me. The reflection. The woman who had my face, and eyes like a shark. "When you … you looked like me?"

I could not look like me. Too much. Little birdie would have stopped beating. Snap. Crunch. Broken.

That was almost – almost – lucid. Even in the midst of my fear it seemed as if she was making more sense this time around. That, or I was getting closer to insanity.

I wanted to speak to you again, *she continued.* Because you survived the first time. I do not always mean to but – snap! – you break so easily. I did not break you, did I? I am getting closer now, though. Do you feel it? Do you feel me coming closer to you? I can almost see your world from here. Almost touch… *A sudden, shocking sound, broken and hollow.* I will be there soon. Soon. Soon I will touch…

"Touch my world?" I whispered.

It used to be mine once. All mine. So pretty. So bright and warm. I cannot go there now. Crunch. Little bones all poking out. I have been in the dark too long. I have. But my pets can get through. Yes. I am close enough now for that. I send them one by one, two by two. A shrill little giggle. Flap, flap. They will find you, you know. They will find my treasure. They have no brains, but they never get tired. They never give up. Sniff sniff. Flap flap. One by one, two by two.

The Shikome.

And the realization was cold as ice sweeping over me and suddenly, just as I knew I couldn't move, I knew who it was that I was speaking to, who it was that had brought me here.

My lips shaped the name. "Izanami?"

Drip, drip, drip.

A soft, ragged moan filled the cavernous darkness – a moan like a thousand years of wailing and begging and tears, a thousand years of grief and sorrow, and loneliness too great for any creature to bear. I couldn't think around it. Couldn't think at all. I lost track of fear. Forgot who I was. Heat spilled down my cheeks, burning in the ferocious chill. My soul wailed for something it had never had.

A tiny hand, icy cold, covered in something sticky-wet, cupped my cheek.

The touch jerked me back to myself. I went rigid, breathing through my mouth. The stink of blood clogged my nose.

Tears for me. *She sighed.* I think … I think I will be sad when you die, Yamato Mio. All things die, and you will not give me what I want. But I will be sorry.

I could almost taste the blood, lying in a furry coppery coat on my tongue.

Dripdripdrip.

The sticky fingers flexed on my face.

He comes.

I jumped, startled by the sudden urgency in her voice.

He is vicious when he is afraid. So vicious! Oh! Beware, little birdie. He is very frightened now…

Light exploded in the backs of my eyes. For a split second, I saw the red forest, Shinobu's shocked dark eyes staring up out of his pale, pained face, and his blood-stained hand clutching at his chest where he lay in the red and gold fallen leaves. I saw a green, leaf-shaped blade flashing down towards him—

Dry-retching, I staggered back, away from the sink, away from the treacherous, dingy grey reflections in the mirror. My spine flopped like over-cooked pasta and I ended up on my knees, hands supporting my weight on the cracked lino of the floor, under the frantically flickering fluorescents.

The iron taste of blood was still in the back of my throat. I could still see that vivid snapshot of Shinobu's shocked face and the green, oddly shaped blade plunging down towards his heart. I could still remember that beautiful dream of lying with Shinobu in the grass in the golden sunlight. Only it hadn't been me lying there with him, had it?

Or had it?

Was it a dream? Was any of it a dream? All of it?

Am I going mad?

With one hand on the side of the basin, I dragged myself to my feet, wobbled to the door, and almost fell out into the corridor. My one thought was to get back to

Jack and Shinobu. I barely noticed the lights in the corridor start to flicker as I passed beneath them, hanging onto the plastic rail fitted to the wall. The katana was still pulsing in its harness, sending discordant jangles of energy fizzing through my skin. *Shut up. Shut up. I get it. Stay away from mirrors from now on.*

Which way was it from here? Had I turned left before or, or...?

The sight of the large vending machine made me sigh with relief. Now I remembered. Straight on. Letting go of the plastic rail, I walked unsteadily past a health-care worker who hesitated in front of the machine, her finger hovering in midair over the buttons. But as I turned, I stumbled. My elbow glanced off her side.

"Oh! Sorry – I didn't..." My voice came out overbearingly loud and I let the apology trail off as two things occurred to me.

First, the hospital had got really quiet. Not silent. I could hear city noises, traffic rushing by outside. But that was all. I couldn't hear voices, machinery, or that terrible moaning from earlier. All the usual hospital sounds were gone. Just gone.

Second, the woman in front of the vending machine was still in her half-bent position, staring at the buttons. She hadn't looked around when I hit her. She hadn't even flinched. I was suddenly, horribly, sure that she wasn't breathing.

With the katana still rattling against my spine, I reached for the woman's shoulder. She didn't respond when I made contact. Her arm was as rigid and unmoving as the arm of a chair. She was frozen.

I had seen people frozen like this before.

Izanami had said: *He comes.*

The Harbinger was here.

CHAPTER 5

LESSONS
IN FEAR

S *hadows and blood...*
This was the third time he had come for me.

Beware, little birdie.

The third time he had come for the sword.

You belong to me. The sword belongs to me. Everything belongs to me. If the sword is lost, you will die, hell shall open, and shadows and blood will devour this world.

I eased my hand away from the too-stiff flesh of the woman's shoulder. Adrenaline flooded my system and my pulse thrummed in my ears like a trapped wasp, trying to get out. Everywhere I looked, there were doorways into wards, offices and nurses' stations. No noise disturbed the unnatural quiet of the hospital floor. No hint of movement. He could be anywhere.

Little birdie in an ivory cage...

He could be with Jack and the others right now.

The lights flickered silently, like the strobes in a club. He was doing this. He was trying to scare me again. *And it's working...*

Acting on instinct, I reached into the loose collar of my sweatshirt and pulled the sheathed katana free from the leather harness. As I took the hilt in a firm two-handed grip, the sword shuddered painfully between my hands. The heat of its energy was spiking against my skin. Even holding it with both hands, I couldn't prevent the blade from trembling. Was it afraid too? Reacting to my fear? Or just eager to be freed?

The desire to unsheathe the sword was almost painful – but the very strength of that desire warned me that I shouldn't give into it. Not yet. I was surrounded by people here, and I didn't know for sure if I could control the sword or its powers.

The safety catch – the sword's saya – had to stay on until I had no choice but to fight.

I put my back to the wall and began to sidle down the corridor in the direction of Jack's ward. The lino floor seemed to stick to the soles of my boots like glue. Each footstep was a laborious, maddeningly slow effort, but Shinobu, Jack and Rachel were completely unprotected. I *had* to get to them. I had to make sure they were OK.

The lights flared suddenly, stabbing my eyes. I squeezed them shut for a split second. When I opened them again, the corridor was black. Pitch black. I froze.

It was the middle of the day. Even with no lights, it couldn't possibly be this dark.

Then the lights came back on. They flickered faster than ever. The katana rattled in my hands.

Some instinct made me cast a glance over my shoulder.

In the corridor behind me there was a blot of coruscating darkness, a black hole in the fabric of reality. It had the shape of a man. Where its eyes should have been were two circular holes, blank and blazing white.

The Harbinger.

I whipped round and pelted down the central corridor. My throat rasped with panicked, shallow breaths. Doorways and frozen people blurred past on either side of me.

The lights went out again. My boots squealed on the lino as I skidded to a halt, too terrified to move. The black air around me pulsed with menace. Where was he? Where was *I*?

The lights flashed back on.

The black shape was directly ahead of me, close enough to touch.

I dived sideways into the nearest opening in the wall. An office. Filing cabinets. Desks. Frozen secretary frowning at a heap of files. *Door.*

Swerving past the woman, I wrenched the door open and found myself in another corridor, almost identical to the first one. I slammed the door shut behind me and ran again, dodging around more motionless people.

A shadow flashed across a Perspex window in the wall ahead. I stopped in my tracks.

He was still in front of me. Between me and the others. What was he doing? Herding me away from them? Holding them hostage?

What if he had already hurt them?

I spun on my heel and ran back the way I'd come, bolting through the office door, out into the main corridor, towards the lifts. At the last second, I turned – nearly tripping over my own feet as my boots snagged on the linoleum floor again – and barged through the emergency fire doors.

The grey-and-white flecked walls of the stairwell closed in around me. My footsteps sounded like a drumbeat as I dashed down one flight of steps, hit the next set of doors and burst out onto the floor beneath Jack's. I shot along the main corridor, skipping and twirling to avoid knocking over the frozen patients and staff. A grunt of pain escaped me as I collided with the emergency doors at the other end of the hall. I broke through them and hit the stairs again, running upwards this time. My leg muscles were on fire now. I laboured up the steps, then pushed open the emergency doors on Jack's floor and ran out. *There.* Jack's ward was on the left, straight ahead.

Where was the Harbinger? Had I managed to outrun him? Was he already here?

Everything went black again.

The blow to my chest lifted my feet from the floor. I flew backwards, the breath whooshing out of my lungs. Something that felt like wood splintered under my weight as I crashed down. The lights came back on and my watering eyes took in a narrow space lined with shelves. A storage cupboard. I had smashed its door. There was no other way out.

I gulped a fiery mouthful of air, then rolled dazedly over onto my front – *too slow, too slow* – and heaved myself to my knees. My skin prickled with awareness as I waited for the next blow to fall. The doorway was empty. I gasped in another breath, easing to a crouch and bringing the katana up.

Was now the time to unsheathe the blade?

Another painful breath.

But Jack was so close. They were all so vulnerable. It wasn't safe.

Still no sign of him.

Was he in there with them right now?

I coughed, gritted my teeth, and launched myself out into the corridor, gaining my feet in a shower of dust and plywood splinters.

There was no one there. I couldn't hear anything. My own heartbeat and ragged breathing blocked out the unnatural quiet of the frozen hospital. The overhead lights flickered manically. The entrance to the ward where I'd left the others was only a few steps ahead – the way partially blocked by an empty trolley, its grey blankets trailing onto the floor. The second I went forward, he was going to attack me again. I knew it. Unless he was already attacking my friends while I stood hesitating.

There were no good choices here.

"Hey!" I screamed. "Where are you, you coward? Too scared to face me?"

This time the blow caught me between my shoulder blades. I flew across the corridor and crash-landed onto the abandoned trolley, which careened into the wall and bounced off. I toppled to the floor. The trolley smashed down beside me.

My eyes had squeezed shut. I forced them open – and saw the terrible dense blackness of the Harbinger hovering above me, just out of reach. *There you are, you bastard.* One of my hands groped and found the metal rail of the trolley lying on the ground next to me. A grunt punched out from between my gritted teeth. I heaved.

The trolley soared up over my head and cleaved through the Harbinger's darkness like a knife. I scrambled to my feet and threw myself the last couple of steps into the ward. There was just enough time to locate the curtained sanctuary of Jack's bed with my eyes. Just enough time to find the narrow opening in the pastel fabric and trace the straight lines of Shinobu's back, and Jack's sleeping face on the pillow. They were where I'd left them. They were OK.

Then the Harbinger was on me.

I didn't scream. I didn't get the chance. Darkness flooded down around me, solidifying into stinging black and gold fibres that wrapped me up like a fly in a cobweb. I was hoisted off the ground, and spun helplessly in the air as the strands writhed over my body, gluing my arms to my sides and my legs to each other. The katana's energy, imprisoned inside the saya, screamed and smoked. Wisps of fire licked out around the hilt. The dark fibres of the Harbinger winced from it, but it didn't matter. I had waited too long to free the blade. I was as trapped now as the katana was.

Something pale glowed in the dark cloud. It was the Harbinger's face, awful with rage and less than an inch from mine. His nose almost brushed my cheek. Icy cold, sickly sweet breath washed over my skin. The blank white eyes were on fire and pulsing in his face.

"*You*. How dare you defy me? How dare you escape me? Vile, ugly mortal. Your stubborn spirit has always been a thorn in my side."

The blackness tightened. My ribs creaked under the strain. "What – what are you t–talking about?" I choked. "Why are you – doing this? I protected the sword—"

He hissed with fury. Something coiled around and

around my throat. It tightened, then solidified into fingers. Bony knuckles jabbed the underside of my jaw as his hands flexed, pressing on my windpipe. I wheezed.

"Protected it? You have unsealed it! For five hundred years it was protected – in less than three days half my work has been undone!" He shook me viciously. My back slammed into something. I was on the floor now, crushed by his weight as he compressed down into the shape of a man again, growing rapidly denser and heavier on top of me. I could feel his bony hips pressing into my thighs, his sharp elbows grinding against my ribs.

He bared his teeth. They glistened like polished metal, the incisors sharp as scalpels. "It is mine! It was always mine! Now it will no longer answer to my voice. This is your doing! If I had known what you would do, I would have ripped your soul in two when I had the chance. If you were not the last of your line, I would do it now. This is your final warning, your last lesson in humility and fear. Attempt to work against me again and I shall exercise no clemency."

Bluffing. Has to be. He needs me, or he wouldn't have wasted all this time on me already. I shook my head. The movement sent his maddened face spinning in my vision.

"Pay attention!" he raged on. "There will be no more mistakes. I shall bind the cloaking spirit to the blade again. I shall seal it anew. All will be as it was! No one wins against me. No one. Not ever!" The words had a desperate, feverish edge. It sounded as if he was trying to convince himself. *Almost as if he's afraid…*

He is vicious when he is afraid.

He took one of his hands from my throat, his long, pale fingers spreading out as shining white energy crackled between the joints. It was too bright to look at. I could barely make out what he was saying now – the blood was pounding in my ears too loudly. Lack of oxygen made my vision fade in and out.

"Come. Come! *Answer me!*"

He was trying to summon the sword – to take it away from me the way he had before. And the katana was fighting. The heat of the sword's power scorched my skin. Every fold of silk on the hilt burned into my palm as the blade vibrated in my grip, its energy tearing the air with a shrill scream of defiance. I would have screamed too if I'd had enough air. But the Harbinger was holding my windpipe closed. Blackness was eating away at the edges of my vision. Nothing remained but a pinprick of light…

And in that pinprick, something moved.

A cloud of curling, toffee-coloured hair. Golden skin. Dark eyes that glinted almost yellow as one small-boned, delicate hand reached out.

No, Rachel, no. Get back. Get away while you can…

Rachel pounced, grabbing a handful of the Harbinger's hair. She yanked his head back with an enraged scream.

His mad, pale face contorted, and his fingers loosened on my neck. I choked on the sudden flood of air. Rachel's other hand curled around the Harbinger's throat, her manicured nails sinking into the pale flesh. White fire bubbled up around the wounds; it dripped down onto me like blood. The Harbinger shrieked as Rachel dragged him away from me, out of my blurry sight.

There was an immense shattering sound: one of the windows running down the side of the building must have broken. Exhaust-scented wind blasted my face. Shocked voices cried out everywhere – sounds of machinery and movement rushed back. *Time warp over...* I rolled up onto my hands and knees, coughing and gasping for breath.

Arms closed gently around me, helping me up. My head lolled back and I saw Rachel's pinched face, her glittering yellow eyes.

"You're OK, Mimi," she whispered. "I've got you. Just breathe. You're OK."

You never call me Mimi, I tried to say, but I just coughed some more and let Rachel take my weight.

A second later we were both through the gap in Jack's curtains. Rachel eased me down and I slumped on the edge of the bed as she nipped the curtains closed again. Outside I could hear nurses and patients exclaiming over the broken window. Inside the flimsy barrier of the curtain there was silence as everyone stared at me. Shinobu's eyes burned like black stars. I winced from them, only to meet Jack's, sunken and fearful in her pale face.

"What *happened*?" she whispered hoarsely.

Another cough raked through my chest. Shinobu rushed to snatch the plastic tumbler from Jack's bedside locker and fill it with water.

"Drink this," he said, taking my free hand and wrapping my palm around the small glass. I was still unsteady. He had to keep his hand there, guiding the water to my lips. The first taste of the lukewarm liquid burned like acid, but the next one was glorious.

"The Harbinger?" Shinobu asked softly, urging me to sip more water. His expression was calm, but his eyes were terrible.

All I could do was nod.

"Rat-bastard," Jack mumbled. Her hands clenched and unclenched on the blanket. "Talk, Mimi."

I took one more sip, then let Shinobu take the glass away. He brushed my cheek, tucking my tangled hair behind my ear. I could feel his hand trembling.

"He wanted to punish me," I said. My voice crackled and broke. It felt like I was trying to talk through a mouthful of sand. "He said … I'd unsealed the sword. Something about how the sword wouldn't answer to him any more. And it wouldn't. He tried to call it to him, but it fought."

I looked down at the sword and realized with a shock

that my fingers were still clamped around the hilt, knuckles standing out purple and yellow with the strain. My hand was numb. The blade lay still in my grasp, without a hint of vibration. Maybe it had exhausted itself.

I tried to open my fingers and couldn't. The effort made sharp cramping sensations shoot down my wrist. This had happened once before – the last time the Harbinger had attacked me. Was it possible that the sword hated and feared him as much as I did? *Am I clinging to the katana right now? Or is it clinging to me?*

Shinobu saw my problem and took my hand in both of his large, warm ones. He chafed at my fingers, deftly massaging the joints until they began to loosen. "The Harbinger hurt you to punish you?" he prompted me quietly.

"Said he was teaching me a lesson. Repeated the thing he said before, too, about how if I weren't the last Yamato he'd kill me. And … and he talked about you, Shinobu. He called you 'the cloaking spirit', but I'm sure he meant you. I think he's the one who did this to you. I think he's the one who trapped you in the blade."

Shinobu's hold on my hand tightened minutely. He stared down at the sword, motionless, eyes screened from mine by the thick fan of his eyelashes. His face was smoothly blank. The very lack of reaction gave me a lurching sensation deep inside. "Shinobu—?"

He gave a little tweak to my fingers and unpeeled them from around the sword hilt. I dropped the katana next to me on the bed with a gasp of relief, flexing my hand. My palm was marked with faint pink lines from the silk tsukamaki, but otherwise unharmed. I could hardly believe the skin wasn't burned to a crisp. There wasn't even a blister.

Jack kicked her legs feebly under the covers, demanding my attention. "Did you ... at least ... cut him up ... this time?" The effort of producing this many words clearly exhausted her and her head slumped back on the pillow.

"Not exactly," I said, hesitantly. I shifted my position to stare at Rachel, who hadn't moved or said a word since she'd closed the curtains and stationed herself at the foot of the bed.

She looked exactly the same as normal. She looked like Rachel Luci, Jack's bossy-but-mostly-OK sister who I'd known practically my whole life. A friend. Safe.

Oxygen deprivation and a whack to the head could make people see things – but I couldn't have imagined everything I saw. I couldn't have imagined what Rachel did. There was no way I would have escaped from the Harbinger on my own, not this time. She'd dragged him right off me. She'd scared him enough that he fled out of the window, freeing the hospital from his spell, which had held every other human in the place frozen, even Shinobu. Rachel had saved me, for sure. But how had she broken free? How had she done any of it? I couldn't forget that strange yellow fire I had seen in her gaze. I didn't know what it meant, but it didn't feel right.

Her eyes were brown again now, the same familiar brown as Jack's. Those familiar eyes were pleading with me. *Don't, don't. Don't make a fuss. Don't say anything in front of Jack.*

Shinobu had picked up on our silent communication and was looking at Rachel warily, clearly realizing that something was wrong. Jack was still lying on the pillow, eyes closed, but she was going to pick up on the silence in a moment.

I bit my lip. Then I picked the katana up and quickly returned it to its place in the harness on my back, before grabbing the metal foot board of the bed to lever myself to my feet. "We have to go."

Jack's eyes flicked open. "What?"

"Whoa, Xena," Rachel said. "Stay right where you are. We don't need you passing out again."

"I didn't pass out before," I said indignantly, even though I was still hanging onto the bed for balance. "Listen, Jack, the Harbinger is focused on me, on Shinobu, and on the sword – but it's only a matter of time before someone else gets caught in the crossfire and is badly hurt. And I'm not helping you or anyone else by just sitting around here, anyway. We need to figure out what we can do to fix this – all of this, the Harbinger, the Shikome – the way we did the Nekomata. There has to be an answer out there."

Shinobu nodded slowly, considering my words. "The Harbinger may have fled for now, but if the sword remains here, he is sure to return. We are surrounded by the ill and vulnerable, including Jack-san. It is not the place for a confrontation."

"Hey," Jack protested. "I'm – fine. I can … come … with you."

"You're not going anywhere," I said, reaching out to grab her hand. Her fingers twitched in mine. She was trying to squeeze back. My knees buckled, and I ended up leaning on the bed with my free hand, desperately trying to keep my expression neutral. My voice came out slightly strangled as I finished. "But nice try, though."

Jack's gaze searched my face. Then she closed her eyes, her head moving in the tiniest possible gesture of assent. "Fine."

"I'll go with them," Rachel said, to Jack's obvious surprise – and my secret relief. I needed to get her alone and find out what was going on with her. "You just need to rest anyway, Jack. You'll be safe here. And if these two clowns are going to do any good at all, they'll need all the help they can get." She dug in her coat pocket and started unloading things onto the top of Jack's locker. "I'll leave you my iPhone and earbuds for if you get bored. Here's Mum's emergency credit card if you want to buy anything, OK? You know the pin. Call me if you need me."

Jack nodded again, squeezing her eyes closed for a

second. When she opened them, they fixed on me. The intensity of her stare made her seem even smaller and more pathetic hunched up in the pale blue hospital gown; the uncharacteristic lack of argument over being left behind drove home to me just how terrible she must be feeling. Jack always fought. Only ... not today.

"What are you going to do?" she asked, a little hoarsely.

"I don't know yet," I admitted. "But I promise I'll figure it out."

CHAPTER 6

LITTLE BIRDIE

I had voted to take the Underground route home from the hospital. I couldn't imagine any huge, winged monsters would be able to get at us on the Tube or in the stations, especially if we lost ourselves in the crowd.

So it was kind of a shock to find there was no crowd.

It was a weekend afternoon, and Christmas was in a few days. There ought to have been tides of bad-tempered people heading out to do shopping or hauling their pre-Christmas-sale bargains home again. Instead, the station felt like an echoey ghost town. When we got on the Tube, there were precisely two other people in our carriage – a woman standing right next to the doors with a scarf pulled up over her face despite the uncomfortable humidity in the train tunnels, and a man sitting on the opposite side, as far away from everyone else as possible, who kept darting worried looks at us. I couldn't tell if it was because Shinobu's presence was playing games with his perception or if we just looked mad, bad and dangerous to know. Maybe both.

Self-consciously, I checked the hood of my father's old sweatshirt, which I'd pulled up in an attempt to hide the rapidly darkening necklace of bruises around my neck. I felt Shinobu, who was sitting on my right side, stiffen as he caught the movement. His gaze flared with the same dark fury I had seen in the hospital, and then dropped to the floor. His big hands clenched into a single fist on his knee.

"They're no big deal," I said, trying for breezy unconcern. It didn't quite work; my throat actually hurt like hell, and my voice was raspy and rough.

"Please do not lie to comfort me."

I sighed. "Well, stop beating yourself up, then."

"This is the second time that you have had to fight him alone." He paused. When he spoke again his voice was nearly as hoarse as mine. "You could have died." His hands flexed and clenched again.

I chewed on my lip for a moment, then haltingly reached out to lay my hand over his. A tingle of the natural electricity that was always waiting between us made my breath catch as Shinobu instantly turned one of his hands over and twined our fingers together. He lifted his eyes from the floor to meet mine.

Maybe now he would listen.

"It was horrible, and I was scared," I admitted carefully. "But he didn't intend to kill me today. He didn't even mess me up that much, and he could have. He still wants – needs – me to protect the sword for some reason. I don't know why. I don't think he really cares that much about the fate of this world, or humans. But for whatever reason, whoever he is, he wants me alive."

Shinobu frowned again, but it was a thoughtful frown now, not a self-loathing one. "If he is invested in the fate of the katana, why does he not simply take it back and protect it himself?"

"Yeah, I can't figure it out. He's way more powerful than me. Look at the way he froze everyone in that place. Everyone except..."

Inexorably, my head turned to look at Jack's sister, who was sitting in the seat on the other side of me. Shinobu followed my gaze. "Except Rachel-san?"

Rachel shifted away from us. Her eyes looked huge and tense. There was a long, uncomfortable pause.

"Rachel?" I said finally. "You want to chime in here? How did you do it? You broke out of his – his freeze-ray effect. You actually managed to *hurt* him with your bare hands."

"I – I ... I'm not really..." Her nervous eyes darted away from us. She looked down, fiddling with the ends of her black-and-white scarf. Pity twinged under my ribs.

Rachel had been through so much in the past

twenty-four hours. She probably shouldn't even be out of bed yet. But what she had done to the Harbinger … that should have been impossible. It was impossible for me, even with my katana-boosted muscles and speed. Something was going on, and I needed an explanation. I tried to put as much compassion into my voice as possible. "Come on, this is me, not the Spanish Inquisition. Just talk to me."

She shoved her glasses up her nose. Her eyes stayed down. "I remember having a really weird dream," she said, her voice barely audible. "I was stuck. I couldn't move or see or hear."

"Right." I nodded encouragingly. "That would have been when the Harbinger froze everyone."

Rachel's trembling hands knotted together. "But then there was this – this voice. This … awful, scary voice." She shuddered. "It said – she said – *The little birdie needs you. Awaken. Move.* And I woke up."

I could feel my eyes bulging. *Little birdie?*

"And then?" Shinobu was leaning into me now, his chest a warm, solid wall against my back.

The announcement for our stop came on the Tannoy. The Tube grumbled to a halt and the doors hissed open. Before I could even get my feet under me, Rachel was up and bolting out of the carriage.

I shouted her name. She didn't look back. I was so shocked that I almost forgot we needed to get off here too.

"Quickly!" Shinobu hauled me upright and out of the doors. But we were already too late to catch a glimpse of where Rachel had gone. We jogged up and down the platform peering through the tiled archways.

"Why would she run away like this? It's pointless. She needs to get on the next train out of here to get home, just like we do." A sudden image of the way we had found Rachel last night – her wide, staring eyes as she fought the Nekomata's bonds – made my stomach do a queasy flip. What if it was all finally catching up with her? She could be having a flashback, freaking out – and who could blame her? I tightened my grip on Shinobu's hand. "Come on."

Now it was me dragging him as I slapped my Oyster card on the ticket barrier. If an invisible man fails to pay his fare in a busy Tube station, does anyone notice? Not this time. We walked out into the blinding orange light of the low winter sun without interference.

The pedestrianized area between the Tube stop and the main train station was lightly scattered with people – not half as many as I would normally have expected, but still enough for someone to hide among. Light glinted off the windows of the buildings towering over us. The Gherkin's sleek form almost blinded me. Shielding my watering eyes, I scanned the crowd, trying to make out Rachel's curly hair and red jumper before she disappeared completely.

"There!" Shinobu pointed.

I saw Rachel's small form almost opposite me. She was hustling up the steps of the main train station, past one of the giant white mushroom-lights that stood in the courtyard.

We wove through the crowd, dodging briefcases and shopping bags. "Rachel!" I yelled.

All around me people turned around to stare. Rachel froze for a second, then sped up.

"Perhaps we should let her go," Shinobu suggested. "She might simply wish for some time to herself."

"Maybe. Yeah, maybe. But…" But we still had no idea what was behind that sudden burst of incredible strength and aggression. And then there was the fact that Rachel had just confessed to hearing a "scary" voice in her mind, speaking the same words I had heard in my dream. Words that might have come from Izanami. I shook my head. "She's panicked and emotional. She might put herself in danger." *She might endanger other people…*

I let go of his hand and put on a burst of speed. Shinobu kept up with me easily, making me realize that he could probably have caught Rachel before, if he'd been willing to abandon me in the crowd. We caught up with her just as she was about to scoot into the giant glass structure that served as the train station's porch.

I snagged her arm and drew her back out of the thin trickle of people between the twin brick clock-towers, firmly ignoring her attempts to shrug me off. It was the sort of move I'd have pulled on Jack. It was only once I actually had hold of her that I realized I'd been a tiny bit reckless, given that Rachel just might be capable of tying me into a pretzel if she wanted to.

No. This was Rachel. Jack's Rachel! The bossyboots who been babysitting and lecturing me about my mess since I was a kid. Remembering that made me feel guilty, which made me mad.

"What are you doing?" I demanded. "Why did you go running off like that? Are you an idiot?"

"Let go!" She struggled, apparently not worried about the curious looks we were getting. "Leave me alone!"

"What do you mean leave you alone?" I hissed, hanging onto her arm doggedly. "What if another Foul Woman turns up, like the one that got Jack?"

She winced. Before I could apologize for my trademark sensitivity, she recovered and poked her finger at my face. "It's none of your business what I do! I don't answer to you, Mio Yamato. I'm an adult, for God's sake! I'm nearly twenty-one years old."

"Then start acting like it! We're on the same side here. We are trying to *help* you."

"How?" Her voice hit a pitch so shrill that it echoed even in the middle of all the deadening sounds of the city. We got a slew of horrified stares. Rachel didn't seem to notice. "How? You have no idea what happened to me!

You have no idea what's still happening to me..."

All the fight seemed to drain right out of her. Her tense shoulders sagged and, to my horror, big, fat tears welled up and spilled down her cheeks.

Well, crap.

Jack and me ... we didn't do this. We didn't cry in front of each other. We didn't do that Reality TV Big Emotional Moment stuff. It wasn't us. If this had been Rachel's sister in front of me, I'd have known just how to handle it – let her turn away, let her get herself back together without trying to help. Jack would already have been sucking it up.

But this wasn't Jack. And Rachel wasn't sucking it up. She was just standing in front of me in the middle of a crowded London train station courtyard, with one arm wrapped around her middle like she was about to fall apart, crying silent, pathetic tears.

Shinobu's face filled with a mixture of sadness and understanding. He made an abortive move to touch Rachel, then stopped and stepped back, as if realizing contact from him probably wouldn't be welcome. "Then you must tell us, Rachel-san," he said gently. "Trust us with your fears. Trust that we will listen and understand."

He gave me an urgent look and mimed a hugging movement.

Thanks. Thanks a bunch.

Feeling stiff and uncomfortable, I put my arms

around Rachel and patted her on the back. "Shush. It's all right now. It's all right."

To my surprise she flopped against me, burying her head in my shoulder as she cried. It was like … like she'd just been waiting for someone to lean on all along. For the first time it really dawned on me that Rachel and Jack were different. Yeah, they had something of the same attitude, a lot of the same mannerisms, even looked alike if you ignored Jack's goth thing – but they weren't the same person. I needed to start seeing Rachel for who she was, not just Jack's Big Sister.

I hugged her a bit tighter, and patted her back with a bit more enthusiasm. "I'm not going to pretend that I understand exactly how you're feeling, because … you're you, and only you can know that. But I can sympathize. Maybe I can even help. Please tell me what's going on."

"I'm sorry I'm being such a bitch," she sobbed into my shoulder. "I don't mean to be, honestly, but I – I feel *different*. I'm so angry. There's this huge bubble of awful stuff inside me and it keeps bulging out."

"You're allowed to be angry. You're not going to drive me or Jack or Shinobu away, no matter how bitchy you get."

She shook her head. "But when I saw that Harbinger guy strangling you, it was like I went crazy. I didn't even know what I was doing. I wanted to rip him up, kill him. I've never felt like that before in my whole life. I'm not saying that I was a saint, but that? That wasn't *me*."

I definitely got that. I'd been just where she was, and only a few hours ago. Which made it easy to get the fact that however freaked out I'd been about what I'd seen Rachel do, Rachel was freaked out squared. With a cherry on top.

"We're not exactly in a normal situation here. You can't expect to react the same way you always do. The last time I got really pissed off, I decapitated something. Does that seem in character for me? You were trying to save me – there's nothing wrong with that impulse."

"You seriously don't get it, do you?" Rachel pulled back to stare at me with watery, red-rimmed eyes. She took a deep breath and grabbed the scarf around her neck. She tugged it down. It took me a minute to work out what I was supposed to be looking at. There was nothing there. Then a few brain cells sparked to life – and I remembered that there *should* be something there.

This morning the sight of Rachel's neck, covered in swollen red punctures from the Nekomata's teeth, had brought me up short. Now that terrible wound was completely healed. Gone. There wasn't a scab or a bruise there, not even a scar.

"Nobody just heals up like that. Nobody human. That thing bit me," she said. "Now I'm changing. It's like a part of it is still inside me. I don't know what I'm becoming."

My blood suddenly felt as cold as ice water, and goose pimples prickled on my skin like nettle stings.

Holy shit. What if Rachel was turning into a Nekomata?

I could feel Shinobu's stare. Rachel was still staring at me too. Waiting. Hoping. Just like last night.

Rachel had been dragged into a supernatural nightmare because of me. She'd nearly died because of me. She'd seen Jack in a hospital bed because of me. I was the one who had brought the Nekomata into our lives. And when I'd had to make a choice between Rachel and the sword … I had chosen the sword. I had hesitated and let her fall.

I couldn't let her fall a second time. Not without a fight.

Slowly, fighting against every instinct that was howling in my body, I reached out and put my arms around Rachel again. The Nekomata's monstrous eyes – Rachel's eyes, the way they had looked in that hospital ward – shone in my mind, and I could almost feel its sharp teeth – her teeth – sinking into my neck. Shivers crawled up my back.

I squeezed her until she let out a tiny squeak.

"Listen," I whispered in her ear. "It's going to be all right, Rach. We'll figure this out. I promise I'm not going to let you down this time."

I heard her gulp. Then she hugged me back.

After a little while, we both straightened and let go of each other. Rachel grabbed the ends of her scarf and rubbed it over her face, scrubbing away tears. "O–OK. I guess. OK—"

We both jumped as a piercing scream rang out behind us. I spun round, moving automatically into a fighting stance as my hand flew to grab the katana's hilt. Shinobu appeared at my side like magic.

A young man had collapsed a few feet away. A girl was crouched next to him, desperately trying to hold him still as she yelled for help. The boy's body sprawled stiffly on the station steps; his limbs twitched and jerked. A thin line of drool leaked out between his lips and trickled over the livid purple rash that spread down his neck.

And there, caught on the collar of his shirt, I saw a dull, greyish wisp. A feather.

A Shikome feather.

In the next instant the wind swirled around the pair, and the feather was swept away.

All around us other commuters were backing away, their faces caught in frozen masks of disbelief and fear. Someone in the crowd broke and fled. Suddenly everyone was running, scattering in all directions, more screams rising up to tangle in the air like smoke.

A lone security officer puffed down the steps, walkie-talkie in hand, and bent over the convulsing boy. She didn't get too close. "Calm down now," she shouted over the girl's screams. "Calm down. I've got an ambulance on the way."

I started forward – and was jerked to a halt as two pairs of hands grabbed my arms to hold me back. "What are you doing?" I asked, looking at Shinobu and Rachel with bewilderment. "That man—"

"Doesn't need your help," Rachel said urgently. "Unless you think having another one of those harpy-things swoop down on him would be therapeutic? One was close enough to drop a feather on him, and they're attracted to the sword, right? We need to go. Now."

My eyes automatically shot up to the metallic win-tery blue sky. I couldn't see anything, not even a cloud, but with all the roofs surrounding the station, a Shikome could be hiding anywhere. I stopped resisting and reluc-tantly let them pull me away under the glass portico of the station.

"… have released the security guard without charge. It's believed the investigation into the break-in at the British Museum, which resulted in the death of assistant curator Belinda Dowling, has been linked to the murders of three security officers at Battersea Power Station last night, although detectives would not confirm how. The investiga-tion into both incidents is ongoing."

The newsreader pursed her lips, her face pale under the regulation layers of foundation and blusher. Her gaze was more than usually fixed as she stared at the scrolling white text on the blue autocue screen. She cleared her throat and launched into her final segment as the producer's countdown ended in her ear.

"And back to today's main headline: Hospitals in the central London area are dealing this morning with a sudden influx of cases believed to be due to unknown, airborne contaminants. Initial symptoms include convulsions and a rapidly spreading rash. The London Primary Care Trust has stated that over the past twelve hours around two hundred patients have been admitted to local accident and emergency departments displaying the same symptoms. However, a source from one hospital puts the correct number at three times as many, with more still coming in."

In her mic'd ear, she could hear the unusual silence in the production room. One of the researchers had a teenage son in the hospital right now. He'd left the house right as rain that morning. Half an hour later he had collapsed in the middle of the street.

Tiny beads of sweat glittered at the newsreader's hairline. She took a deep breath and continued. "Health Secretary Daniel Anders has urged the public to remain calm. In a statement given just a few moments ago, we were told that there are no official plans for a quarantine of the city at this time. Emergency measures are already in place, and specialist teams are hard at work to discover the source of the contaminants. However, it is advised that the public avoid all non-essential travel, and if possible stay in their own homes.

"The prime minister, on day three of his official visit to India, was unavailable for comment, but is said to be preparing to return home early. Public health officials urge..."

The newsreader paused, blinking rapidly. The white writing was wavering in front of her eyes. In her ear, the programme's producer made urgent noises as her silence stretched on. She cleared her throat again.

"Health officials urge anyone showing symptoms to contact..."

The newsreader shook her head, but instead of clearing it, the movement sent the bright lights of the studio into a dizzying whirl around her. She sucked in a sharp breath.

"Contact the NHS helpline for—"

The lights were moving too fast. She felt sick. Oh God, she couldn't be sick on national television. She would never live it down; her career would be over. She tried to turn away from the hulking shape of camera one, but the chair skidded away from under her and the next thing she knew, she was flat on her face, cheek crushed into the ugly grey studio carpet.

"Helpline..." she whispered. "Help."

People were shouting and running around her. Hands grabbed the back of her Chanel suit and tried to turn her over, and suddenly the whirling lights exploded in her head and she screamed.

By the time someone cut the live feed, four million people had witnessed the newsreader's seizure and the spread of the purple rash that appeared, like dark magic, on her face.

But no one noticed the tiny wisp of a grey feather that clung to her teased blonde hair.

CHAPTER 7

AND THEN THERE WERE THREE

We were all tense and wary on the walk back to the house from the Tube station, stopping frequently to duck into doorways and check the sky.

Just how stupid were the Foul Women? That was what I wanted to know. The one we'd seen had only made those strange seagull cries – *could* they talk? Did they have the intelligence to lay a trap for us? Or were they really like animals, who had no conception of the future, and would just flap around London following all the different trails of the sword's scent until they caught me out in the open somewhere?

Our house, warded against supernatural attack with the collective powers of the entire Kitsune Kingdom, was the one safe refuge we had. The idea of a Foul Women – maybe more than one this time – hiding somewhere, lying in wait for us to return, made my heart pound unevenly. I was intensely conscious of the katana humming in its harness. I thought it would warn me if we were about to be attacked, but that was concerning in itself; I didn't want to rely on the sword.

We paused at the turn-off to my road. "If there had been more than one of the Foul Women here this morning, I am sure they would have attacked together," Shinobu said reassuringly. "We must have killed it before it could call any others of its kind."

"Let's run anyway," Rachel said uneasily. "Even if they are birdbrains, they still might get lucky and spot us from the air."

We took the pavement at fast clip and reached the house with no sign of any winged monsters. I slammed the front door shut behind us and made for the living room, ripping my dad's sweatshirt over my head as I went. One smooth movement had the leather harness off and the katana free. My right hand found its place on the hilt, the left gripped the saya. I slid the saya back – just a little – an inch. Then two. The sight of that beautiful black-and-silver blade, marked with the long flame-shaped ripples, eased me in some way I couldn't name.

Mio... The blade's silvery voice breathed into my mind.

I gently snicked the lacquered sheath back into place before the sword could speak any more. This was enough. I sat down where I was, rocking gently as the sword's energy drifted around me like the steam from a hot bath, touching my face and twining around my arms.

The silence in the room finally penetrated. I looked up to see Rachel and Shinobu both staring at me. Shinobu was stationed in the doorway, on guard despite the wards on the house. Rachel had slumped tiredly on the arm of the other sofa. They couldn't have looked more different, but their expressions were identical.

I hadn't even realized until that moment what I had just done. I stared down at the sword as if it was a snake that might bite me. But even then I couldn't quite bring myself to let it go.

"You really meant it, didn't you?" Rachel said, voice hushed. "You're like … like an addict craving a fix."

"I think it's getting stronger," I admitted with an icy thrill that might have been fear – or excitement. *What is the sword doing to me?* "The compulsion. The connection." Those words didn't seem strong enough any more. It was more like an obsession, hardwired into every part of me.

"So what does that mean? For you?" Rachel asked.

"I don't know," I confessed. My gaze strayed to Shinobu. His dark eyes were unreadable in that particular way of his that forced me to look away. *What is he thinking?*

"Rach, what you said before … about the scary voice you heard when you were frozen—" I began tentatively.

"Mio, no offence, but I don't really want to talk about it right now, OK?" Her tired smile robbed the remark of any bite. She got to her feet. "I'm heading up to change into my own clothes and check on the flat. You probably don't feel like it, but we need to eat – it's been hours. Order us some food? I'm not in the mood to cook."

I forced myself to rein in my curiosity, and nodded. She headed towards the stairs. There was a door on our first floor that led to the old servants' staircase. Normally it was locked, but Beatrice must have given Rachel the key. I had the feeling that she was desperate for a bit of time alone to process what had happened.

I could sympathize.

After she was gone, silence fell over the living room like a heavy cloth. Shinobu was still looking at me, but I found myself retreating from his gaze as if our eyes were two sets of positively charged magnets. This morning I had admitted to him that I thought I was falling in love with him, and he ... he hadn't said it back. Maybe he had meant to. But how was I supposed to know? It hadn't seemed to mean anything at the time. Now it meant a lot. If only we hadn't been interrupted. I'd felt something click between us then, in that moment, as if we were about to get to wherever we needed to be to *know...*

Because I didn't really know anything. Not about Shinobu. All I "knew" – about his first life, and his family, and who he had been – was what he told me himself. I didn't think for an instant that he'd lied to me, but it had been obvious, with every word, that he was holding back. How could I blame him for that? It had to have killed him to remember everything he had lost, everyone he was never going to get back. I was sure there were a hundred things he hadn't brought up – things that were too hard to talk about. Too private. Things I didn't need to know.

Of course he hadn't told me about some other girl that he had known then. A girl that he had laughed with and lain in the grass with. A girl whose hair he had touched and played with, the way he always seemed to want to touch mine... He hadn't told me because it didn't matter. Love wasn't a zero-sum game. The feelings he'd had for someone else – might still have – didn't somehow invalidate whatever he felt for me.

Whatever he felt.

What matters is now, I told myself. *And the rest of what you saw. You saw her. You saw the Goddess of Death. Izanami.*

Little birdie. That was what she had called me. That was what Rachel had repeated. Could Izanami's inter-ference explain what had happened to Rachel? What if Izanami had woken Rachel out of her frozen sleep and sent her to help me?

But why would Izanami want to protect me against the Harbinger?

All these unanswered questions were starting to give me a headache.

In an effort to distract myself, I managed to peel one

hand off the katana and grab my phone out of my pocket, carefully avoiding any glances in Shinobu's direction as I turned it back on. I hadn't been sure if you were allowed to have mobiles in the hospital.

The sight of several missed calls from a number that I hardly ever saw made my eyebrows go up. "What does *he* want?"

"Whom?" Shinobu asked. His voice was neutral, giving no hint as to what was going on in his head.

"Er – my father. He's called me four times since this morning." I stared at the logged calls intently, and not just because it gave me an excuse to avoid Shinobu's gaze. "How can I have managed to annoy him from all the way across the Channel?"

"Maybe he wants to check that you are all right."

I snorted. "Not bloody likely."

I'd probably catch hell later for not calling him back. But I was already going to catch hell for so much stuff anyway – there seemed little point in adding to my current stress level. Instead I opened my web browser and squinted at my emails. Two from Mum. One was from yesterday evening, the other lunchtime today. There was no subject line on either – Mum always forgot – but it wasn't hard to guess what they were about. I opened the first one and sure enough it was a short, chatty email about the hotel and the gorgeous dinner they'd had. Reassurance and caring glowed brightly between the lines. She was still worried about me.

I managed to squeeze out a few cheerfully untruthful lines about what was going on here in London. I told her I missed her, but resisted getting too mushy. Even the best parents know that's a sign they need to get suspicious. When I'd closed the email with a few kisses, I decided I'd deal with the second message from her later. I didn't have any more generic perkiness in me right then.

What I really wanted to do next was combat my sense of helplessness by fetching my laptop and Googling "Shikome/Foul Women", "Systemic anaphylaxis – treatments" and anything else that might possibly offer us an idea about how to help Jack. But realistically, I knew it would be a waste of my time. Wiki wasn't designed for this sort of scenario. And Rachel was right; we needed to be grown-ups and feed ourselves. I was shaky, headachey and a bit dizzy already, and none of that was going to improve if I refused to eat. Then maybe we could have some sort of a brainstorming session or something...

I dialled the nearest takeaway place, and ran into a brick wall. A recorded message said they were closed for the foreseeable future due to the current health crisis. The next nearest takeaway didn't even pick up. Tucking the katana under my arm, I went into the kitchen – aware of Shinobu silently shadowing me – to try the menus pinned to the cork-board on the wall.

No answer. Recorded message. Recorded message. Number out of service.

I dropped the phone onto the breakfast bar and rubbed my forehead tiredly.

"Is there a problem?" Shinobu asked, still in that careful tone.

"Not really. Just … things must be worse out there than I thought. Everywhere's closed. I can make us something."

I put the katana carefully down on the edge of the worktop. It glowed against the plain wood surface like a black star. *Like Shinobu's eyes when he's angry...* I shook that thought off and made a shooing gesture in his direction. "Go and sit down in the living room."

"You look tired." It was a statement, not a question, but I wasn't fooled. I could hear the unspoken questions – the same ones he was always asking – jostling under the surface. *How are you coping? Are you all right? How do you feel? What will you do next?*

Involuntarily my nails began to beat out a rapid tattoo on the counter. I knew he wasn't the cause of my frustration and anxiety, but … I was the one who'd been tossed around like a rag doll in that hospital ward. I was the one who was trying to figure out the sword's influence on me. I was the one hanging in there, waiting for some sign of his feelings that he apparently couldn't be bothered to give. I had enough problems. Why was I constantly having to tiptoe around reassuring him that I was fine?

What if I wasn't fine, dammit?

"Mio," he said heavily, reclaiming my attention. "We need to talk."

Apprehension tingled through me. I made myself turn to face him. "Well, that sounds like fun."

My sarcasm bounced off without leaving a dent. "Earlier today – before Jack-san was attacked – I meant to speak then, but I did not have the chance."

Earlier today when I told you that I loved you? I took a slightly shaky breath. "Yes?"

"I can sense that something has changed."

I nodded. "OK."

"Things have altered between you and the sword. You said that the compulsion is growing stronger, but I think it is more than that. I am right, am I not?"

It was like stepping into what you thought was a warm shower – and being drenched with ice water instead. I let out a choked, incredulous laugh. "That's what you want to talk about?"

"Please," he said gravely. "Tell me how you defeated the Nekomata alone. Tell me what happened to you after I ... when I fell."

The scaffolding pole broke through his chest, blood gushing up like a red flower...

The green blade flashes down in the red light—

I flinched, then sighed. "Nothing. Nothing really ...

happened. We fought. I won."

His eyes were fixed on me like lasers. I could almost feel the burn on my skin. "I do not believe that is all."

I drummed my nails on the countertop again. "I don't know exactly. After ... after I saw you go down, I got angry. Very angry. And I screamed your name, but I think the sword took it as an invitation because it spoke to me again, but it didn't ... *do* anything. I mean, it didn't blast the Nekomata into smithereens or open a wormhole and suck it into space. The blade caught flame, and I suppose it probably boosted my strength and speed again, but ... I had to use what Ojiichan taught me. I had to do my own fighting. Then after I'd killed the demon, the sword tried to talk to me about making some kind of deal and I told it to piss off and shoved it into the saya. And I haven't taken it out since. Even though I really, really, really want to." I stopped abruptly, breathing hard, and looked him in the face for the first time since I'd started talking.

He was staring at me with horror. "You communicated with the blade? You ... made some kind of – of *bond* with it? Why did you not tell me?"

"Why would I?" I asked defensively. "Look, it's not like there's anything you can do about it. I messed up, I get it. I let the sword in somehow. I didn't mean to. What more do you want?"

"I want you to talk to me!" he snapped. "Tell me what

is happening and how it affects you! This is important. I had a right to know!" He slapped one hand down flat on the counter. It made a sound like a gunshot. The katana rattled.

I jumped in surprise and reached out to put my hand over the hilt before it could fall off onto the floor. As my fingers closed around the silk wrappings, I felt the angry thrum of the sword's power and suddenly my own temper ignited.

"What. The. Hell?" I snarled. "You have the *right to know*? You don't have the *right* to know anything about me. It's not like I know everything about you! You don't get to decide what I should and shouldn't do because you've appointed yourself my bodyguard. I don't belong to you! I don't owe you anything. If I wanted this kind of crap, I could have phoned my damned father."

The look of surprise and – yes – hurt on his face was oddly satisfying. "That is not what I—"

"No, you've said enough. Get out of my face. Go away. I don't want to look at you right now." He hesitated and it was the last straw. "GET. OUT."

Without another word he turned on his heel and stalked back into the living room. I put the sword back down onto the counter, ripped the fridge open and furiously started grabbing the ingredients for sandwiches, which was what I had intended to do before Shinobu came in and started throwing his weight around.

Seriously? Seriously, he was going to take that attitude with me? I slammed a plate down and started buttering bread with a fury. *I'm supposed to tell him everything when he tells me nothing? He can't even bring himself to tell me that he* likes *me!*

Maybe he didn't like me. He'd never said that. Ever. All he'd ever said was that I was important to him because I was the one thing he had when he was trapped in the sword. He might still be in love with *her*, for all I knew. I sliced a sandwich in half with a vicious movement. The knife skittered over the chopping board.

Maybe he's just … clinging to me now that he's out. The way that someone who's drowning will cling to any old chunk of wood that floats past in the sea. The way a man lost in darkness will cling to his last candle.

The way a boy who lost his entire family in a single moment might desperately fight to protect the one person he has left…

Shit.

How could I have forgotten that? How – Jesus, *how* – could I have completely ignored the fact that for Shinobu, it was only yesterday that his world disappeared forever? It was barely an eyeblink since he died protecting them, and he knew he would never see them again. Never get to say goodbye. He was completely adrift in a different time, in an alien world … and I was all he had.

He was scared it would happen again. The fact that he had lost his last girlfriend would just make that even worse. If I had gone through what Shinobu had, I would be a psychotic mess. But Shinobu wasn't. He wasn't even that overprotective. He'd never tried to stop me from fighting. He just wanted me to be honest with him.

And I'd turned round and annihilated him for it.

Oh God. Oh God, what did I just do?

I dumped the butter knife in the sink, grabbed the sword and rushed into the living room.

Shinobu was standing with his back to me, staring out of one of the living-room windows into the street. His hair hung over one shoulder, leaving the line of his spine looking exposed and somehow ... vulnerable. One hand was knotted into a tight fist on the wall above his head. He was utterly motionless. Like a rock.

The sight was horribly familiar. He'd gone like this once before. Only yesterday, actually, after I'd accidentally reminded him of everything he'd lost. He'd sort of curled into himself, curled around the pain, frozen as if one unwary movement might shatter him. And now I'd done it again, but this time it wasn't just an ignorant mistake. I'd deliberately hurt him.

That time I'd left him alone. I'd walked away and left him to deal with his feelings by himself.

Well, not this time.

I swallowed hard, and slowly, slowly bent over to place the katana on the sofa. My fingers spasmed and twitched, fighting me as I forced them to release the warm, gleaming lacquer of the saya. It took a lot of effort to straighten up again and leave the sword there. I was shaking as I walked across the room to stand behind Shinobu, but I forced myself to ignore the need to turn back. This was about Shinobu now, and I had to focus on him.

He gave no sign that he had heard me come into the room or approach him. Slowly – even more slowly than I'd moved when I put the katana down – I reached out and put my arms around Shinobu's narrow waist, leaning into the warm, dense muscles of his back. I pressed my lips between his shoulder blades, resting my palms flat on his chest. The warm pines-and-smoke scent of his hair and skin met my nose.

Immediately I felt the nearness of him affect me. My heart pounded harder than it did when I thought the Shikome might be lying in wait for me. I couldn't get control of my breath. I rested my forehead against his shoulder and squeezed my eyes shut against the heat of tears. But at the same time, I could feel a terrible, cold tension easing out of me. Like I had come home. Like I was where I was supposed to be, and I was safe.

Shinobu always made me feel safe, even when my feelings for him scared the crap out of me.

At first it was as if he didn't even notice me embracing him. Maybe he'd gone somewhere so far away that he really didn't. I just held on, tight, pressing myself into the hard planes of his body in wordless apology.

Come back. Come back to me. I've got you. I won't let you go.

I won't let go.

I felt a little shudder go through him – a ragged breath dragged into his chest. His hand unclenched and dropped from the wall to his side. And then it lifted to touch mine; a tentative caress of his fingers across my knuckles that became more confident when I didn't move away. He laced our fingers together, his big hand cradling my smaller one.

"You have it completely wrong," he said finally, his voice so quiet that I could barely hear it. "I do not ... I have never felt that you belong to me."

My heart throbbed like a wound. "Why not?"

"Because it is the other way around. I am yours. Completely." He stopped, sucked in another uneven breath. "You own all of me. Forever, for as long as you live. And as long as I may stay by your side, I will have all that I need. Everything that I need."

And I had wanted some pat twenty-first century declaration of love?

The tears spilled over and I turned my face to the side so that they wouldn't soak through his T-shirt and give me away. Something tipped him off, though. He turned suddenly and took my face in his hands. His thumbs stroked the tracks of moisture away.

"I'm sorry," I said. "I don't know why I said all that

to you. I was wrong." My voice trembled and broke, but I forced myself to meet his eyes.

They were dark and very serious, and full of silvery grey shapes like clouds. But his lips quirked up on one side into a crooked smile. "Not completely wrong. I had no right to shout and demand answers, and for that I am sorry too." He stopped, and I knew he was waiting.

I sighed, a long painful exhalation. "The katana wants something from me. I don't know what, not really. It said 'freedom', but ... what does that mean to a sword? It can't get at me while it's in the saya, but I can still sense its energy. Pushing at me. Pushing constantly, trying to get in. When I fight with it, I hear it in my mind, talking to me, trying to influence me. And when I say its true name ... that's when things get really scary because I'm not always sure what thoughts, what feelings, are mine and which are..."

My voice trailed off as I remembered touching the sword, its grip, at the exact second that I had flown off the handle just now. But the blade had been sheathed. And I had already been annoyed and touchy. It couldn't influence me that much through the saya. It... I ... I couldn't face that possibility.

Shinobu drew me closer, pressing his forehead against mine. "We must find out how to break the compulsion and free you, before it damages you in some way that is irreparable."

"I can't waste time on that. No, listen, Shinobu – I'm as desperate to be rid of the sword and the compulsion as you are to have me rid of them, believe me. But everything I said to Rachel before still stands. Helping Jack and getting rid of the Shikome is more urgent than anything else. And we need the sword to do that."

His arms were almost crushing me. I felt his lips against my hair. His voice shook when he spoke. "Then fight it, Mio. You must fight it with everything you have."

"I will," I promised, even as the deep pull of need was already drawing me back to the place where the sword rested on the sofa.

"Euw. God save me from lovey-dovey teenagers," Rachel said from the doorway. I hadn't even realized she was there.

I blinked a few times and cleared my throat, dazed from the intensity of the moment.

"Remember what I said," Shinobu said softly. With a last touch to my cheek, he reluctantly released me.

Rachel gave us a sly grin, so like Jack's that my heart stuttered in my chest. I scurried away from both of them, snatching the katana up from the sofa en route to the kitchen, where I retrieved the sandwiches and some bottled water.

When I came back, Rachel had flicked on the overhead light in the living room, making me realize how dim it had grown. She had the TV remote in her hand and was frowning down at it.

"Turn it on," I said quietly. "Try to find a news programme. I have a worried feeling about what's going on out there. We need to know how bad it is."

Rachel nodded and switched on the set, flicking channels for a minute before coming across what seemed to be a press conference. A woman stood outside the front door of Number 10 Downing Street, surrounded by microphones, her face lit with constant photo flashes.

"Health Secretary Anders is unable to carry out his duties due to illness at this time," she was saying. "The prime minister has authorized me to take over."

"Can you confirm the reports that Mr Anders is in a coma?" one of the reporters shouted.

"It would be inappropriate for me to divulge any confidential medical information about Mr Anders," she responded primly. "Next question."

Another reporter called out, "What can we – the general public – do to protect ourselves from this disease?"

"Firstly, it is not a disease. It is an allergic reaction. Secondly, current information shows that around ninety-eight per cent of those admitted to hospitals with these symptoms today were outside, either when they were taken ill or immediately before. We are urging Londoners to stay inside their homes unless their journey is essential. If you are currently at work or travelling, we advise that you head for your home or the home of a friend or family member, whichever is closest."

"How many people have been affected?"

The woman looked grim. "We need to focus on helping one another at this time, not on numbers."

"What about the risk of infection from person to person?" the same reporter demanded.

"I repeat, this is not a disease. It is not infectious. There is no evidence – I repeat, none – that these contaminants are transmitted through person-to-person contact. Please do not hesitate to welcome friends and family into your home." The woman drew herself up, raising her chin. Her voice took on a rolling, pompous tone as she continued. "London is an ancient, proud city which has survived plague, fire, flood, and the *Blitzkrieg* of World War Two. I am sure that Blitz spirit will remain with its people today, and we will pull together, and work to get through this crisis—"

Rachel made an exclamation of annoyance and jabbed the remote with her finger. The TV screen went black. "They're as useless as normal," she said. "But the question is, how many of those Shikome are out there? They must have infected a lot of people for the government to be doing a public statement."

One by one, two by two… If it really had been Izanami in my vision, and if she had told me the truth, then she was somehow getting "closer" to the mortal realm, and the closer she got, the more of her Foul Women she was able to push into our world. Their numbers had to be increasing – but how quickly? How many of the Shikome would it take before the situation reached critical mass and so many people were infected that the city just fell apart?

"Hello?" Rachel interrupted my train of thought. "Are you listening? Please tell me that you have *some* sort of plan?"

I set the sandwiches and water on the coffee table and sat down on the floor next to it, shoving my hair back behind my ears. "The plan is, we're all going to eat something so none of us pass out at a crucial moment. And then I'm calling in my favour from the Kitsune. Whether they want my help or not, they still owe me theirs."

Rachel pulled a face. "They ignored you this morning," she pointed out. "What makes you think it'll be any different tonight?"

"This time I won't let them ignore me," I said grimly.

CHAPTER 8

DOWN THE RABBIT HOLE

Shinobu waited patiently, leaning on one of the extension's glass panes while Rachel wandered around the messy kitchen, not tidying so much as rearranging the mess. I stood in the back doorway, yelling for Hikaru. Then shouting the name of every other Kitsune I knew. I called for the king. I even tried a formal "summoning" in stilted Japanese that Shinobu taught me to repeat parrot-fashion when it was clear things were getting desperate.

Hikaru didn't answer.

No one did.

I didn't give up easily. It took a good couple of hours for my voice to give out. Or maybe it was my hope that failed first, not my throat. Finally I had to admit that I wasn't doing any good. That was when Rachel lost her temper. "Those sneaky, lying, ginger b—"

I glowered at her. "Stop it. They're our friends."

She folded her arms in the now-familiar defensive posture. "You are such a child, Mio. Just because people say 'I promise' doesn't mean they're your friends."

The condescending tone tweaked a nerve, and when I spoke again it was through gritted teeth. "Can you give it a rest, please? I know that you're older than me – you point it out every three seconds – but you don't know everything. When it comes to this world, you are the kid and I'm the adult."

"Excuse me?" she demanded. "What does that mean? I should be seen and not heard?"

"That'd be nice actually, yeah,"

Rachel let out a tiny scream of frustration. Vivid yellow sparked in and then flooded the dark brown of her eyes. She spun round and kicked at the pile of debris that was the ruined kitchen table. A splintered piece of wood – one of the table legs – flew up and embedded itself in the wall.

I found myself plastered against the glass of the extension. My fingers, wrapped around the hilt of the katana, were twitching with the need to pull the blade free. Shinobu rocked forward on the balls of his feet, face tense.

"Rach?" I whispered warily.

Slowly she turned round. Her expression was miserable and her eyes were clear brown. The tension eased out of me with a long shudder.

"Sorry," she muttered.

"No worries." I forced my fingers to loosen their grip on the sword, slowly letting my hand drop. "The room's a mess anyway."

I didn't quite pull off the pretence of unconcern, and Rachel's expression didn't lighten. She shoved her glasses up her nose. "I'm... I'll call the hospital again and check on Jack."

She hurried out of the room, leaving me staring at the still-vibrating chunk of wood, sunk at least a handspan deep in the wall.

"She kicked it away from us," I whispered when she was gone. "She wasn't trying to hurt us."

"This time," Shinobu said equally softly. "Has she always been prone to sudden fits of temper?"

I hesitated for a second. "I don't know. She doesn't take any crap, like Jack, but she's ... together, normally. I think. I guess, even though she's always been around, I don't know her all that well. We weren't ... friends."

But we were now. After everything we'd been through together, Rachel was no longer just Jack's bossy big sister. She was my bossy friend. And she was in trouble.

"Rachel needs a friend now. More than she realizes," Shinobu said, unknowingly echoing my thoughts.

I didn't have any answers. I sighed and changed the subject. "Why aren't the foxes responding, Shinobu?"

"You were right. Something must be very wrong

there. The Kitsune do not break their word. It is not in their nature."

I thought about the Kitsune. Daredevil Hikaru was surprisingly kind beneath his reckless façade. Hiro was clever and funny, and you never quite knew where you were with him. Araki was serenely competent, and solid as a rock. Poor Araki. I was never going to forget that awful noise she had made the last time I saw her. And even though the king scared the pants off me, he had still proved himself to be an honourable, decent ruler. What was happening down there that prevented them from at least answering me?

We needed their help desperately. Right now they were the only viable resource we had. But I was equally keen to help them if they needed it – and I had a bad feeling that they did. With me stuck here in the mortal realm, help in either direction was impossible. It was infuriating.

I plopped down on the threshold and set the katana across my lap. "Maybe they're just … busy," I said dismally. "Really busy."

Shinobu sat on the floor next to me. His arm brushed against my shoulder, and our knees bumped. "I hope you are right."

I stared at the shadowy space of the back garden, my fingers restlessly tracing the lines of the katana's hilt and saya. The lack of streetlights at the back of our row of buildings meant the whole garden was practically black, and the horrific, tangled-up remains of the Shikome were impossible to make out. I could feel the presence of the creature's body out there, though. It itched at my awareness like that sore sensation you get just before a giant spot erupts on your skin.

I'd never been scared of the dark. Not like Jack. Not even as a kid. I don't think I had enough of an imagination. But since I'd taken the sword out of its hiding place, I'd had a crash course in all the terrible things that liked to hide in the dark places. I had every reason to be terrified of shadows these days.

If things keep going wrong like this, what will I do? What if … what if there's no end? What if this darkness I'm in now stretches on forever?

"You're starting to shiver," Shinobu said. "Come back to the other room."

"No, I want to wait."

"Hikaru is capable of knocking on the door to get our attention if he suddenly appears."

I shook my head stubbornly. It was probably irrational, but I was determined not to budge from this spot. Not to give up on them. The Kitsune would come. They had to come. I would be waiting.

Shinobu sighed. "Very well."

He got up and walked out of the kitchen. I stared after him in shock, struggling with the urge to follow and apologize again. But ... no. I hadn't done anything wrong this time. It was his choice whether he wanted to wait with me, but he didn't get to decide what I was going to do.

Two minutes later he reappeared. His arms were filled with two of our big squashy tapestry cushions, Mum's angora throw and the old woollen crocheted blanket from the back of the sofa.

He quirked an eyebrow at my look of surprise. "Must we freeze to death as well? You did not mention that part."

I couldn't resist the smile that twitched at the corners of my lips. "Shut up."

He smiled back at me for a moment, then seemed to shake himself. "Rachel talked to a nurse in Jack's ward. Jack is stable."

"But she's not getting better, is she?"

He looked grave, but only said, "Rachel is going to try to rest. She says she will sleep on one of the sofas in the living room, and keep the telephone with her in case Jack or the hospital call." Bending, he arranged the blankets and pillows into a cosy nest, and then pulled me into his arms. "Is this acceptable?"

"It'll do." I sighed, letting my head rest in that oh-so-comfortable hollow in his shoulder. "Thank you. Again."

His hand found mine, which was wrapped tight around the hilt of the katana, and clasped it wordlessly.

He does care for me. He loves me, even if he can't say it yet. Even if he never says it.

"I wonder if the neighbours heard me screeching," I said into the quiet, after a while. "They must have heard something over the past couple of days. I bet they think gang members have taken over the house while my parents are away, and killed us all."

"They have not called the authorities," Shinobu pointed out.

"That's not all that surprising," I said. "No one ever wants to get involved – especially not when the city's practically on lockdown. They're most likely too busy barricading their doors and windows."

I heard Shinobu's frown in his voice. "That does not match with what the woman was talking about on your television set. She said people would pull together in times of crisis. What did she call it? Blitz spirit?"

"Hmmm." I let my head fall sideways so that I could look up at a partial view of his face. I smiled a little as his arm shifted to curl around my back. "My dad doesn't believe in Blitz spirit. He thinks everyone likes to look back on wars as golden times, and say that people all pulled together, and everyone was noble and brave. But really? Crime rates rise by, like, a hundred per cent during wartime. People loot bombed houses, and buy black-market food, inform on their neighbours. Dad said you can't expect people to act noble and brave when they feel powerless. You can only expect them to act in whatever way seems most likely to ensure their own survival. The more powerless they feel, the more desperate to save themselves they'll get, no matter what they have to do..."

My voice trailed off as my dad's words struck me anew. Just how powerless would I have to feel before I got that desperate? And how was I supposed to change things?

"Your father is cynical," Shinobu said, faintly disapproving.

"He likes to think of himself as practical. Doesn't believe anything if he can't see it with his own eyes. If he'd been here to see what we have, his head would probably explode."

"My father – my adopted father – was the opposite," he said softly.

I went still, my attention suddenly riveted on his quiet voice in the darkness. Shinobu had only spoken to me about his life with his lost family once before. "The opposite, how?" I prompted after a couple of seconds.

"He was … incredibly honourable and idealistic. He had seen many terrible battles, had killed in the course of his duty, but his faith in people and his sense of right and wrong were unwavering."

"He sounds really nice," I said wistfully.

"He was a great man." An almost noiseless sigh slipped through Shinobu's lips. I felt it move through his chest. "But he was not perfect. His idealism sometimes made him unrealistic. I did not see it then. It makes me feel disloyal to think it now. But I wonder ... if he had let the frightened villagers attack the newcomer to our village and drive him out as they wished to, would that have driven the Nekomata away also? The creature came at the same time as the newcomer did. Perhaps he led it to our lands. Perhaps..."

Now it was his voice that trailed away.

Perhaps none of this would ever have happened.

Perhaps Shinobu would have lived out his mortal life happily.

Perhaps our family would never have had the katana.

Perhaps we would never have met.

A pang of misery went through me at that last thought. But I knew it was selfish to feel that way – and I knew what Shinobu meant. What would I be doing right now, if things had been different? Hanging out with Jack and Rachel, getting ready for Christmas, laughing and messing around, living a normal, carefree life with no idea of the darkness that lurked out there. I would never have had to know this pain, this fear, all this guilt and sadness.

Or maybe not. The tiniest of changes in history could have massive effects. I had seen enough Doctor Who to realize that. If Shinobu had lived, everything might be different. Maybe the Yamato family would have made entirely different choices, or died out centuries ago, and I would never have been born. There was no way of knowing. There were no certainties.

I would have given a lot for some certainty right then.

I have the katana. But even if I could figure out how to unsheathe it and unleash its energy without letting it inside my head, I still don't know how to control it and make it do what I want instead of what it *wants. It's almost useless to me, except as a way to destroy things. It healed me after the car accident, and made me stronger, but I had no choice about either of those things. The sword does what it wants, and I'm powerless to stop it.*

How can it be right that I possess the weapon so many creatures are willing to die to get hold of, and yet I'm the one who's running and hiding? I'm the one that's afraid and powerless...

Give me what I want, the sword had whispered into my mind. I heard it now so clearly that it was almost as if the sword was speaking to me again. *I will give you power. Such power as mortals have dreamed of since the dawn of time.* Only I didn't want power or strength. Not unless they would let me fix what I had done when I took the sword from its hiding place. I just wanted to set everything right and end this nightmare.

The katana throbbed heavily under my hands, its warmth rippling against my skin in a strange, beguiling rhythm. For an instant my instincts urged me to fling it away from me. But it was so warm and comfortable in the nest of blankets, curled up next to Shinobu, and I was sleepy. Before I could even move, the knee-jerk reaction had passed, fading away as if it had never been.

I let my eyes fall closed.

The girl is waiting for Shinobu.

The woods are still and silent, their vivid red colour dimming as the sun dips below the horizon. Standing on one of the smooth stones in the garden, she shivers in the evening shadows, eyes straining against the dusk for any sign of him. Through the rice-paper screen she can hear her mother and father speaking, their voices low and tense with worry. She knows what they are saying, even though she cannot make out their words. "He should have been back by now. He should have come back."

They are right.

I should have fought harder.

I should not have said those things.

I should never have let him go alone.

A sudden wind stirs the leaves, chilling the girl to the bone as it whips around her, sending long strands of hair into her face. She brushes them aside impatiently – and something moves under the trees. Her heart leaps with fear and hope.

But it is not him. In the next instant she knows it. That is not his shape, not his walk.

I should not have let him go alone.

I should have held on…

It is another man who walks towards her out of the gathering darkness. She recognizes his long, pale face and dark robes. It is the newcomer, the wanderer Yoshida-sensei. He carries something in his hands, and when she realizes what it is, the knowledge strikes through her like a knife. She jams her knuckles against her lips to hold in a cry of denial. My sword. *The sword that Shinobu took with him when he ran away from her to fight alone.*

I should never have let go.

Suddenly the vision shifts. The tree limbs dance, their colours blurring, growing dim before my eyes. I am lying on my back, my hand clasped over my heart. The heat of my own blood pours through my fingers, scorching me. I am grown so cold, so numb.

Mio…

I hear footsteps crunching in the fallen leaves. Something moves in the corner of my eye. I twitch, but I cannot move. I catch a glimpse of a pale face, eyes glowing bright with excitement. Too bright. The light makes me flinch. Yoshida-sensei? What is that in his hand? What is it that he lifts above me?

Mottled green-brown, curved like a leaf, it gleams in the red light of the setting sun.

Why? Why, when I am already dying…

The green blade flashes down in the red light—

A gentle shake of my shoulder had me jerking bolt upright.

"Who – what?" I flexed cramping fingers around the katana's hilt, rubbing my face with my other hand. For a second, vivid, disturbing images from my dream danced in front of my eyes. They shredded away from me before I could make sense of them, leaving me with nothing more than the familiar feelings of sorrow and frustration. *Argh. Stupid dreams.*

"How long was I out?"

"Most of the night. It is nearly dawn," Shinobu said.

"Never mind that!" Rachel's voice broke in excitedly from somewhere above me. "Look."

I took my hand away from my eyes and gasped when I saw that Shinobu's face was lit with dancing copper light. The whole kitchen shimmered with it. We cast long black shadows over the wreckage strewn across the floor. Rachel was pointing to the garden. I turned to look.

My eyes skipped uneasily past the body of the Shikome to the unruly mulberry bush that grew by the garage. It was glowing, incandescent with all the shades of autumn. Red and gold and bronze rays pierced the foliage, and the leaves tossed wildly, as if there was a high wind in the garden. Their movement made the copper light flash like the neon displays at Blackpool Pier.

I'd only seen this light shining from the mulberry twice before. Both times Hikaru had stepped out of the bush within a few seconds. But there was no sign of any of the Kitsune now. The bush just sat there, glowing and rustling and flashing.

"What are they waiting for?" I muttered.

"Maybe…" Shinobu said slowly. "Maybe they want us to go to them."

I looked from him to the urgently blinking lights.

"But you need someone to create a rift in the veil between this world and the spirit realm. You need someone to hold it open while you pass through." *And you need to be sure that whatever is waiting for you on the other side is something that doesn't want to eat you…*

"Maybe there are other ways," Rachel suggested, shifting from foot to foot impatiently. "Come on, we have to try! The Kitsune might know how to help Jack!"

She was right. If those lights went out while I was hesitating, I'd want to drown myself.

"OK." I kicked blankets away from my legs and got up, adjusting my grip on the saya and hilt of my sword as I did so. Shinobu picked up his katana and wakizashi and shoved both sheathed blades into his sash.

"You go in the middle," I told Rachel. "And go quickly. We don't know what else might be waiting out there."

She nodded jerkily. "One, two…"

"Three," Shinobu finished.

We squashed through the doorway together. My head wanted to tilt back to check the sky, and my ears strained for the telltale thunder of wing-beats. I fixed my eyes on the light and ran. I reached the glowing mulberry bush half a step ahead of Rachel and two ahead of Shinobu.

After skidding to my knees in front of it, I crammed myself under the spiny branches, shoving the katana in ahead of me. A twig nearly poked my eye out, and I hissed as it scraped my cheek but didn't slow down. As I was ferreting my way under this bush, Shinobu and Rachel were stuck out there in the open, unsafe space of the garden.

Shinobu was stuck alone with Rachel…

I kept crawling forward, twigs scraping my scalp and back, wet soil squelching under my knees, and the stink of cat pee in my nose. I was expecting to take a tumble at any time. Last time we'd done this, the ground had dropped right out from under me and sent me plummeting helplessly into the earthy darkness of Between – a sort of airlock space that the Kitsune conjured up whenever they opened a gateway into the spirit realm, to stop anything nasty making a run for it from either side.

Come on, where are you? Where's the rupture?

A huge earthy paw reached up out of the ground and engulfed me.

The air left my lungs with a squeak, my vision swam with distant silvery shapes, and I thought my eardrums were going to burst. I could feel myself moving, but I was immobilized, trapped and powerless.

Then, with a sound exactly like a belch, the paw released me.

I landed face down in soft, sweet-smelling grass.

For the space of a few relieved gasps I lay there, letting the water stream from the corners of my eyes onto the mossy cushion of greenery under my cheek. There was another belch and a thud, and I turned my head to see Rachel flat on the grass beside me, looking as messed up as I felt. Her hair stood out around her head in a fuzzy halo, and there was a long streak of mud across her chin.

"What – what was—?" she gasped, making no effort to move.

Then Shinobu popped up through the grass in a sort of wave of soil that broke under him and then rolled over, flattening out to smooth green as if it had never been there. He crouched alertly, his eyes darting from me to Rachel. "Are you both unharmed?"

Rachel shrugged.

I nodded limply. "What about you?"

He took a deep breath, moved his shoulders experimentally, and nodded back. His hair had tumbled down out of its plait, and he had a dirty smudge on his cheek.

"Hikaru did tell us last time that it could've been worse…" I muttered.

"My ears are burning," a familiar voice called out dryly. "I hope you're saying nice things about me."

A glossy, copper-coated fox with a bright white blaze

on his chest and a white-tipped tail was approaching us. His eyes – a vivid, unforgettable green that I'd never seen on any human, but which somehow looked perfectly natural on him, even like this – glinted at me.

Hikaru in his fox form.

I managed a smile for him. "We were just wondering if you'd managed to get out of those white leather trousers on your own, or if you needed help. And a shoehorn."

"He is probably still wearing them, under the fur," Shinobu said, dead-pan.

Hikaru let out a hoarse barking noise. Fox laughter. I took the opportunity to heave myself to my knees and look around properly. We were in a tunnel. Not surprising, as the entire Kingdom of the Kitsune was underground – the Underground actually. It occupied the space scooped out by London's Tube lines and stations. But this place was vastly different to the soggy, shadowy chambers we'd passed through last time.

The walls and ceiling that curved around us were made of massive swathes of vivid purple-and-white flowers. The blossoms looked a little bit like wisteria, but the petals were much bigger and more deeply coloured. They stirred gently as I watched. Silvery white light shone around and through them. The tunnel extended as far as my eye could follow, both in front of and behind us. It felt like being inside the giant stone in Jack's prized amethyst thumb ring.

"Where are we?" I asked.

"A place I'm pretty sure no other humans have been allowed to visit," Hikaru said, sitting down with his front paws placed neatly together. "This is the entrance to His Majesty's palace. It took a butt-load of hard work to get you here, and we don't have all day. Jack needs to hurry up and get her sweet self through that rupture."

My breath caught and suddenly, stupidly, my eyes prickled with tears. I realized that some part of me had been waiting for Jack to appear here too. Since we'd become friends, Jack had been a part of every adventure, every mess I got into, either one step ahead of me or one step behind. She was always *there*.

I blinked rapidly as I glanced at Rachel. Her face was stony. Clearly it was up to me to break the news. I took a deep breath. "Jack's not coming."

Hikaru's ears and whiskers drooped. His unrequited crush on my best friend was still burning bright. "Why?" he blurted out. "I mean – is she busy or something?"

Rachel's eyes narrowed. She opened her mouth.

I jumped in hastily. "Jack's sick. That's partly why we need your help."

Hikaru's head jerked up, his jaws gaping open to reveal sharp fangs. It was the first time I'd ever seen him speechless. Then he was on his paws, tail lashing the air behind him. Tiny sparks of white lightning crackled up and down the thick brush of copper fur. "Please tell me it's just some stupid human disease. Something she ate — or — or — a headache or something, right?"

I shook my head wordlessly.

"She has the taint of the Shikome?"

"Taint?" Rachel repeated, as if the word offended her.

"A Shikome attacked her," I said slowly. "She's in the hospital."

A bolt of lightning crackled out of his tail and disappeared into the flowers overhead. Thunder rumbled through the tunnel, and the purple flowers shivered.

"Come on," he said urgently. "The king is waiting for you."

CHAPTER 9

BLITZ SPIRIT FOX

Rachel, Shinobu and I trotted after Hikaru through the corridor of flowers. An imperceptible breeze stirred the petals around us; I heard silvery bells chiming in the distance and high, sweet voices singing songs without words. The flowers had a pleasant, vanilla-ish scent. Beneath that there was another smell, a strong, salty odour a bit like the beach at low tide. The strange light rippled and ebbed through the walls of the corridor as if we were under water.

Holy crap, maybe we were under water.

Don't think about it. You don't want to know.

I asked Hikaru, "Where were you earlier? We shouted for you for ages – I was really worried."

"And how did you learn that the Foul Women had invaded London?" Shinobu put in.

"How do you think?" Hikaru responded brusquely.

"Our scouts encountered them. Hurry up."

I frowned. "That still doesn't explain why it took you so long to answer me. Hikaru, what is going on in the Kingdom? Are you in trouble too?"

Before Hikaru could reply, a new voice broke in. "I am the one who should answer that question, sword-bearer."

The intense power carried in those soft, musical tones made my legs quiver with the desire to fall to my knees. *The king.*

Hikaru stopped in his tracks and turned to face a section of the flower wall that was shivering and dancing as if someone had turned on a wind machine behind it. He sank down into a prone position, planted his nose in the grass, and rolled one bright eye at us.

I suddenly remembered that there were different rules in the Kitsune Kingdom. I made a hurried "Get down!" gesture at Rachel and then, trying not to feel ridiculous, bowed formally, fixing my eyes on my feet. Shinobu followed Hikaru's example and knelt, placing his forehead on the backs of his hands, which he pressed flat to the ground. Rachel stood stubbornly for a moment, then grumped under her breath and finally knelt down next to Shinobu. She bowed her head, but didn't lower it fully. Putting my frustration with and worry for her to one side – had she always been so bloody stubborn? – I focused on the task at hand.

"Your Majesty. Thank you for agreeing to see us."

"There is no need for such thanks. Not from you. Rise, please."

Hikaru, Rachel and Shinobu got to their feet, and I slowly straightened up.

It was all I could do to keep my jaw attached to my face. It wanted to hit the floor. Hard.

The thick layers of purple blooms had twisted up into swirls and knots overhead, revealing a gargantuan opening – the size of a double-decker bus – in the side of the tunnel wall. Beyond that was a cavernous chamber, nearly as big as the Kitsune amphitheatre we had visited last time. Its ceiling was clustered with slender, spiralling stalactites that looked exactly like the white horn on a unicorn's head. Except that these were about twenty feet long. Dozens of blue fox lights danced in among the pale spears of rock. The floor of the cavern was flooded with a glassy expanse of water, so dark and still that it looked black. Smooth white rocks, splashed with vivid yellow, orange and blue lichens, ringed the pool. But the cave, beautiful as it was? Was nothing compared to the king.

The king stood at the edge of the pool, in human form. And that human form, unless I needed glasses … was a she.

Like some of the older Kitsune I'd seen in their human shapes, he – she – looked very young. If I'd seen her – him – in the street, I'd have thought I was looking at someone about the same age as me or maybe younger.

Straight hair fell in a coppery waterfall to her shoulders, framing a delicate, heart-shaped face, with a dusting of golden freckles across the nose and cheekbones. She was a little shorter than me and built like a greyhound, with limbs and waist so tiny they looked like an angry stare would snap them. She was wearing a pretty white linen sundress. It had a wide green ribbon tied at the waist. The bow sat at the small of her back, and just below it, her luxuriant tails – all nine of them – poked out of a carefully shaped hole in the linen. They fanned the air gently.

The dress, which bared not only her thin, freckly shoulders and arms but quite a lot of her chest, made it impossible to believe that the king was cross-dressing for a lark today. She was definitely all woman. I'd have been tempted to believe that I'd misunderstood somehow, and this was another one of the king's subjects I was meeting – except for those eyes. Acid-green, and glowing with age and power, they were unmistakable. Meeting them was like trying to push an elephant over. After the first second, it took everything you had just to stay upright.

While I tried to work out if I'd somehow imagined everyone calling the king "Grandfather" and referring to her as "he" and "His Majesty", the king picked her way delicately across the white stones towards us. Green enamel earrings, shaped like apples, swung at her ears. When I glanced down, I saw that her tiny feet were bare, and the toenails were painted a matching shade of pale green.

"My apologies for the delay," she said, arriving in front of me. She inclined her head in the smallest possible bow. It was still a huge concession from someone so much older and more powerful than me. A tiny arc of blue electricity fizzled between two of her tails. "My people are unable to enter the mortal realm at this time. I was forced to create a rupture that would bring you through Between safely without a guide – a time-consuming task."

I cleared my throat. She might look like I could pick her up and toss her across the tunnel with one hand, but she was still a ruthless, extremely dangerous immortal who had nearly caused Jack's death the last time we came here. Favour or not, I had to get my brain in the game. *And stop staring at her boobs!*

"Apology accepted, Your Majesty," I said. My voice sounded a bit shaky – that was nothing new. "But can you tell me *why* your people can't enter the mortal realm? Is it to do with the Shikome?"

The king let out a nearly soundless sigh. "Walk with me, sword-bearer. I find movement helps me to think." She gestured for me to follow her into the cavern.

"Grandmother," Hikaru began urgently. *Oh,* now *it's Grandmother.* "My friend Jack—"

The king silenced Hikaru with a look that held equal

parts sadness and warning. "I heard what was said. Let me speak to Yamato-dono, Grandson. The two of us have much to discuss."

Hikaru snapped his mouth shut, his expression one of foxy dismay. I sympathized; I wasn't sure I was looking forward to this private chat too much myself.

Shinobu gave me an encouraging look.

I pulled out a smile for him and Rachel, then followed the king into the cavern. Behind me, the ropes of flowers unravelled with a faint papery whisper, veiling the entrance again.

Her Majesty walked between me and the deep green-black stillness of the pool, her face as enigmatic as the water. One of her hands reached into the pocket of her sundress and then jerked out towards the pool. White crumbs scattered from her palm, hit the pool, and sank without a ripple.

"The Kitsune are immortal," she said quietly, as if continuing a conversation we'd already begun. "In theory we can live … forever. Time does not touch us, except to bless us with greater wisdom and strength. But in reality, most fox spirits never achieve even their half millennium. Do you know why this is?" Her hand flicked out again. Again, the crumbs sank without a trace.

Great, a test. And I didn't revise…

No. Wait a second. I know this.

I'd once seen a line of hardened Kitsune warriors go

145

down as if they'd been clothes-lined. The spell which had done it had rolled right off me. Not long afterwards I'd seen them bleed and scream with pain as they did battle with the Nekomata's army of feral cats. Kitsune were not invulnerable.

"Because," I said slowly, "you can be killed. Your people are vulnerable to magic and violence, just like mortals."

"Observant," she said with dry approval. "And what other things are mortals vulnerable to?"

It took me a second, but then the light bulb flickered to life above my skull. "Disease," I breathed. "This … taint, Hikaru called it … Kitsune are affected the same as humans? That – that poor girl who came through the portal just before we left here. Was she—?"

The king's tails lashed behind her. Blue sparks flashed and then faded at their white tips. She came to a halt, staring into the water. Her hand reached into her pocket and flung out towards the dark pool for the third time. This time as the crumbs began to sink, something stirred beneath the surface. I saw slow, sinuous movements – something silver that glinted and flashed in the jellylike depths of the water.

Suddenly a long, supple neck rose up out of the pool, snapping at the air with narrow jaws that bristled with jagged ivory fangs. Opaque white eyes glared blindly. Its feathery tail slapped at the surface, churning it up. The king threw more crumbs. The water-creature writhed and whirled, as graceful as a silk ribbon moving in the wind, dived, then came back up again with a crash of water as a second white head rose beside it. The two creatures – water dragons? – darted and snapped at each other, now entwining, now struggling apart.

"She was only one hundred and four years old," the king said, dragging my attention away from the duelling serpents. Their noise wasn't enough to hide the king's soft voice from my ears – but I was sure that no one outside the cavern would be able to overhear us, even with sharp fox ears. "It was a routine scouting patrol. They were unprepared, unafraid. She had no chance at all."

"I'm sorry," I whispered. The words felt plastic and meaningless, but they were all I had.

She went on as if I hadn't spoken. "So long as the Foul Women fly outside their rightful realm, no human can recover from their taint. Only with their banishment will the spread of the plague be halted and reversed. But for a Kitsune, there is never any hope of recovery at all. My people have no defence against the illness that Izanami's Handmaidens spread. Once tainted, death is almost instant."

For people that could hope to live for thousands of years, how terrifying would it be to face an illness that wiped you out, just like that? An illness that none of your magic or your wisdom could fight?

"I must protect my people," she went on, a hint of steel in her voice. "Even with my strongest calls, some of those who were in the mortal realm when the Shikome appeared have not returned. I do not know how many of them are already lost to us forever – but I will lose no more. Not one more. I will hold this kingdom together."

There was the Blitz spirit, all right. I wanted to say that I was sorry again, but the implications of what she was saying were sinking in, and they made me feel cold and numb.

We were on our own.

The Kitsune were trapped here in the spirit realm. There would be no help from them this time around. No fearless fox army to march with us against the unknown numbers of Foul Women swarming on London. No sardonic Hiro or competent Araki to back us up. No Hikaru. If we intended to fight the Shikome, we'd be doing it by ourselves. Involuntarily my fingers tightened on the katana's sheath. The sword's energy pulsed irregularly in my grip, warm but ragged, like a panicked heartbeat.

I can do this. I can still do this. I defeated the Nekomata alone in the end. I can do what needs to be done. I swallowed a couple of times, trying to get some saliva back into my dry, sticky mouth.

"But they *can* be banished? You said… Can the Shikome be destroyed or sent back to Yomi?"

The king nodded, her gaze on the antics of the white water-creatures.

"How?"

She looked me in the face. "I was younger than Hikaru is now the last time that my people encountered the Foul Women, in the old country. We lost my father to them, and countless other friends and relations, before they were finally banished from the mortal realm. I was too small and too distressed to truly understand what was happening then. But I do know that we Kitsune had nothing to do with our own salvation. A greater force – some even whispered that it was a divine force – intervened and returned the Foul Women to the Underworld. As to how it was done ... I do not know."

It was like the roundhouse kick to the gut that finishes you off. I took an unsteady step back, my breath whistling out between my teeth.

What do we do now? What are we supposed to do? How am I going to fix this?

I wanted to scream and stomp and kick and hit out at anything or anyone close enough to touch. I kept myself still with an effort that made me tremble. I'd been threatened with the king's lightning bolts before – I didn't want to repeat the experience.

As I stood there, my body singing with tension, she turned fully away from the pool for the first time. Behind her right shoulder, I saw the white serpents drifting on the dark surface of the water. They were braided around each other with their sharp muzzles touching. But what she said next made my gaze snap back to her face. "Do not despair. I think I know a way for you to find the knowledge you seek, sword-bearer."

"Then please tell me," I begged.

"You must realize by now that the blade you carry is more than a mere weapon. Whatever its true nature and wherever it came from, it has powers that I have never seen before. Such powers may be strong enough to banish the Shikome, if anything can."

I looked down at the katana, my eyes absently following the black-and-gold patterns that I knew by heart as my mind whirred with the king's words. Ever since I had called the sword's true name, seen its column of light pierce the sky, watched universes blow out and die in that light's shadow, I had known the sword was more than just a weapon.

It was The Weapon.

But even if I could somehow hunt down and kill every Shikome that had invaded London, the way I had the Nekomata, that wouldn't stop Izanami from sending more. It wouldn't banish the illness that the monsters spread with their infected feathers. And I had no idea how to summon or control whatever other powers the sword might have, the ones that might allow me to truly banish the creatures or help the people they had infected.

It wasn't like I could ask the katana; it wanted to be in the driving seat, not put me there.

"Maybe you're right," I whispered. "But this thing didn't come with a handy how-to guide, and based on my track record so far, whatever I try is only going to make things ten times worse." My breath hitched in my chest and I realized with horror that I was on the verge of tears. Again. Jack would disown me if I kept this up.

"You need instruction."

I risked a glance up, hoping my eyes hadn't already gone red and watery. The king was still staring at me, unblinking.

I nodded. "Yes."

"There are locations in the human world where the energies of other realms strain against the veil more strongly for some reason, where the veil itself seems thinner and more permeable. In those places even normal humans, who lack the ability to see yokai and spirits or to sense magic, as you can, feel the difference. Humans call them fairy mounds, cursed woods … haunted houses, if any mortal was so unwise as to attempt to build there. We call such a place a nexus. There is a very powerful nexus in London. We believe that several realms – not only the mortal and spirit realm – are present in that place. This nexus is occupied by someone who calls himself a man. He has the appearance of a man, dresses and lives and eats just as a man might, so that he draws no attention to himself. But he is not a man."

"Then what is he?"

"Old. Very old. The nature of this being is hard to ascertain. It is cloaked by the overwhelming energy of the nexus, which may be why he chooses to live there. But the savour of his power is something close to that of your sword – close to the very eldest of my kind that I have met. I think he is powerful. And, to live as he does, drawing so little attention, wise too. He has dwelled in that place since long before I brought my people across the sea from our homeland. He never leaves."

"You think he might know how to control the sword's power? How to use it to banish the Foul Women?" I said.

She nodded.

"But why would he want to help us, even if he could? If he's that powerful, he probably isn't scared of the Shikome or their taint."

"He may refuse to venture outside of his den, but we have observed him nonetheless. He is known to have a fond feeling for young ones. When homeless children shelter from the weather in the doorway of his home, they always leave healthy and healed, and often experience sudden, inexplicable turns of good fortune. Once, he was visited – purely by chance – by a family which included a small child who had been undergoing treatment for a human malaise called leukaemia. The child was very ill. Within two days of that visit, she had miraculously recovered. She lives to this day."

"So you think he's ... good?"

"It is a mistake to label any being of power in such a way. Let us say that he may be willing to take an interest in your plea and is unlikely to attempt to harm you," she said wryly. "That is as definite as I care to be. But if you want his aid, you must go to him."

"To this nexus place?"

"It is situated beneath an occult bookshop called The Avalon. The being runs this business and lives in an apartment above it. The shop is on Museum Street."

I'd never heard of the shop, but the address was unexpected. "Museum Street? That's maybe a mile from my house, if that."

"An intriguing coincidence." The king paused. "If that is what it is."

"It has to be, doesn't it?" I said, not really protesting but struggling to make sense of it. "My family only came to Britain from Japan a few decades ago. You said the – being – had been here for centuries before that."

The king flicked more crumbs into the water. Instantly the entwined dragons wrenched apart and turned on each other, snarling. The water of the pool thrashed and turned silver with bubbles as the monsters fought. "But your family carried the sword with them when they came," she said softly. "And a meitou as powerful as yours can often have a strange way of … *influencing* those who wield it. Your sword may have its own agenda. That is a fact, Mio-dono, that you would do well to bear in mind."

I took in a slow, steadying breath and nodded to show that I had heard and understood. "There's … there's one more thing, Your Majesty. It's about Rachel. Jack's sister. She is the one your Kitsune helped us rescue from Battersea. While the Nekomata had her, it – it fed from her. And now she's—"

"Changing," the king finished. Her profile was mournful as she stared at the water. "You are beset by sorrows, are you not?"

I swallowed past the tightness that clutched at my bruised throat. "You already knew something was wrong with her, didn't you? That's what you meant when you warned me to keep my eye on her."

"Few humans survive a Nekomata's bite, sword-bearer. Very few. The ones that do … sometimes live long and happy lives. Lives where they might, perhaps, be known for their unusual speed or strength, or even simply for their excellent night vision. Sometimes. But sometimes they are not so lucky. Sometimes they succumb to the venom that flows in their veins. They mutate. They lose control. And then…"

"They die?" I whispered.

She gave me a sharp, sidelong look. "People like you must kill them."

CHAPTER 10

AND THEN THERE
WERE TWO

T he thick curtain of flowers fell shut behind me, hiding
the king and the pool cavern from view. Hikaru and
Shinobu were waiting where I'd left them. Rachel had
paced off a little way to the side, but came hastily back as
I emerged. Shinobu moved towards me, his fingers reaching out to run lightly down my arm. As I met his eyes his
brows creased, and he stepped into me, slipping his arm
around my shoulder as if he thought I needed support.
Maybe I did. I let myself lean against him, taking comfort
from his steady presence.

"What?" Hikaru said uneasily. "Hey, it's rude to have
silent conversations, you know."

A similar thought was clearly going through Rachel's
mind. She lifted her eyebrows at me expectantly. I rubbed
my free hand over my eyes, blocking out her face. It was
a struggle to get my thoughts in order. The first thing

that popped into my head – no, not the first thing, but the first thing I could safely say – was "You could have warned me the king was a woman."

Hikaru blinked at me. "Huh? Why?"

Now it was my turn to blink.

"Who cares? Focus!" Rachel said. "What did she say about Jack?"

How much am I allowed to say? How much can I bear to say?

"Short answer," I said finally. "They're in a tough situation and they can't really help us right now."

"What?" Rachel's voice escaped as a squeak. She stared at me in disappointment and disbelief.

Hikaru groaned. "Damn. I thought for sure when we went to all that trouble to get you here that Her Majesty had something up her sleeve. I'm sorry."

I fought off the urge to bend down and stroke him comfortingly. He wasn't a family pet. Anyway, it would have been more for my comfort than for his. Oh God, how could I explain everything to Rachel? How could I even look her in the eye when I knew that all I could do for her was wait and see? It just wasn't enough. It wasn't enough.

"Mio, what are we going to do? Tell us everything the king said. There must be something!" Rachel demanded impatiently.

"I – um, apparently, there's someone else who might

be able to help us, or at least give us more information," I said, and gave them a bare bones explanation, finishing with, "Any humans who are infected should get better, if we can just banish the Shikome before..." *Before they all die.* Somehow that didn't exactly seem like good news.

I was startled to see Shinobu's face light with dawning excitement. The drifting grey clouds in his dark eyes seemed almost silver in the strange light of the flower tunnel. "If Her Majesty is right, this could be an extraordinary opportunity for us," he said. "This being could answer so many questions. He may even be able to tell us—" He broke off abruptly, but his arms tightened around me, almost painfully. What had broken through Shinobu's calm like this?

Knowledge, I realized. This might be our chance to find out how Shinobu's spirit had been bound to the blade – and why – and whether I was right about the Harbinger's involvement. Shinobu could finally learn why this terrible thing had happened to him. Make sense of it all.

A terrifying feeling swamped me. A feeling I'd experienced once before, when Jack and Shinobu and I stood in Battersea Power Station in the pitch-black, waiting for the Nekomata to find us. *It's all changing. Everything's changing. I can feel it.*

For a dizzying instant I was the epicentre of a massive

quake, but the thing that shifted wasn't the earth under my feet. It was reality itself. Vast, unseen powers whirled around me, ripping the universe apart and reordering it. When the sensation faded, as abruptly as it had come, I was sure that the world had changed in some way, great or small.

I just didn't know how.

"So there might be a way to help Jack after all? Help all of us?" Hikaru was asking.

I tried to arrange my expression into something blank, something normal. Or at least not bat-shit crazy, which was how I felt. "Yeah," I managed to say. "We've got a chance, I think."

"Then we should go," Shinobu said decisively. "You can tell us more when we get back to the house."

Rachel nodded in agreement, and Hikaru got up. "I'll take you to the rupture site."

The singing behind the flowers was louder and more mournful now; the bells sounded like something from a funeral dirge, and underneath there was a sound like quiet weeping. It sent shivers down my spine.

"What is it with the sound effects?" I asked Hikaru irritably, unable to ignore it any longer.

Hikaru looked back over his shoulder. "What sound effects?"

Shinobu raised his eyebrows at me. He was just as clueless as the Kitsune. Rachel kept walking, too absorbed in her own thoughts to respond.

"Right," I mumbled. "Never mind."

Hikaru came to a halt in a part of the tunnel that looked the same as all the rest to me, and sat down in the grass.

I looked around. "Is this it?"

Hikaru nodded, his front paws kneading uneasily at the grass. "Look, before you go, I just... Is she...? How did it happen? To Jack?"

Rachel stiffened. I sighed. My head was aching and full of uncertainties and questions with no answers. There were so many complicated feelings that needed to be dodged around here – including mine, even. The last thing I wanted was to talk about that awful moment in the garden when Jack had turned from my anchor in the storm to the weight on my back. I didn't even want to think about it.

But we owed Hikaru. All of us. He had listened to Jack when she asked for his help, and gone out on a limb to get us an audience with the king. He'd helped us navigate the spirit realm and the political intricacies of the Kitsune Court. He'd stuck up for us against his own family and risked the king's anger – and much as the king clearly liked his youngest descendant, he did *not* play favourites. Without Hikaru, we would never have got Rachel back, and the Nekomata would still be rampaging through London.

Rachel turned away as I began, "It was this morning – yesterday morning now, I suppose. She'd gone out into the back garden of our house—"

"Alone?" Hikaru interrupted, tail lashing. "She knew it wasn't safe out there! I told you both that our protections only covered the house."

"We didn't know about the Shikome then," I said, the familiar stab of guilt making my tone sharper than I'd intended. "The Nekomata was dead and I'd told Jack that I thought something was wrong with you guys. She wanted to make sure you were all right."

Hikaru went very still. I waited to see if he was going to say anything, but he just stared at me, his eyes unnervingly like his grandmother's.

I went on, "I don't think she got the chance to call you. We – we heard her yell and went running out. By the time we got to her she was already down and it was—"

"Too late," Hikaru finished in a whisper.

Rachel whirled around like a tiny, curly-haired hurricane and stabbed her finger through the air towards Hikaru. "Do not say that. Do not say *too late*. Jack would kick your ass for that attitude. She's alive, she's fighting, and she's got us, all of us, looking out for her. It isn't too late for *anything*."

I took a deep breath, then nodded firmly in support. "Damn right."

Rachel gave me a grateful look. There was no sign of

the Nekomata on her face, just protective big-sister fury. I patted her awkwardly on the shoulder.

"Sorry," Hikaru said, a little shaken. "Really. I didn't – I really didn't mean it like that."

"Just don't go giving up on her that easily, all right?" I said.

He flashed me a tiny, foxy grin. "I never give up."

Something boomed through the tunnel, making us all jump. I leapt away from Rachel and half-drew the katana before I realized what I was doing and hastily shoved it back in its saya.

"Hikaru, do not delay our allies any longer," the king's voice said sternly, echoing among the flowers. Petals drifted down onto the grass around us. "They have much to accomplish, and much of what they must do is vital for Kitsune as well as mortal."

Hikaru looked chastened. "Sorry, Grandmother."

"You are forgiven," the king boomed, from wherever she was. *Magical intercom?* "Sword-bearer, before you leave – I have been remiss. Despite our present situation, it is still our intention to fulfil our promise to you. It grieves me to turn you away with so little aid today. If you are able to free London of this taint which has fallen upon it, the Kingdom of the Kitsune will owe you another debt. One which can never be repaid. Banish the Shikome, and you will become an adopted daughter of the foxes. Banish the Shikome, and the London Kitsune

161

will honour you and your descendants always. Banish the Shikome, sword-bearer."

"I'm going to try," I said. *I'll die trying if I have to.*

A sizzling ring of blue-white lightning sprang up on the grass a step away from me and Shinobu. Hikaru danced back quickly, just avoiding getting his paws scorched. The long tendrils of lightning twined and pulsed, growing until the ring was big enough for a person to pass through. The grass within the lightning ring disappeared, leaving a dark hole. We stepped forward to stand on the edge.

"Geronimo?" Shinobu murmured.

I nodded. Rachel stepped off the edge and disappeared. Shinobu and I jumped into the darkness together.

"Good luck!" Hikaru shouted after us. "And remember – don't die!"

My first instinct on walking through the kitchen door was to keep going straight out the front one, and then on until we found this mysterious bookshop and its owner. But common sense – and a strong need to pee – got in the way. A glance at the clock over the sink in the kitchen showed that it wasn't eight o'clock in the morning yet. Would the being open his doors this early? Would he even be awake?

I ran to the loo and tidied myself up a bit, then found the katana's harness in the living room where I'd left it last night. I fitted the sword into place and buckled up. When I came back, Shinobu was waiting for me in the kitchen, alone. I turned to him questioningly. My face must have given away my anxiety.

"Rachel is using the bathroom upstairs," he assured me quickly, stepping forward to take me in his arms. "She seemed normal. Calm."

I let out a long sigh, leaning my head against him and feeling myself relax, just a tiny bit. "Good. That's … good."

"What did the king tell you?" Shinobu asked very quietly. I knew he wasn't asking for more details about the bookshop owner this time.

"Nothing useful," I admitted. "She – she basically said we had to wait and see. God. If I—"

I heard light footsteps on the stairs and shut my mouth hurriedly as Shinobu and I broke apart. Rachel popped in a second later with a casual greeting. She'd washed her face, changed her T-shirt, and pulled her hair back into a neat French plait. She looked tidy, healthy, and totally herself. There was no reason for the sight of her to send that quick chill down my spine.

I don't know what I'm becoming… she had said.

I opened my mouth with no idea what I was going to say, but before I could speak, a tinny, annoying tune suddenly filled the air. "Wind Beneath My Wings"? It took me a blink to realize that it was my phone. At some point Jack must have reprogrammed my ringtone again. I fumbled it out of my pocket. *Euw, don't let it be my dad...*

"Hello?"

"Hey, She-Ra." The voice was low and bruised-sounding, but there was no mistaking my best friend.

"Jack!" Shinobu and Rachel both hurried to my side as I went on. "How are you doing? Are you OK?"

There was a muffled cough. "Great. Perfect. Place is like..." She stopped, sounding as if she was trying to catch her breath. "You know, a spa. What are you up to?"

Rachel prodded my arm. "Let me talk to her."

"Wait a second," I said. "Sorry, Jack, just Rachel being bossy. We just got back from the spirit realm. We talked to the king."

"Sounds like ... fun," she said raspily. "How did that work out? No – wait – turn video call on?"

I obeyed, beckoning Rachel and Shinobu to stand behind me so that when I turned the phone sideways and held it up, Jack could see all of us.

My phone showed Jack lying back in her hospital bed, hair standing up in uncombed tufts around her face. Her skin had a funny, chalky quality. It made her look almost grey, especially next to the livid purple rash on her face. There were deep shadows around her eyes and under her cheekbones, which stood out painfully sharply. It had been less than a day since I'd seen her last – how was it possible that she had lost so much weight?

"Hi, guys. How's it going?"

I bit my lip, trying to get my reaction to Jack's appearance under control.

"Fine. What's going on there?" Rachel asked, surging into the silence I had left. "Are they treating you OK? Do you need anything?"

Jack shrugged a little, sending the neckline of her hospital gown slipping off one shoulder. I could see the ugly purplish marks spreading down over her chest. "Like I said. Fine—"

Her voice cut off as she started coughing again, turning her face away from the screen. For a second all we had was a blurred shot of a hospital pillow as the phone jerked in Jack's hands. Harsh, dry coughing barked down the line, followed by ragged breaths.

Rachel turned away with a muttered swear word. She pulled the band from the end of her plait and yanked her hands through the wavy strands of her hair so hard that I was surprised she didn't pull half of it out. My own fingers had gone bloodless as they clutched at the phone. The plastic case let out an ominous crack. Shinobu reached out and steadied my grip before I could drop it or crush it.

"Jack-san?" he asked gently. "Are you still there?"

"Wait… Wait. I'm … here." Jack's face came back into view. Her voice was even rougher and she was clearly fighting for air, but she acted like the coughing fit had never happened. "You ... find out anything useful ... from the Kitsune?"

"Yeah, we think so. We're about to head out to do some investigating. We'll figure it out soon," Rachel promised, her voice unnaturally cheerful.

Jack's sunken eyes seemed to brighten. "Really? Good work ... team. Be careful ... out there ... though."

"Don't worry about us," I said firmly, finally getting my voice back. "I'm a badass, remember?"

She snorted feebly. "Says ... who?"

"Says the Nekomata. Except – oh, it can't, because I lopped its head off and threw it in the Thames. Booyah."

Jack let out a tiny laugh. *Success.* Then the laugh turned into a short, nasty cough and I felt worse than ever. After a couple of gasps, Jack nodded. "Yeah ... all right. You can pull ... the badass thing ... off."

"I will keep an eye on both of them," Shinobu promised, solemnly.

"Yes. You just worry about taking care of yourself," Rachel said. "Call us again if you need anything."

"Will do. Catch you later ... space cadets. Good ... luck."

The screen went dark.

We all stood, motionless, staring at the blank screen of the phone, for a long moment. Finally I lowered my hand and shoved the phone back into my pocket.

"She looks so..." Rachel said softly, moving behind

the island to collapse down onto one of the kitchen stools.

"We did not lie to her," Shinobu said. "The Kitsune King has given us a valuable piece of information, and we will follow it wherever it leads us."

"But she's all alone there, and she's so sick." Rachel stared blankly at the floor, then raised her eyes to mine hopefully. "I feel a lot better. Almost like normal. I could go back to the hospital and visit her."

"No!" The protest shot out of my lips like a bullet. I saw Shinobu wince, and cleared my throat. *Shit.* "I don't think that's a great idea. We need you with us."

Rachel's eyes, which had gone wide when I shouted so suddenly, slowly narrowed. "You want to keep me away from Jack."

"No, it's not that." I stopped. "Well, maybe a little bit. We agreed she was better off without us there, right?"

There was another humming pause as Rachel got off the kitchen stool and stood facing me from the other side of the breakfast bar. "What did the king tell you about me? I'm not stupid, Mio. I know you asked her, but you haven't said a word. What did she say?"

I forced myself to meet her eyes, even though I wanted to squeeze mine shut. *You can't be a coward as well as an idiot.*

"Well?"

I thought frantically, trying to present the king's words in the best light. "She said … not many people survive a Nekomata bite. The ones that do sometimes develop strange abilities, like strength or speed, or even just really good vision."

"And?"

I hesitated.

"For God's sake!" She spoke through gritted teeth. I could see tiny yellow sparks swirling in her eyes. "For once in your life stop trying to spin everything and just tell the truth!"

"OK. I'm trying, OK?" I said slowly, lifting my hands in a calming gesture. "She said that some people – they – they mutate. And there's no way to know if it'll happen to you. If it does you might start to … lose control."

"That's it? That's all she said? I don't think so." Her eyes went far away, drifting past me as if she was seeing something else, something in her own head. "She told you I could turn into a monster, didn't she? It's going to happen again. Just like before. Me and the Nekomata all alone, together, in the dark – only this time it's inside me … and I can never ever get away…" She put her hands over her face.

My eyes swam with tears, turning her into a blur. I moved around the breakfast bar towards her, hand outstretched. "Rachel."

Shinobu caught my shoulder and jerked me back as the katana let out a furious buzz of energy against my back. I staggered and clutched at the end of the countertop for balance. The tears trickled down my cheeks, clearing my vision.

One of Rachel's hands still covered her eyes. Her other arm was fully extended, hand fisted in midair – on the air where my face had been one second before. Curving obsidian claws protruded grotesquely from the ends of her delicate fingers. The soft brown hair curling over her shoulders began to move as I stared, squirming around her head like a nest of worms.

"Don't. Touch. Me." The words came out on a low, guttural snarl. Her hand slid away from her face to reveal blazing yellow eyes.

Shinobu was pulling at me, trying to drag me away from her, but I couldn't go. I couldn't leave her alone. Not again.

"Rachel—"

"This is all your fault!" she hissed. "You did this to me!"

"No, no, no—" I didn't even know if I was denying Rachel's words or just begging the world for this to stop, for time to turn back, for this all to be a bad dream.

Rachel surged up onto the breakfast bar, sending plates and tea mugs flying. Her hair – black and glossy now – was writhing around her head. Both hands bristled with claws. Veins of darkness arrowed out around her eyes, as if her blood was turning black inside her.

"You…" she growled low in her throat. "You have to *pay*…"

She sank down into a catlike crouch, horrifyingly alien – and sprang at us. Shinobu dived left. I spun to the right.

The black claws grazed my cheek, opening lines of fire on my skin. Rachel landed in that same cat-crouch on the ground. Her talons dug into the floor, gouging chips out of the ceramic tiles and leaving a smear of blood – my blood – there. Warm rivulets slithered down my cheek.

Shinobu darted between us, his hands held up in a futile gesture of peace. "Do not do this, Rachel-san. This is your home. This is your family. You are loved and safe here."

"Liar!" she shrieked. The word hit a high, yowling tone. It was the Nekomata's voice coming out of Rachel's mouth. My whole body jerked in reaction.

"Get out of my way!" She lunged at Shinobu. There was a wild confusion of movements that I could barely follow – Rachel striking and slashing, Shinobu blocking and dodging and struggling to hold her back without hurting her. One of Rachel's arms seemed to elongate in the air, bending in a way no human joint could. He ducked. She knocked him off balance and surged past.

The next instant she was at my throat. The sheer weight of her – too great for her height and frame – slammed me back into the breakfast bar. One of her hands dug painfully into my hair while the other clamped onto my neck. Her claws pricked at my skin. Not quite piercing the surface. Not yet. She smelled familiar and homely, like Jack but with a bit more soap. Yet her breath, ghosting over my face, was the Nekomata's breath. Hot and sickly sweet with decay.

The yellow intensity of her gaze found mine. The hate and fury and triumph burning there was terrible. But the misery I was sure I could see lurking behind them was so much worse. *Oh, Rachel, I'm sorry, I'm sorry, I'm so sorry…*

Slowly her yellow eyes lost their deadly focus on my face. A frown of confusion pinched at her brows. Her gaze slid down to where the narrow silver smile of my katana rested against her belly.

One twitch of my hand. The faintest pressure. That was all it would take for my blade to slice open her stomach.

The katana hummed eagerly in my hand. I couldn't hear its voice in my head yet, not yet, but I could feel its desire, its yearning to strike out, to kill.

Tears streamed down my face, mixing with the blood. I didn't relax when the yellow eyes finally lifted back to meet mine, even as their vivid cat colour leached away into a soft, natural brown. Her hair still snaked around her face, and the dark veins still showed on her skin.

"Sorry," she whispered. "Sorry."

"Me too," I breathed, not daring to move.

Rachel nodded, setting tentacles of hair shivering, jellylike, over her shoulders. I felt the sharp points of her claws retract into blunt human fingernails and her grip ease. "Take care of Jack."

"Wait—"

She let go of me, whirled round, and ran for the back door, limbs blurring with speed. The door flew open. She was through it before it had banged once, gone before I could even lower my sword.

"Rachel!" I stumbled forward, staring at the empty garden in disbelief. She couldn't have disappeared so fast! "Rachel, come back! Please…"

Shinobu stopped me from plunging outside. "It is no use now."

"What?" I turned on him furiously. "How can you say that? We have to go after her and bring her back!" The intensity of the sword's energy was flooding my body with adrenaline, heightening all my feelings of guilt, of horror, of rage. I *would* go after her. I would *make* her see sense. I would force her to—

"How?" he asked, as if he was responding to my thoughts. "The only way to get her back into this house would be to fight her." He gestured to the naked blade in my hand. "Whichever of you won, you would both lose." His jaw clenched and I realized that he was struggling with his own feelings. He let out a short, ragged huff of breath. "Sometimes the only thing you can do is let go."

The scaffolding pole broke through his chest, blood gushing up like a red flower…

The green blade flashes down in the red light—
Don't let go!

I exhaled, forcing myself to stand still, to resist the urge to stalk out of the room after Rachel. Slowly, with a great effort of will, I reached up and pushed the katana back into the saya on my back.

The moment the blade rested in the saya, I felt my emotions settle under my control once more, and my mind clear. *It's getting stronger. It's getting worse. Oh God.*

Don't think about it now. You can't break down now. Focus on Rachel and Jack.

Focus on what you have to do.

"You're wrong," I told Shinobu finally. "Letting go isn't the answer. If this being on Museum Street is so ancient and wise, he can tell me how to save Rachel as well as Jack. Because I'm not abandoning her. Not again."

She ran. She didn't know where she was going – didn't dare stop long enough to look, or even to try to recognize the buildings that wheeled dizzily past her eyes. Some panicked remnant of common sense led her into the shadows. She scuttled down alleyways, hid behind rubbish bins, and ran – always ran – from the sight or sound of people. She muffled her painful, gulping sobs with both hands over her mouth, terrified of what would happen if someone heard. If someone saw. If someone tried to help.

There was no help.

She would never, ever forget Mio's face. Covered in blood – covered in claw marks – eyes huge and dark with fear. Not fear of Rachel.

Fear *for* her.

Mio could have killed her at any moment. Rachel knew that. She'd seen Mio fight. But Mio had only wanted to help Rachel. She'd let Rachel hurt her without even trying to defend herself. And Rachel had nearly killed her for it. She had *wanted* to.

Kill. Slash. Rend. BITE.

"No," she whimpered, and kept running.

The urge to keep going, to get far, far away from home, from anyone she cared about, drummed in her blood, echoed in every heartbeat. She focused everything she had on it. It was all she had left.

She found herself on scrubland. Some abandoned building site, the chain-link fence half-fallen down into the litter of rubble from demolished houses. Everything was covered in nettles and ivy. Instinctively she headed for the shelter of a tumbledown corrugated iron shed. Graffiti was sprayed over the walls like blood. Inside it was crawling damp, and the floor was heaped with old fag ends, crumpled beer cans and broken bits of drug gear. It stank of vomit and urine.

It was safe.

She huddled in one corner with her arms wrapped around her body, rocking gently. *Don't go back. Don't ever go back. Stay away. Don't go back.*

Her gums itched fiercely. So did her hands and face. Shudders ripped down her back. It felt as if her flesh was squirming, as if something was … was bubbling up underneath. Trying to shed her humanity the way a snake does its old skin.

Hunt. Bite. Drink…

No!

"Hey, bitch! What you doing in here?"

The voice was young, male and aggressive. The kind of voice that would have made her breathless with anxiety – would have made her hurry away without looking back – on any normal day. Now she curled into a tighter ball and dug her burning fingers into her upper arms.

"I'm talking to you! This is my place – get your ass out now."

An eerie laugh, high-pitched and hiccuping, leaked out of her lips. "Go away."

"What did you say?" The voice cracked with surprise and indignation, revealing the speaker's youth. "You're gonna regret laughing at me, bitch. You just made the worst mistake of your life. I'm gonna cut you up."

She raised her head. A boy, no older than fifteen, stood against the light. She got a vague impression of a pasty, belligerent face, and knock-off gangsta gear. He clutched a tiny flick-knife in one hand. The other hand was hanging onto his baggy trousers. They looked like they might fall down any minute.

175

But it wasn't his looks that interested her. It was the smell. The rich, delicious smell that flooded her nostrils, like no flavour she'd ever experienced before. It was irresistible and beckoned her, forcing her out of her miserable huddle into a tense, ready crouch. The scent of anger. Fear. Human blood.

Drink…

The laugh that spilled out of her this time was different. It was deep and gloating. It was the laughter that had haunted her nightmares. The Nekomata's laughter. The boy's expression twisted with terror as he caught sight of her properly for the first time.

Strike. Claw. Bite.

The itching in her fingers sharpened into a fierce, satisfying burn as black claws unsheathed themselves. She scraped the air, stretching her hands out luxuriously.

His knife trembled in the air. "What – what—?"

"Hmmm…" she purred, bouncing on her toes. "What if I cut you up instead?"

The boy let out a choked squawk. The knife hit the concrete with a tiny ping. He turned and fled.

Chase. Tear. BITE.

CHAPTER 11

HAPPINESS AVENUE

I fetched the kitchen first-aid kit from under the sink, and Shinobu quickly sponged the drying blood off my face and neck. He applied antiseptic and then a pad of gauze and some tape. The dressing covered most of my cheek. Even so, it had to be less eye-catching than the trio of deep claw marks Rachel had left, slashing across my face. They stung like mad, a constant reminder of the torment Jack's sister had to be feeling right now. There was no time for a hospital visit, stitches, or any other fussing. I just had to hope I wouldn't scar permanently.

The top the Kitsune had given me – God, was it only the day before? – was soaked with blood over the whole left arm and shoulder. There was no way I could wear it out of the house, but I didn't have anything else. I already knew that none of my old clothes was going to fit me.

Mum's things had been too small since I was twelve, and my dad's were way too big.

The only wardrobe I could realistically raid was Jack's.

I rummaged in the key drawer and found Dad's keys to the old servants' staircase, as well as his spare keys to the flat. Silently, Shinobu and I headed up the stairs. I didn't bother trying to tell him that he didn't have to come with me. It wouldn't do any good. Anyway, I wasn't sure I wanted to do this on my own.

Jack's room was in chaos. The duvet had been ripped off the bed and flung into a corner. The huge pile of books and magazines that had reached nearly halfway up the wall had either fallen or been pushed over and was scattered all across the floor. Random objects had been tossed everywhere. Books, DVDs, old cuddly toys. One of Jack's karate trophies had left a big black dent in the purple wall and then broken into three pieces on the carpet.

A stuffed toy – a grizzled, grey animal with a long stripy tail and a missing ear – sat in the centre of the pillow on the bed, leaning against the headboard.

"Ringo the Ringtail," I whispered, recognizing him.

I was looking at the panic and fear Jack had felt after we realized the Nekomata had taken her sister.

"Are you all right?" Shinobu asked.

I jerked my head at him – not sure if I was trying

to nod or shake. Jack didn't even know what was happening to Rachel. She had no idea. She was lying in a horrible hospital bed, alone, waiting for me to save her. Waiting for her best friend and her big sister to come back, any minute, and fix all this. And Rachel? She was alone too, lost and afraid, traumatized and changing and out of control. I'd failed so badly. Failed them both, lost them both.

It might already be too late for Rachel. And I didn't know how much time Jack had...

A large, warm hand came to rest on my back, between my shoulder blades. Shinobu didn't speak, or ask me if I was all right again. He just waited: a calm, reassuring presence, demanding nothing, there if I needed him. I forced myself to breathe calmly, waiting for the wave of emotions to pass over me. After another moment, I nodded. "I'm OK. I just want to get this over with."

The massive wardrobe, decorated with stickers and posters of Jack's favourite bands, stood in the corner. I went to it and opened both the doors – then stepped back in amazement.

It was like something out of a fashion spread. Footwear was aligned in two perfectly straight lines along the bottom of the wardrobe, with boots at the back and shoes at the front. Each pair was polished and had a pair of socks folded up in the left shoe or boot. Above the shoes, Jack's clothes were hung up on fancy padded hangers, organized by colour going from black through grey, white, pale pink, dark pink, purple and then blue. One quarter of the wardrobe was taken up with closet shelves, where every item, from T-shirts to jeans to scarves, was folded into a perfect geometric square that I wouldn't have been able to achieve with two helpers, a ruler, and sticky tape.

I turned my head and looked at the chaos of the room. Then I looked back at the wardrobe.

No wonder she never let me see inside before.

"Jack, you big fat fake." I let out a laugh that was half sob. "Look at this. Look! She's the worst neat freak of them all, and I never even knew. I never even knew..."

Trying not to mess anything up too much, I searched through the neat piles of T-shirts until I found what seemed to be a plain, scoop-necked white top with short sleeves. I pulled it out, but when I unfolded it, there turned out to be a tattoo-style design on the front: a skull sitting on a bed of gleaming emeralds, with a green snake poking out of one eyehole. In Gothic lettering underneath, it read WELCOME TO MALFOY MANOR.

Typical Jack, I thought, hugging the shirt to my chest for a second. *Pretending to be cool Slytherin when she's actually swotty Ravenclaw through and through.*

I found a long-sleeved black T-shirt and sent Shinobu out so that I could put it on with the white one over the top. Then I finished the outfit off with a loosely fitting dark purple hooded fleece, which hid the katana and its harness as well as anything could. There were tiny vampire bats on the lining of the hood, but otherwise it was about as regulation as Jack got. I checked myself in the full-length mirror on the inside of the wardrobe door.

Well, I was clean. But that was about the only positive. Even fully zipped up, the fleece only partially concealed the necklace of darkening bruises around my throat. Another, older bruise on my jaw was vivid blue-black, while the scratches I'd picked up over my right eyebrow were red and ugly. Shinobu's white gauze bandage finished the picture of a girl who had been in some kind of horrible accident. How could anyone safely blend in looking like this? I sighed, poking at the gauze.

The katana pulsed suddenly. A wave of heat undulated up my spine, snapping my back ramrod straight. The heat intensified, rippling out through my body to shoot down into my arms and legs. When it reached my face, it seemed to explode, sparks tingling as they travelled across my skin to all the places where I was hurt. I gasped.

The bruises, the scratches, every sign of trauma, had disappeared. Nothing ached, stung or throbbed. For a few heartbeats, as I gaped at the mirror, I saw – I was – a Mio who was completely healed. I saw the Mio I had known before all this began.

Unscarred. Innocent.

Normal.

I clapped my hands to my face – and felt the healing cuts and grazes protest. Instantly the pain of my injuries fell back on me. It was like being caught in a cascade of bricks. I had to lean on the wardrobe door again to stay upright; everything seemed to hurt twice as badly as it had before that second or two of release.

When I opened my eyes, I saw that the image of a perfect me was gone. Gone as if she had never existed.

A hallucination?

An invitation?

The katana hummed. I could feel its energy pushing at me, trying to get into my mind. I shivered, straightening up despite the stiffness and aches.

It doesn't matter if you were … tempting me or – or punishing me. I don't trust you. I won't make any deals with you. If I have to use you, it will be on my terms. You don't control me.

You don't own me.

I turned away abruptly from the mirror and pushed the bedroom door open. Shinobu frowned when he saw my expression.

"What—"

"I don't want to talk about it. Let's go."

He lifted his eyebrows at me, but didn't argue.

A few minutes later we headed out of the front door, stopping briefly to cautiously check for signs of anything hinky before we stepped over the threshold. The sky was a blinding bright white, the thick high clouds like an opaque paper cone thrown over the city. An icy wind whistled down the street, abrading my exposed skin without disturbing the menacing sense of stillness that lay over everything. But it seemed the Shikome, however many of them there were out there, were still searching for us elsewhere. I turned to lock the door behind us, trying to ignore the uneasy itch on the back of my neck.

"All these tall buildings worry me," Shinobu said from the step below. "The Foul Women could be anywhere. We must be very alert. And walk quickly."

We had already agreed that we had to walk it. The bus or Tube would take us miles out of our way and we couldn't afford to lose any more time.

Shinobu had both his blades at his waist again, and he had buttoned my dad's long coat up over the top to hide them. In the black leather, with his hair severely braided back and his eyes sharply scanning the sky, he practically shouted *Armed and Dangerous*. I was very much hoping that, at least for today, his invisibility still held.

I clung to the shelter of the doorway for another breath before turning away to march down the steps onto the street. Shinobu fell into step behind me, placing himself slightly to my right. I guessed that was so he wouldn't get in the way of my blade if I needed to draw it. Which made me feel incredibly conspicuous. I'd walked around London all my life without ever catching, well, *anyone's* attention. Up until a few days ago I was just Mio Yamato. An average schoolgirl with a cute, honest face. Patently harmless. The kind of girl that little old ladies stopped in the street to ask for directions. I'd never been in a real fight. I thought of myself, carried myself, like a non-combatant.

But I was different now.

I *wasn't* harmless any more. The extra height, speed and strength were the least of it. Now I knew what I was capable of. I knew that I could fight. That I would kill.

What if people could tell by looking at me?

I flicked a glance back at Shinobu and saw that he was scanning the street with focused, intent eyes. One hand rested on the button of his coat, ready to rip it open and grab his blades at any minute. Seeing him made me realize that my own hands were hovering at my sides like a gun-fighter from the Wild West, ready to hit out or draw the katana.

If I'd seen me coming towards me in a dark alley? I'd have run like hell.

"Shinobu, please can you walk next to me like a normal person?"

He opened his mouth on what was clearly destined to be a protest. Then he met my eyes, and his frown eased into a look of understanding. He moved alongside me and held out his hand. I pulled my left hand out of my pocket and let him take it. He twined our fingers together.

"If you watch the streets, I will keep my eyes on the sky," he said.

My knotted-up shoulders unscrunched from up under my ears, and I squeezed his hand in gratitude. "OK. Thanks."

We crossed the road hand in hand. I tugged him around the corner onto the shortcut I'd planned across Lincoln's Inn Fields. Shinobu squinted up at the empty sky, and then turned his attention to me as we walked. "Will you answer a question?"

"It depends what it is," I said warily.

"Last night, you said something that ... surprised me."

"Oh. Was it my dad's Blitz spirit speech? Because I'm kind of thinking that was a load of—"

"No. Actually it was something you said in your sleep."

My gaze glued itself to his face. "What? What did I say?" *Please God, don't let it have been a sexy dream...*

"It was shortly before I woke you. You became disturbed, struggling in your dream. You said a name. Yoshida-sensei. "

My embarrassment faded, to be replaced with puzzlement. "I did? I have no idea who that is."

"You have not heard the name before?"

"Not that I can remember." I frowned up at him. There was a deep crease between Shinobu's eyebrows and his

185

eyes had that distant look. "But *you* have. Haven't you?"

Shinobu hesitated. "Yes. It was the name of the stranger in our village. The newcomer. The one who taught us about the Nekomata, and sent me to fight it."

The green blade flashes down in the red light—

I flinched as the strange vision burned itself on the back of my eyes again. "You never told me that. Am I – am I dreaming your dreams again? Still? How is that possible?"

"Possible and impossible are relative terms for us," he said dryly. "Can you remember what you were dreaming about?"

"Well, I still dream about you – about your fight with the Nekomata – a lot. Sometimes I see other things. Fragments. You know how dreams blur together, and you seem to know things in them, but when you wake up none of it makes sense? I thought I was imagining, maybe. What it was like to be you. Lying there in the red leaves, looking up at the sky. I dreamed about … about being someone in your family. Someone who loved you and was waiting for you to come back. Wishing I hadn't let you go…"

His lips pressed together into a thin line and he turned his head a little, as if to hide his expression from me. I shut up, mentally cursing myself as we left the park and crossed the road to head into a quiet area filled with red-brick buildings and parked cars. At least, at first glance it looked peaceful and quiet. Until you noticed that two of the cars had been attacked, their paint scratched, their windscreens smashed and tyres slashed. One of them, I saw as I got closer, was partially burned.

The large, posh houses around us also showed signs of trouble. Some had boards nailed across their windows on the inside and starburst cracks in the glass. One house had black scorch marks streaking the front door, as if someone had set a fire on the doorstep. Debris crunched underfoot. Rocks, crushed cans, and smashed glass.

What in the world had happened here? It looked like there had been some kind of riot.

As we passed by the Lincoln's Inn Fields sign onto a narrow, shady road where the buildings on either side had deep arches of greyish-white stonework, a woman turned the corner onto the pavement ahead. She was the first person I had seen outside – not flying by in a car or other vehicle – since we left the house. She did a double-take as she caught sight of us. Then she whipped round and ran in the opposite direction. A moment later I heard a door slam.

My dad had always said that fear makes people do strange things. Bad things. Suddenly my head was filled with a selection of awful possibilities as to how the Shikome's taint could have sparked this violence. What if someone had asked for shelter here and been turned down – and in their terror they tried to break in?

What if people got ill here and no one would come out to help – and someone tried to punish them for it? What if, what if...? There was no way to know for sure. But this couldn't be a coincidence; it wasn't just my life that was falling apart. The whole of London was starting to seem frighteningly like a war zone. A war zone packed full of unknowing, unprepared people who were still capable of hurting themselves – and others, too – in their fear.

Shinobu squeezed my hand. "Mio, tell me more. Tell me what else you have seen in your dreams."

I took a deep breath, forcing my attention back to our conversation. "I keep dreaming different versions of – of you dying. Sometimes I see it from the outside, looking down at you, with you staring up through me. Sometimes I'm inside you, seeing what you see. But the last few times I saw – there was a man there, bending over you. Most of his face was hidden, but *you* recognized him. He had a sword in his hand. It wasn't shaped like a regular sword. It was sort of like a leaf, thin at both ends but fatter in the middle, and it was green. And then the blade came down and everything went dark. That's where the dream ends."

Shinobu let out a shuddering breath. His fingers had slowly tightened on mine until his grip was almost painful. "I don't remember that. I don't remember anything after I looked up at the sky and thought of..." His voice trailed off.

"Look, maybe I did imagine it. Maybe it isn't real," I said. But even as I said it, I knew that I was talking rubbish. Shinobu's decisive head shake just confirmed it.

"That cannot be. You spoke his name. I had almost forgotten it myself. That means Yoshida-sensei was there when I died. He precipitated my death. But I cannot understand why. Why follow me into the woods? Why murder a dying man?" He paused. "And ... what else might I have forgotten?"

That was a question I would have liked answered, too. Why could I never remember my dreams properly? Why did they always fade as soon as I woke up, leaving me with only vague feelings and disturbing fragments that made no sense? I needed to start trying to piece them together, to make sense of them. I had to be seeing these things for a reason...

A sudden cold shiver raked down my back. My senses ratcheted up to high alert; spinning in place, I caught sight of the dark shape the second it flashed into the sky above us. I shoved Shinobu with all my strength, pushing him back into the shadows of the nearest archway. My momentum slammed me into him as he hit the stone. Swallowing a grunt, I craned my neck to try and keep the monster in sight.

Shinobu's arms wrapped around me and he swiftly reversed our positions, caging me against the wall with his larger body. He whispered, "Shikome?"

I nodded, my eyes fastened on the sky like grappling hooks. The massive winged shape was darting in and out of sight above the road. For such a huge creature it was incredibly agile.

The thing disappeared. I leaned sideways, trying to catch a glimpse.

"Is it still there?"

"Wait," I whispered, my instincts still screaming. My hands tightened on Shinobu's shoulders.

The Shikome dived into the road.

The thundering of its immense wings blasted the air below it, a force-ten gale tainted with the burned-hair-rotten-garbage stink of the monster. My hair and Shinobu's flew around my face. My ears were filled with the deafening sound of dry, desiccated feathers chittering together. Dead leaves, dust and litter spun around our feet. The monster's huge paws grazed the buildings on either side of the street as it shot along the narrow gap, sending chips of brick and tile and cement raining down onto the tarmac below. Only the narrowness of the gap stopped it flying lower and seeing us. I closed my eyes and hid my face in Shinobu's shoulder, breathing through my mouth. His arms crushed me against him.

The sound faded away. The wind died down. The icy-cold tickle on my spine dried up.

"It's gone," I said, opening my eyes.

He blew out a relieved breath. "You saved us both."

"You're welcome. But don't think I didn't notice your little bodyguard manoeuvre just now. You have to stop putting yourself between me and danger like that. I don't need you to protect me any more."

One corner of his mouth quirked up as his eyebrow lifted. He probably didn't even know the phrase, *Girl, please,* but his expression said it for him.

"Look—"

He leaned down and kissed me.

For about half a second I contemplated smacking him for trying to derail the discussion. Then I decided it could wait.

His fingers cupped my face, cradling my cheek and jaw as if I was made of glass. I found a handful of his soft hair and wound my fingers into it, while curling my other hand into the shoulder of his leather coat. My heart hadn't even stopped thundering from the Foul Woman's presence. Now it was thrumming against my ribs again, too fast to count the beats. I did something I'd always secretly wanted to and bit down, very gently, on his beautiful bottom lip. Shinobu's breath shivered into my mouth, and he pulled me closer.

I was taller now, but not tall enough. Tiptoes didn't bring me where I wanted to be either. I jumped and hauled myself up the steel pillar of his body, wrapping one leg around his hip. The big, warm hand on my waist slid slowly down the thin fabric of my trousers to cup my thigh, supporting my weight. His other hand was clenched in my hair. A wave of almost painful excitement and yearning crashed through me, and sent me into a full-body shudder that I had no chance of hiding. A tiny moan popped from my lips straight into his.

"Mio. Oh, Mio…" His shaking voice echoed in my ears, mixing with words in Japanese. I recognized some of them. *My beloved. My Mio.* He pressed his mouth to my eyelid, my cheek, the edge of my jaw, the skin beneath my ear.

There was a loud tearing noise. We both froze.

Abruptly I was aware of the wall against my back, and the tremble in my thigh from hanging onto him like a demented spider monkey. I swallowed and blinked as Shinobu eased back, letting my feet drop to the pavement again. Our eyes met.

"What just…?" I asked.

He cleared his throat. "I think – my shirt."

I looked down and saw that at some point I'd traded my grip on his hair for a handful of the T-shirt and jumper under his jacket. My fingers had gone straight through the thin wool and made a nice tear in the cotton beneath that too.

"Darn super-strength," I muttered.

Shinobu's lip twitched up at the corner again. I snatched my hand away from his ruined clothes and clapped it over his mouth. "No laughing at me," I said, only half joking. "Not at a moment like this. Romance will die forever and it'll be your fault."

He peeled my hand off and pressed a kiss to my palm. "Where are we now? What is this place?"

"Um … Remnant Street, I think."

"No. From now on it will be Paradise Street. Heaven Road. Happiness Avenue."

"You big cheese-ball…" I muttered, putting my arms around his waist and hugging him tightly.

"What?"

"Never mind!" I grumped, then sighed. "I wish we could stay on Happiness Avenue a bit longer…"

"But we can't," he finished. "It is all right. I promise we will come back whenever you want."

CHAPTER 12

LOOKING FOR AVALON

Museum Street.

It was another narrow road, made narrower by the motorcycle rank that took up half of the tarmac. On the corner there was a cafe with its white awning still out, although the window and door were shuttered and the little metal tables and chairs you'd have expected to see outside were missing. A hairdresser's and the Japanese restaurant on the other side of it were both obviously closed too. But next to the cafe, and to the right of the hairdresser's, there was a shop with a dark blue-green façade. Its large display window was unshuttered and an OPEN sign hung on the door. The plate glass was painted with swirling golden lettering that declared:

AVALON BOOKS

OCCULT AND ANTIQUARIAN BOOKSELLERS

EST. 1977. PROPRIETOR: L. LEECH

I read the words aloud, then repeated, "Nineteen seventy-seven."

"That must be incorrect. The king said this being has dwelled here for centuries."

I waved that away. "I suppose he'd have to change his name and business every now and again, to stop people getting suspicious. It's just … seventy-seven was the year my grandfather came here from Japan with my dad."

Shinobu eyed the lettering with more interest. "Perhaps it is a message?"

"If it is, that means he's been waiting. For me. Waiting since – since – before I was born. And…" I gulped and squared my shoulders, "the only way to find out is to go in there."

I moved forward. Shinobu quickly stepped in front of me and pushed the door open, holding it for me while making sure that his body was between mine and the interior of the building. *Bodyguarding me again, damn it.*

Then we were both inside, and the door had snapped quietly shut behind us.

The first thing that struck me was how big the place was. Not exactly TARDIS-like, but a lot larger than I'd been expecting from the exterior. This row of buildings had three storeys, and the height of the ceiling in here seemed to suggest that someone had taken out the second floor to create a double-height space for the shop.

The ceiling was painted the same vivid blue-green

as the outside. Some really talented artist had mixed the darker shade with subtle swirls of silver and pale greens and blues, until you felt like you were looking up into a deep ocean. The walls were hidden behind fitted, crammed-full bookshelves of sand-coloured wood that climbed to about seven feet, and the space between the tops of the shelves and the ceiling was filled with … fish tanks. They ran, uninterrupted, from corner to corner. The things must have been custom-made to fit the gap. I squinted at them, expecting to see bright exotic fish or something. Instead I realized that the clean, sparkling water was filled with… Were those jellyfish? All different kinds of jellyfish, ranging from tiny white blobs barely as big as a button, to one vivid red umbrella-sized one with trailing streamers as long as my leg. They drifted through the tanks with that peculiar halting motion, in apparent harmony with one another.

"This is … unusual," Shinobu whispered.

More bookcases – these ones without aquariums on top – formed three wide corridors, dividing the space in the middle of the shop. Shinobu indicated the middle one to me with a questioning tilt of his head, and I nodded again. We moved forward into the aisle together.

The faint watery swishing from the tanks overhead blocked out the sounds of the outside world, making the room feel quiet in a way that was more oppressive than true silence. I shifted to put my back to the shelves, unzipping my hoodie. Shinobu unbuttoned his long coat and pushed it aside so that he could reach his swords. My fingers were trembling with the desire to grasp the hilt of the katana sword, but I refused to give in – for now.

There was a long wooden counter at the other end of the aisle. As we got closer, I saw an antique-looking metal till and ancient Bakelite dial-phone taking up one side. A tiny teacup – the kind made of bone china so thin that the light actually shines through it – sat in a saucer next to the till. The green liquid inside was steaming gently. The other end of the counter held a display of books piled into a geometric pyramid shape, with a yellowing human skull sitting on the apex. The top of the skull had been removed and a brass plant pot, holding some lush green plant with heart-shaped leaves, stuck out. OK, now *that*? Was officially Grade-A creepy.

Something stirred to Shinobu's right.

The sheathed katana was out of its harness and in my hand before the first syllable of the words "Watch out!" formed in my mouth.

Shinobu was even quicker than me. He whirled and drew his short wakizashi blade in a single, flowing movement.

Then we all froze.

I stared, trying to make sense of the still scene that had resolved itself out of the flurry of motion.

A short, plump man, with a slightly hunched back,

his scalp shining through sparse wisps of grey hair, stood in the gap between the last bookcase and the counter. He was leaning on a polished dark wood cane. The round silver top gleamed between fingers that were swollen and bent.

The man had heavily lined skin with the soft, silk-like quality which only comes from extreme age. His eyes were dark, and his features were obviously east Asian. The most striking thing about him was the absolutely beatific smile on his face. It pulled his cheeks up into round little balls and made his eyes twinkle.

The tip of Shinobu's short blade was about a milli-metre from his throat.

"You know, it's rude to point," the old man said. His voice had a faint accent that I couldn't place, and was as rich and fruity as Christmas pudding. "Or don't they teach young people that any more?"

This man had none of the overwhelming, crushing presence of an immortal like the Harbinger or the King of the Kitsune. He didn't make me feel sick or cold, like the Yomi creatures. And unlike every other ancient super-natural I'd met, he was making no effort to look young. My eyes and my spidey-senses both told me that I was looking at a harmless little old man. I quickly slid the katana and saya back into the harness on my back.

Shinobu lowered his own blade and resheathed it at his waist. "My apologies ... Mr Leech?"

"Well, at least they taught you to apologize nicely. Were you two looking for something in particular today?" he asked, eyes twinkling.

Shinobu and I shared a helpless look. This was the right place. This *had* to be the right man. Being. Thing. And yet … he wasn't playing his part. How were you supposed to just ask someone if they were an ancient immortal?

"Goodness, was it that difficult a question?" Mr Leech asked, letting loose a deep, boozy-sounding chuckle. "Don't look so worried, my dears." He limped away from us and took up a place behind the counter, leaning his walking stick against it so he could pick up his tea. He slurped it loudly, still looking at us with those calm, twinkly eyes.

"Um, I'm really sorry if we – we were rude," I said hesitantly. "It's just that there's lots of weird stuff happening in the city lately. I don't know if you've noticed?"

"Mysterious allergens in the air. Unsolved murders. Shady happenings. A storm brewing," he said with relish. "I can check the BBC News website just like anyone else, you know, young lady."

"Well, I was told that you … might be able to help."

He chuckled again. "Really? And who told you that? Your tall acquaintance here?"

Would the king be OK with me bringing her name into this? Or should I make something up? Before I could think of a way to answer, Shinobu sucked in a deep breath. "You saw me straight away," he said in a tone of dawning discovery. "And *you can still see me now.*"

Crap. I can't believe I missed that.

The old man grinned like a kid caught out playing a trick.

"You're messing with us, aren't you?" I said.

"I have been accused of having an unfortunate sense of humour. But when you reach my age, most of life becomes either unbearably funny or unbearably sad," he confessed.

"What is your age, exactly?" Shinobu asked, moving smoothly towards the end of the counter.

"That would be telling," the old man said, still smiling like a plump-cheeked little baby.

"I don't care," I said, finally out of patience. I took two swift steps forward and leaned over the till into the old man's space, meeting his gaze without flinching. "I don't care how old you are or who or what you are. I have questions that I need to ask. You have information that I think you want to share. So why don't you give the games a rest and we can get on with it?"

Mr Leech stared at me consideringly, and I stared back. I could see it now: the only flaw in his disguise. Close up his eyes were more than just the twinkling eyes of a funny old man. Behind the ordinary brown, there was light. A soft brilliance that seemed to come from a long, long way away. Those eyes were like a gap in a cloudy night sky that lets the distant glow of the stars shine through.

"You are exactly like her, aren't you?" he said quietly.

I frowned suspiciously. "Like who?"

In the corner of my vision Shinobu made a sharp, jerking movement. I flicked my gaze to him for one second. His face was expressionless, but his fists were clenched.

"Never mind," the old man said. "I think you'll do. You'll do very well indeed."

"Do for what?" Shinobu asked.

I interrupted. "Don't. He can probably keep talking in riddles all day. Mr Leech, are you going to help us or not?"

The old man snapped his cane up in a deft movement that his swollen fingers ought to have made impossible and turned away from me towards a door behind the counter marked STAFF ONLY. "Follow me upstairs. I think we're going to want a little privacy. Come along now, what are you waiting for?"

Taken aback, I looked around blankly. "But – what about the shop?"

"Oh, don't worry about that. People don't notice it unless I want them to, you know."

Just like I'd never noticed it before.

Sidestepping Shinobu's attempt to go first, I followed

the old man out of the shop and into a tiny, dingy lobby, crammed with piled cardboard boxes and old newspapers, and up a flight of shaky, rusty, iron stairs. At the top, we waited a couple of steps down from Mr Leech as he unlocked a peeling plywood door.

"What kind of tea do you prefer?" he called as he disappeared into the room beyond.

"Um … PG Tips?" I moved cautiously into the space and looked around as Shinobu shut the door behind us. He kept his hand on the handle.

The place was tiny and looked as if it hadn't been redecorated since about 1900. A vivid pink floral carpet was almost hidden beneath heavy, dark furniture that was way too big for the room – a massive, peeling red leather sofa and two wing chairs, a Welsh dresser taking up most of one wall, a sideboard and about three sets of those little nesting tables. Every available surface was covered in what Jack would have called "Old Lady Bling": china figurines, commemorative plates, glass paperweights, silver candlesticks. The two tiny windows were veiled by blindingly white net curtains.

"Would you like a soft drink, perhaps?" Mr Leech's voice floated out of an alcove to the left, where I could just see the edge of what looked like a kitchen cabinet. There was a clattering noise, as if he was searching through cupboards.

"Don't go to any—" I began.

The old man stepped out of the alcove with a sword in his hands.

It was sheathed, and he held it flat between his palms as if he intended to offer it up, rather than draw it. I could see, even in the dimness of the flat, that the sword was old, and well used. The plain black lacquer saya was scratched and chipped in places, and the black silk wrappings worn and frayed. It was a wakizashi: a short blade like the one that Shinobu liked to fight with. There was a click as the old man caught the edge of the saya with one thumb and slid an inch of gleaming steel free, his bright, youthful eyes fixed on me.

My katana throbbed. The hot energy burst through my back, making my muscles judder so badly that I squeaked. Shinobu let out a strange, choked gasp.

Then he crumpled to the ground at my feet.

"Shinobu!"

I dropped next to him, grabbing his shoulders. He had doubled up over his knees and was clutching at his chest with one hand. His other hand clawed at the flowery carpet. His skin was waxy pale and his eyes had gone black, opaque. I called his name again; he didn't respond.

A scarlet droplet oozed between his fingers and trickled across the back of his hand.

"Take the blade," Mr Leech rasped out. I looked up to see him standing exactly as before. "Take it," he repeated.

"What are you doing?" I demanded. "What is that? What are you doing to him?"

"He doesn't matter," the old man said impatiently. "The wakizashi has been hidden for half a millennium. Now that it is out even the nexus's energy cannot conceal it any longer. Your enemy will know it is here. He will come for it. You must take it and unsheathe it."

A dark, sticky stain was dampening the fabric between Shinobu's fingers. He fell sideways onto the carpet, his breath hacking harshly.

I surged to my feet and ripped the katana from its sheath in the fastest draw of my life. Ghostly white fire sputtered to life along the cutting edge as I stepped towards the old man. His eyes widened.

"You're killing him!" I said.

"He is already dead!" He sounded almost pleading. "Take the blade now and this can all be over."

I brought the tip of the katana up until it pierced the air directly in front of the old man's chest. The blade's flames flared between us. "Whatever you are doing to him, stop it right now. If you don't, I swear on my grandfather's grave, I will gut you."

In that heartbeat, with the sword's power flaring around me, I meant the threat absolutely.

Mr Leech stared at me for another split second. Then he closed his eyes in defeat, bowing his head over the wakizashi. His swollen, bent old hands slid together and snapped the saya back into place. As his fists met, there was a burst of blinding, rainbow white light. I jerked my head away, eyes squeezing shut. When I looked again, his hands were empty.

Shinobu sucked in a long, deep breath. It sounded more like wind howling down a long tunnel than any human noise. It stirred my hair and set the net curtains fluttering. I spun round in time to see him sit up. His hair fell in messy hanks around his face as he stared down at the dark red blood staining the palm of his hand. I shoved the katana hastily into the saya on my back, nearly tripping over my own feet in my rush to get to him, and grabbed at the hem of his sweater. I yanked the material up.

His chest was smooth, golden, and unmarked. Thick, almost black streaks of blood were drying on his skin. I laid my palm over his heart, nearly sick with relief as I felt the strong, steady beat thundering under his breastbone.

Not again. I can't ever watch him die again.

I'll never let go.

I turned on Mr Leech fiercely. "What did you do to Shinobu?"

"I was trying to help," he said in an infuriatingly melancholy tone. His cane was back in his hand and he was leaning on it heavily.

"By magically punching a hole in him?"

My voice broke on the last word. Shinobu put his

palm over mine where it still lay on his chest. I could feel the stickiness of his blood smearing against my skin.

"I did not know that would happen," the old man said, shrugging a little. *What's a mortal injury between friends?* "How was I to guess that when you brought the sword to me, your friend would be walking beside you in this form? How was I to guess that you would already love him? All my plans in ruins…"

"What plans? I don't understand anything that just came out of your mouth," I told him bluntly. "Are you saying that you didn't mean to hurt him?"

"I had no idea he could *be* hurt." He turned a stern look on us. "I don't think you realize that the being sitting beside you is not a person. He is a spirit. In a very real sense, he has been dead for five hundred years. For him to allow you to love him in this state … it is cruel. And he knows it." His tone was condemning.

Shinobu's jaw tightened, and I was infuriated to see his gaze drop from the old man's. I turned my blood-smeared hand over and gripped his fingers hard.

"We didn't come here for relationship counselling," I said evenly. "Shikome are swarming on London. Hundreds of people are ill, including my best friend. And her sister was bitten by a Nekomata and is mutating. I was told that you could give us the information we need to banish the Foul Women. To use the sword for something good for once, to help all the people who've been hurt by this situation. I hoped you might tell me how to heal my bitten friend. But so far all you've done is double-talk and nearly kill Shinobu. So just tell me – can you help us?"

If anything, the old man's face grew even sadder. The more depressed he got, the younger he seemed to look. His face was less lined now, and I could have sworn that he had more hair.

"That would depend," he said.

"On what?" Shinobu asked apprehensively.

The old man gave me a look that drenched me in icy apprehension. "What are you willing to sacrifice?"

CHAPTER 13

INEVITABILITY

The old man's words hung in the air for a long, tense moment. Then he seemed to shake himself. "What's done is done. But we don't have much time now, not after the amount of energy you and I just unleashed in these rooms. The one hunting you will sniff it out, probably in the next few minutes."

"Hunting us? You mean the Shikome?"

He shook his head. "Those foul things are mere puppets, the least of your worries. You are caught between two sides in a great battle which goes back thousands of years, long before either of you, or your family, were involved. It is a war between Yomi and its mistress, she who was once called Izanami-no-Kami, and her once-husband, the father of the gods, Izanagi-no-Kami."

I felt Shinobu tense by my side, his grip nearly crushing my hand.

Little birdie.

Shadows and blood...

The old man went on, "You, Mio, have been visited by both these beings. The weak echo of Izanami has sought to influence you in your nightmares, just as the one who calls himself the Harbinger – whose true name is Izanagi – has terrorized you in the mortal realm since you took up the sword."

"I don't – this can't be – the Harbinger is a *god*? I can't – I don't understand how..." My words stuttered to a halt and I clutched at my head with my free hand.

The old man sighed. "Let me make it as simple as I can. Five hundred years ago Izanami learned of an uncanny weapon of power – a blade which had been discovered in the belly of a serpent. She believed it might be powerful enough to break the curse that held her trapped in Yomi. But the sword belonged to Izanagi. And so she sent out all her creatures to track him, attack him, hound him, and steal it from him by any means necessary. Irked by their constant onslaught, Izanagi hid the sword with your family under a dense shroud of seals that gave it the appearance of a normal katana, a katana that had belonged to the Yamatos. The strongest concealment laid on the sword's power was the trapped spirit of a human boy – an adopted son of the Yamato family – which obscured the light and scent of its power from all but the sharpest of supernatural senses.

"For a time this deception worked. The Yamatos hid and protected the blade, because Izanagi had bound them to it with their own love for their fallen son, and this love passed down in their blood long after the memory of Shinobu's death had faded. But your actions, Mio, have begun to unravel Izanagi's plan and his protections on the blade. First, Shinobu's spirit was freed from the katana, making the scent of its energy easily detectable to supernatural creatures. Then you figured out and used the first of the sword's names, breaking another seal on its power. Izanagi seeks to bind Shinobu's soul to the katana once more, and to break your spirit so that you will think only of running and hiding from his former wife's monsters, instead of fighting them with the sword. Meanwhile, Izanami has sensed the blade's power after centuries of waiting, and she is desperate to win it this time, before it slips away again."

My face felt as if it had frozen. I knew I was gaping at Mr Leech with horror, but I couldn't make myself stop. *Ojiichan, what have you got me into?*

"There's no way," I whispered finally. "Humans can't win against gods. They'll rip us to shreds."

"Oh, rubbish!" Mr Leech said fiercely. He stumped his way through the crowded furniture and sat in the wing chair next to us. "Rid yourself of fairy tale notions of what these creatures are. They are powerful, yes, but they are neither omnipresent nor omnipotent. Most have no particular virtue and no particular intelligence. Many are damned useless fools!"

While I blinked at this, Shinobu protested, "But the legends – all the stories say—"

The old man jabbed his stick down, hitting the carpet with a dull thud. "Myths and legends! Who believes in those? The beings we're speaking of are Kami, you understand? Nature spirits formed in the wild storm of energy that was the beginning of this world, when all the powers of the universe collided. They are natural forces – natural disasters, like hurricanes, volcanoes, tsunamis. Izanami is a broken, insane shadow of what she once was, and Izanagi a coward who has been running from the consequences of his own selfish actions for millennia."

He paused, gasping for breath after his outburst, and I squeezed my eyes shut as I struggled to sort through the barrage of information. There were hundreds of questions I wanted to ask. Where had the sword come from in the first place? What were its true powers? Was it possible to break the frightening bond I felt to it?

But he'd said we didn't have much time – and there were two questions that I had to know the answers to, no matter what. "Can you tell me how we can banish the Shikome and destroy their taint? And what about saving someone who is transforming after a Nekomata bite?"

Mr Leech clasped his hands together on the top of his cane. "You carry the cure on your back."

My free hand darted back to touch the hilt of the katana. "So the sword really can do more than just destroy things?"

"The sword saved your life that night in the road," Shinobu reminded me. "It must have some healing powers."

"The sword certainly has *power*," Mr Leech said dryly. "Incredible raw power. Whether it uses it for healing or not, that is another matter."

"I have the sword's true name," I said hesitantly. "It answers me when I call it."

"You have one of the sword's true names – and if I am not mistaken, you have already used it. Tell me, did the sword's energy manifest itself obediently and safely when you did that?"

I shook my head wordlessly.

Mr Leech gave me a commiserating grimace. "You will not be able to summon the sword's full power using its first name again. That seal is already broken. And while the sword does seem to have allied itself with you for the moment, it is foolish to believe that you command it. It has its own will. Even once you break the next seal on its power with its second name, it has to be *controlled*, or the sword will simply use its new strength to invade your mind and enslave you. Your friends, those you wish to save, would be none the better off. And you would be a witless puppet, wielded by the blade."

Shit. I knew it. Oh God, I knew it... That was what it meant by "freedom" all along...

The buzz of the sword's energy down my back made my skin crawl. I rubbed at the goose pimples that jumped up on the back of my neck.

"Only if the sword's energy is contained and channelled by someone with an unbreakable will, by someone with the closest possible relationship to the blade, can the Shikome be banished and their taint erased. You, sword-bearer, do not have the ability to do that. Not yet, anyway. The sword has too great a hold on you and your emotions. As far as I am aware only one person in the world has ever done so."

The old man gazed at us, expression pitying.

And now the ice that had been nipping at me ever since Mr Leech used the word "sacrifice" clamped its jaws down over my heart. I heard the echo of Shinobu's voice in my head. Not warm, and real and present, like now, but distant and ghostly, the way it had been that night. The night I nearly died.

The night Shinobu saved me.

"Take my hand..." he had said. *"It will be all right. Take my hand."*

"I'm sorry," Mr Leech said quietly.

"Why?" Shinobu's gaze flicked between me and Mr Leech. "Do you mean—?"

His voice cut off as realization made his eyes go wide.

His fingers, still twined with mine, tightened until his grip almost cut off the blood. I squeezed back just as hard.

"It was the katana's energy which knit your skin and bones back together, Mio. But it was Shinobu's will that channelled that energy into healing instead of destruction. His soul was wrapped so tightly around the blade that the katana's energy had to pass *through* him, and in his desperation to save you, he forced it to do as he wished. Even here, halfway across London, I felt it happen."

"But it was a fluke," I said desperately. "A – a special case."

Shinobu murmured, "Mio…"

I used Shinobu's grip on my hand to pull him towards me, and rested my forehead against his. His hair fell around my face in glinting black strands. I felt his eyelashes brush my cheek.

"The sword is yours. You have the right to unseal its power with its true name," Mr Leech said inexorably.

I wanted to turn around and scream at him to shut up.

"The sword has the power to banish the Shikome, and erase their taint. But only Shinobu – whose very spirit is bound to the blade, even now – has the ability to *make it happen*. If—"

Please. Don't say it.

Don't say it.

Don't.

"—he is bound to the katana again. If he gives up his physical form and bonds with the blade, as he did before. That is the only way."

I didn't look away from Shinobu's set, grave face. "That's impossible."

"Is it?" Shinobu asked softly.

"We have no idea how you got out. We have no idea how to put you back again."

I can't. I won't let you go again.

Shinobu cupped my cheek with his hand, then turned to look at Mr Leech. Mr Leech opened his mouth.

Please. No. Anything, anything, but not that.

My hearing disappeared into a high, thin whine as the carpet leapt up and smacked me in the face. Shinobu threw himself across me. His mouth was moving – he was shouting – but I couldn't make out a single word. Dust and chunks of plaster rained down over us as another impact made the ceiling dance.

The tip of Mr Leech's cane thumped down an inch away from my nose. I peered up to see him standing steady on the rolling floor, gesturing urgently with one hand. I didn't need my hearing to make sense of what he was trying to say. The signs for *Get up!* and *Come on!* are pretty universal.

I staggered to my feet, not sure whether I was

helping or hindering Shinobu. Another impact shuddered through the flat and nearly sent me to the carpet again. Mr Leech seized my arm in a steely grip and towed us out of the crowded wreckage of the living room into...

"Seriously?" I muttered. I still couldn't actually hear myself, but I could imagine the tinny sound of my voice echoing in the dim orange-and-olive tiled bathroom. There was just enough room for me and Shinobu in the space between the toilet and the bath. "Why here?"

The old man slammed the door shut behind us, locked it, then he squeezed past and jammed himself into the gap next to the sink. He pulled the cord on an orange fabric blind, sending the material flying up to reveal a wide, frosted-glass window above the sink. Another impact rocked the floor beneath us. Shinobu grabbed the cistern of the toilet for balance. I clutched at the wall. A massive crack zigzagged up the wall above the bath, shattering the grout and sending tiles smashing down into the olive tub. The ringing in my ears was beginning to fade in and out. In among the crunching of bricks and the sounds of smashing downstairs, I could make out a voice booming up through the floor.

"DESTROY! Rip free of... Yomi will swallow ... this world ... dead and barren... UNGRATEFUL WHELP!"

I read Shinobu's lips as he mouthed: *The Harbinger.*

"Izanagi!" Mr Leech corrected. I could tell he was shouting to be heard, but the word reached me as a squeaky whisper. The old man unlatched the window and flung the sash up, before shouting again. "… only way – rooftops! – be safe!"

"You want us to climb out there?" I asked incredulously.

The old man gave me a look that clearly said, *Well, do you have a better idea?*

Great.

Mr Leech gestured for Shinobu to go first. Shinobu climbed up onto the olive pedestal sink, putting his hands on the narrow plank of the wooden windowsill for balance. He turned diagonally to wedge his broad shoulders through the casement, which suddenly looked a lot smaller. For a blink, I was sure he was going to get stuck. A shattering explosion from below sent me stumbling forward. Another crack arrowed through the wall above the window frame.

Shinobu jerked sideways. Suddenly his shoulders were through. I saw him reach up above his head, and then he was outside and somehow kneeling on the other side of the window. He held out his hand for me.

I huffed out a breath between my lips and waved his hand away. There was barely enough room as it was, and I didn't know what he was kneeling on out there. I scrambled up onto the sink after him, sending a desiccated bar of soap and a plug flying, and crawled over the windowsill.

We were at the back of the row of shops and flats. Below me was a row of tiny concrete courtyards, vivid green with lichens and mould. Ahead was a jumble of rooftops and, in the corner of my vision, the road. The only windows facing us now were curtained. That was good. The supernatural attack on the building would probably escape the notice of the non-magical citizens of London. But Shinobu and me clambering out of a third-storey window in the middle of the day? That looked enough like an ordinary burglary for someone to see us – or at least me – and decide to call the police.

Shinobu was kneeling on a narrow, white, stonework ledge that ran the length of the red-brick building under the line of windows. He had found a handhold above the window on a section of lead pipe. As he shuffled sideways to make room for me, I reached out and grabbed it too, then leaned down to offer my hand to Mr Leech in the same way Shinobu had done for me. He *was* going to need help getting out. Shinobu grabbed the back of my fleece to balance me as I poked my head through the window. "Come on!"

Mr Leech took my hand in that surprisingly strong grip and leaned over the sink to put his mouth close to my ear. "Thank you – offer. No need – can't – fear—"

Huh? "I can't hear you!"

The old man shook his head at me. "Go – too old – running about. I'm – danger."

"Mr Leech, we can't leave you here! Please. I promise we'll protect you."

He smiled the stunning, angelic smile that made him look so ancient and so innocent at once. "I don't – need – protection," he said slowly and carefully. His hand tightened around mine in two urgent squeezes. "Mio – katana's second name – listen…"

I don't want to know!

The green blade flashes down in the red light—

The walls of the building vibrated. An almighty crash echoed through the floor. Mr Leech released my hand and I jerked back just in time as the sash window fell down between us, thudding home hard enough to crack the glass. The orange blind dropped, hiding the bathroom and the old man from view. I waited a second for the blind to lift again. It didn't.

Shinobu yanked lightly on the back of my top and gave me a questioning look.

I shook my head. "He's not coming!" I hesitated for a moment. "I think we need to go."

We picked our way carefully along the ledge. Twice we had to stop and cling to the wall, the pipes and each other, as the building shook again. Finally we reached the corner, and were able to shin a few feet up the drainpipe to the peeling asphalt roof above, where it felt marginally safer. I could still hear distant howls from the Harbinger – Izanagi – and feel the roof heaving underfoot. The old man must have some really bloody powerful magical protections down there or Izanagi would have demolished this whole place by now.

We set off on a jumping, sliding, skidding journey over the rooftops, moving as fast as we could. I craned over the edges of the buildings, trying to make sure that we were heading in the right direction – towards the only possible sanctuary, my house – expecting all the while to see the Harbinger suddenly appear in hot pursuit. Shinobu was scrutinizing the sky, checking for signs of Izanami's Handmaidens.

With every step, I was hyper-aware that we were fleeing from our one source of information about this whole mess. We had brought danger to his door, and then left him behind, and although part of that was his own fault, I honestly felt sure that he had meant us no harm. There was so much more that we needed, *needed* to know, and so little time to find out. My stomach churned with frustration and worry.

After about half an hour of clambering over the rooftops, we hit a flat concrete roof liberally scattered with metal air-conditioning vents. I signalled to Shinobu that I had to stop, and bent over, leaning my hands on my knees and taking deep breaths.

"I cannot understand why he would not come with us," Shinobu mused out loud. I caught what he was saying this time, although my ears were still ringing a little.

"All I could make out was that he didn't want our protection. I think he said he didn't need it. He must have some pretty strong mojo of his own. It's kind of weird how he chooses to look like that, live like that. The king said he never even sets foot outside the shop."

"Did he say anything else before we left? You had your head in the window for a while."

"Mio, this is the katana's second name. Listen…"

Don't tell him.

Just don't say anything.

Don't say it.

For God's sake!

I closed my eyes.

"He told me the sword's second true name."

I felt Shinobu's gaze snap to my face. We stood there in silence as the wind whistled around us.

I couldn't figure out what I needed or wanted to say. Abruptly I was exhausted, so overwhelmingly tired that I could barely think straight. Slowly I slid down to sit on the concrete, with my back to one of the metal vents. After drawing my knees up, I wrapped my arms around them and hid my face. There was a tentative footstep and a rustle of clothing, then Shinobu's shoulder leaned against mine as he sat beside me.

Mr Leech could tell us that the gods – Kami – were damn useless fools all he liked, but they were still terrifying, powerful, impossible to predict, and *after me and the katana*.

What would Izanami do if one of her monsters finally

managed to get hold of the sword? It didn't take much imagination to figure out. She'd break the remaining bindings on it and break out of her Underworld prison, bringing all her demons with her. The mortal realm would become a nightmare battle zone as she went after Izanagi and revenge.

If Izanagi got his hands on it? He'd bind Shinobu back into the sword again. It was obvious now that was what he'd been trying to do the first time he came after me, when he'd skewered Shinobu to the floor with those bolts of white energy. Then he'd ... "break my spirit", Mr Leech had said. I shuddered at the thought of what that might mean. But in the end I'd still be the sword's protector, still be compelled to guard it, still never be safe. And Izanami would continue sending her monsters into the world to hunt the sword, threatening innocent people wherever they went. Innocent people like my family. Like the ones I loved.

Izanami was clearly as crazy as a sackful of ferrets. She gave me the creeps all right. But Izanagi? He was way worse. He was sane and he knew what he was doing – to me, to London, to Shinobu. He just didn't care. Izanami's monsters could wipe out the whole city and he wouldn't lift a finger to stop them, so long as he was safe. He'd successfully evaded the consequences of betraying his wife for all these years and clearly had no intention of stopping, regardless of how many innocent people got hurt.

"Mio," Shinobu began quietly.

"Don't."

"Mr Leech gave us an answer. It was not … the one we were hoping for. That does not mean we can pretend we never heard it."

I ground my forehead against my knees. "Don't."

"Mio—"

"I can't talk about this." The feelings boiling inside me were too much. I couldn't articulate them, couldn't even fully comprehend them. It was too much. I needed it all to stop. I just needed it to stop for a minute and let me *think*. "We have time, OK? We have some time to figure something else out, so we don't have to talk about this."

"We do have to talk about it," he said, his voice a mixture of pleading and resolve. "Look at me. We have to – to try to decide…"

A choked noise burst out of my throat and I slammed my fist down on the concrete beside my hip as I looked up at him. "Decide what? *What?* How to kill you? How to put you back in the dark, but this time forever? Shinobu, there has to be another way. Some way out of this. There has to be. Do you honestly think I could do that to you? Just take away your life? It would be murder! I can't – I can't even…" The words dried to dust in my mouth as I stared at his face.

It was a stranger's face in many ways, with unfamiliar expressions and changing moods that often seemed

223

to lie before me like some undiscovered country, waiting to be explored. But at the same time, it was already as beloved, as familiar to me, as the sky or the sun, or my own reflection. Shinobu's dark eyes were tormented now – shadowed with sorrow and despair and something more. I had never seen that expression on his face before, not even when he lay dying alone in the red forest. And I realized that he was afraid. As afraid as me.

A terrible pang went through my heart. I shook my head wordlessly. *No. I won't let go.*

He took my hand and ran his fingers gently over my knuckles. "You know that the choice … this choice is mine to make. Not anyone else's. Not even yours."

"What's wrong with you?" I whispered. "Why are you just accepting this? Why won't you fight? It's like … like you want to go back into the dark. Like you want to die."

As soon as the words left my mouth, I wanted to call them back. But it was too late. Shinobu dropped my hand and straightened away from me, his face hardening.

I could still never have predicted what he would say next.

"I am already dead."

I jolted as if he'd stuck a live wire into me. "That – that's not true."

"It is. You know it is," he said. His voice was quieter now, but somehow more emphatic for that. "You saw it for yourself. A piece of metal thicker than your arm pierced my heart and I walked away from it without even a bruise. Since I entered this world again, I have not slept. I have not eaten or drunk. Hardly anyone can even see me. *I am dead.* I have known this since the moment I opened my eyes on the floor of Battersea Power Station, and you have known it too, even if you would not admit it to yourself. I am a sundered spirit, walking the earth in human form. This state of things cannot endure. I cannot endure. This – the end – was always inevitable."

Inevitable.

The word echoed through me like a deep, inescapable rumble of thunder. Everything I thought I knew fell away.

I got up and, wheezing shallowly, I staggered away a few steps. I couldn't speak. I couldn't even look at him, although I could sense him getting to his feet, coming after me.

One of my hands jerked up, palm facing him. He stopped dead.

"That's what – that's what you think? The whole time? The whole time we've been with each other that's what you thought?"

For however long I may stay by your side, I will have all that I need. Those words had seemed so romantic to me. I thought he was telling me some pop-song sentiment about how love was the only important thing to him. But he'd meant the exact opposite.

He didn't expect to be around long enough for anything to count.

Something burst open inside me. I whipped round, both my palms smashing into his chest. The blow shoved him back a step, but his face registered no shock, only sadness. That made me even madder.

"I knew?" The words were a scream. "I was supposed to know? I didn't know! I thought we were going to have a future together! You kept everything – you kept all this – a secret. You pretended it was *real*! You let *me* believe it was real!"

"Mio-dono—"

"Don't call me that! You let me believe in us. How could you do that if you never believed yourself?"

I went to shove him again. He grabbed hold of me and dragged me against him, wrapping his arms around me. "My beloved. I'm sorry." He whispered raggedly into my hair, speaking in Japanese.

"What? What are you saying?" I demanded, struggling furiously. "Speak English!"

"*There are lies that are sweeter than the truth*. I am sorry, Mio. I let you believe because I wanted to believe. I let you hope because hope was all I had." His fingers clenched in my hair almost painfully as I tried to pull away.

"Let go of me, you—"

"Listen to me! Do you think I want to go? How can you think that? All I have ever wanted is you. A life with you. I would do anything to stay. Anything. *I love you.*"

The words sounded like they had ripped out of him, dripping blood. It was obvious that it had taken everything he had to say them. I couldn't doubt him. He was telling the truth. That almost made it worse.

"You're so selfish." I hit him half-heartedly in the back with my fist, then again, a little harder. "How could you do this? How could you kiss me? How could you let me fall in love with you?"

He laughed shakily. I felt him kiss my hair, his arms tightening even more. "You are right. I am selfish. I do not deserve you, Mio. I never did. After Battersea, when I knew that I had come back as something different, I should have drawn away from you for your sake. But all I could think was that if I had died then, at the Nekomata's hands, I would have died without ever touching you. Without kissing you. Without having you in my arms like this. I would do anything to stay with you – but I cannot change my fate. I cannot change what is. And if I have to go back into that prison, back into the darkness and the cold, I want to take the warmth of you and the light of you with me in my heart. Without it, I won't survive."

Love and fury and sorrow roiled inside me until I could barely see straight. "We don't *know* how to put you back. There has to be another way. There has to be another way. *There has to be another way.*" That was all

I knew right then, my only truth. "Maybe Mr Leech is wrong. He admitted that he doesn't know everything – he didn't know about you being alive and out of the sword! Maybe I *can* control the sword! I'm stronger than he thinks. I could try. Maybe I don't have to use the next true name at all. I might be able to get enough power just with the first one. I'd have a better chance then. Or … or … and, anyway, we don't know how to put you back."

He cleared his throat, letting me pull away a little so that he could look into my face. "These dreams you have been having are not just dreams, we both know that. I think you have been seeing these things for a reason. I think … I think that … when the time comes … you will know what to do."

The green blade flashes down in the red light—

Frost prickled down my spine. My eyes shot to the clouds, where a pair of birds circled downwards, growing bigger. And bigger. *Those aren't birds.*

I screamed, "Foul Women!"

We hit the concrete as the first monster swooped down on us.

CHAPTER 14

DIVINE INTERVENTION

Jack forced her head to turn on the pillow despite the pain in her eyes and neck and stared at her sister's phone lying on the locker next to the bed. It was too far away. It hadn't seemed that far a couple of hours ago when she dropped it there after calling Mio and her sister, but it was now. She just couldn't find the energy to roll over and reach out for it.

The problem was that she had a feeling.

It had been getting worse for a while now, the weird, sinking sensation in the pit of her stomach that said, *Something's Wrong. Something's Wrong.* She thought she might be sick if she didn't get hold of Mio again and make sure that nothing bad – well, worse – had happened to any of them.

Stop freaking out, she told herself. *Rachel's safe. Shinobu's safe. Mio's safe. They're all together and they're*

229

working on figuring this out. Everything is going to be OK.

But the sickening feeling kept on getting worse. Jack clutched a pillow to her stomach. Maybe she was just imagining these spooky feelings. Maybe she felt sick because she was going to hurl. That would have been a relief, actually.

The patient in the bed on her left began to sob softly.

Somewhere further away – at the other end of the ward – a high-pitched, shrill note rang out. A heart-monitor alarm. A couple of seconds later several sets of footsteps thundered past. Metal rings clattered as someone dragged back the curtains around a bed.

"Get the crash trolley! Page Doctor Amadine!" a woman shouted.

Jack squeezed her eyes shut, trying to mentally block out the sounds of the nurses' attempts to resuscitate the unknown patient. This was the third time someone had flatlined in the last two hours.

The longing to be out of this place, away from the terrible noises, the stinging smells, bright lights and pastel colours was intense. She wanted to go home. She wanted her own stuff, and Rachel, and her mum. A small, long-denied part of her even wanted her dad. Not that he would care, the bastard. He'd never pick her up in his arms and carry her to her bedroom and tuck her in again, even if he was here, instead of living it up in California with a girlfriend who was only eight years older than Jack. He'd checked out of being a father way before he actually had the guts to pack his stuff and leave. And she didn't care.

She didn't.

She didn't…

She could imagine herself back in own room and her own bed, with her skull duvet and Mr Ringo the stuffed lemur waiting for her. The thought made tears prickle in her eyes. *Am I delirious?*

She reached up to brush the tears away—

A small hand snapped closed over her wrist. Jack opened her eyes to stare incredulously at…

"Rach? What are you … doing here? What…?" Jack's voice trailed off as she took in her sister's appearance.

Rachel stood motionless in the gap between the curtains, her face as blank and expressionless as a wax doll's. Her hair was … different. Black and stringy. Wormlike. Was it – was it moving? It seemed to shift and curl as if it had a life of its own. Her eyes were closed. Dark, veinlike marks spiralled out from the delicate skin of her eyelids, giving her face a sick, bruised look.

The small hand tightened on Jack's wrist. "Ow! Rachel!"

Rachel's eyes opened.

They were black. Absolute black. No visible pupil, no whites, nothing. The eyes of a shark. Or something worse.

Jack could feel the blood draining out of her face. Her head spun. Now she really did feel like she was going to hurl. *Shit, shit, shit.*

231

"Rachel Elizabeth Luci," she said, voice trembling. "You … you stop it with this *Exorcist crap* … right now or I swear to God … I will tell Mum."

Rachel slithered forward, her movements boneless and yet somehow awkward, as if she wasn't at home in her body. Her mouth gaped open and stayed open, unmoving, as a thin, plaintive voice echoed from inside her throat. "Don't scream."

That isn't Rachel.

Jack gritted her teeth. "I'm not screaming."

"So frightened. Poor little birdies, flutter flutter – crunch. They always scream."

"Hey! *I'm not screaming.* Now let go … of my arm."

There was a long pause. Rachel's mouth stayed open, her eyes remained wide and unblinking. A tiny frown creased her brow. "You are … not afraid?"

Actually I'm about three seconds away from peeing my pants, but I'm effed if I'll admit that to you. "Are you kidding? I've seen … scarier shit than this … in the Harry Potter films."

Rachel's fingers slowly uncurled from their painful hold on Jack's wrist. Jack wrenched her arm away and cradled it protectively against her chest, feeling the deep throbbing in her skin that meant she was going to have bruises. More bruises.

Rachel's head tilted slowly sideways, the black eyes still staring, her mouth still gaping open.

Jack's eyes flicked to the curtains. They felt like a barrier, but they really weren't. She could fall off this bed and roll and two seconds later she'd be out in the ward in public, screaming her head off, surrounded by people.

But Rachel would still be here. And that thing, whatever it was, would still be … possessing her. How had this happened? She was supposed to be with Mio. She was supposed to be safe! "Who – no, *what* … are you? What do you want?"

"Ah … you don't know." The voice trailed off into a ringing, unnerving laugh.

A shiver shuddered down Jack's spine. It showed in her voice when she spoke. "Obviously not … so why don't you … tell me?"

"Your friend knows. The little one – not so little any more – such an angry little birdie. She's stronger than she looks. She might survive all of us. Or … maybe not." The strange laugh trilled out again.

Jack could feel her face scrunching up. "Mio? You're talking … about Mio?"

"I tried to talk to her again. I can almost touch her now. She's warm. You are all so warm, and I have been cold for so long. But I cannot reach her mind just now. I need her to know. Things. Things about my beloved, my captor, my king. He tells everyone lies about me… I want her to know the truth. I want her to know why I need the grass-cutting blade. It is the only thing that can free me."

The sad little voice trailed off and Jack felt a weird stirring of pity.

"So – you came into … Rachel's body to tell me that so I can tell Mio?"

"Yes. This one, this body, you see … my servant supped upon it. Now she is open to me. So useful."

My servant…?

Oh my God. The Nekomata.

Pity dissolved in a surge of horror, and then both of those were eaten by fury. Jack's hands curled into claws and she tried to lunge forward across the bed. Her body flopped weakly, legs caught up in the covers. She thrashed, her own heartbeat deafening her.

"Get out of her," she panted. "Get out … of my sister! You've no right! Get out, get OUT!"

Pain ripped down Jack's aching neck like a hot wire. She tried to scream again, but she couldn't get enough breath. Her heart felt as if it had swelled up in her chest, pressing into her ribs, crushing her lungs. Dimly she heard the sound of the heart monitor beside the bed going crazy.

I have to calm down, she realized. *I have to stop. I have to lie still.*

But her legs wouldn't stop kicking. Convulsing. Her whole body was shaking now. She tasted blood as her teeth gouged into her tongue. Her head snapped back so hard that white sparks flew across her vision. Then everything went dark.

Thrashing wings engulfed us in shadow, blasting the vile stink of burning hair and decay down onto us. I squeezed my watering eyes shut and tried not to retch as the Shikome's vicious, yellowing talons ripped through the air above where Shinobu and I lay.

The Foul Woman shrieked. The momentum of its dive shot it over the edge of the roof.

I flipped to my feet, swiping a forearm over tear-filled eyes. My hand flew back to my sword hilt, then checked. Conflicting instincts screamed at me: protect the blade, hide it, draw it, kill with it. It was the only weapon I had, yet the thought of using it scared me for so many good reasons, especially after what Mr Leech had told us. But Shinobu was on his feet next to me now, both blades bared. I couldn't let him fight alone.

I gripped the katana's hilt, preparing to draw it as the first Shikome circled.

A second monster dropped out of the sky right on top of me. Shinobu shoved me aside and struck in a whirl of silver and black, opening a long cut on the Foul Woman's flank. This one moved fast. Its flailing talons rent open the arm of his leather coat. Livid red sprayed out, splattering over the ground. Shinobu made a muffled noise of pain and dropped his wakizashi. He drove the Shikome back with a vicious jab of his katana. It shot up in the air with a squawk.

Then the first one was on me again. I ducked beneath the wild slash of its claws without even trying to engage. My eyes were riveted on Shinobu. He had ended up a few metres away, with his back pressed to an air vent. One hand clutched the wound on his shoulder. Blood bubbled up through his fingers.

The first Foul Woman dived at me again, coming in even lower than before. Its feet gouged the roof. Chunks of the concrete surface flew up in two huge lines as the monster headed right for me. I flung myself sideways, skidded, and banged to a halt against the air vent next to Shinobu. The Foul Woman skimmed over the edge of the roof, dropped and then gained altitude again, flapping mightily as it joined its wounded sister hovering above us.

"Shinobu, you're bleeding so much," I panted. "Can you tell how bad it is?"

His face was ghastly white and stark with pain. "Bad. I need a bandage—"

One of the Foul Women swooped over the vent where we were crouched. We both ducked as the monster's back paws hit the metal with a deep, gong-like sound. The top of the vent buckled. Amber liquid – the monster's blood – spurted down over us. It flapped back into the air, squalling.

"At least they are not as clever as the Nekomata," Shinobu said grimly.

I stripped the katana's harness and the fleece off

quickly, wrestled Jack's white T-shirt over my head, then pulled the other things haphazardly back on. Shinobu was trying to draw the leather coat down over his arm to get at the injury. I helped him, grabbing the edges of the torn leather and yanking them apart to give us room to work.

My breath stuttered out in panic when I saw the jagged gash that gaped in his flesh. Something yellowish had been exposed – bone or muscle, I wasn't sure – and the blood was still gushing out around it. It wasn't healing. It wasn't closing up. I tore Jack's T-shirt in half, and on Shinobu's orders, I bound the wound painfully tight, desperately trying to stop the flow of blood. Shinobu's clenched jaw and his suppressed grunt of agony made me bite my lip. The first strip of fabric was soaked before I even managed to bind the other half over the top, and I could still see new blood trickling down his fingers. Why wasn't it getting better? Had something changed? Oh God, what if he had to actually die before his healing ability kicked in? We'd never tested it.

We had to get away from this rooftop, away from the Foul Women. Right now. But how was I supposed to fight monsters that could fly?

I need to fly too.

In that final fight with the Nekomata, it had literally picked me up off my feet and thrown me at a wall, expecting me to be smashed to a pulp. Instead, with the sword's help, I had bounced off the bricks – and then …

then I had *flown* back at it and killed it, powered by sheer rage and the katana's energy. It could be done.

The pool of blood under Shinobu's hand was still spreading. It was frighteningly dark. Arterial blood.

The Shikome were stupid. They swooped down one after the other and then circled for height. It was a repeating pattern – and it had an opening. A weakness.

But for me to use it, I would have to draw the blade. I would need to call its first true name.

I had no other plan, no other ideas. I just had to pray that I would be strong enough to resist the sword, at least long enough to get us to safety.

I eased myself into a runner's starting position, bracing my free hand on the roof.

"What are you doing?" Shinobu demanded, his voice slurring.

"Getting us off here," I said, my eyes on the Foul Women. *One … two…* "Just stay down."

Three.

The Foul Women skimmed over opposite edges of the roof, and for a moment both of them were too far away to be a threat.

I pushed up and ran, shooting across the roof straight at an air vent on the opposite side. At the last minute I jumped, bounced off the vent with both feet and then went airborne, ripping the sword from its saya as I flew.

I hadn't realized until then how truly strong I had

become. The power of my leg muscles propelled me up into the sky, my body carving through the air like a knife. The returning Shikome scattered around me in birdbrained panic, shrieking. For a split second I felt completely weightless.

Then gravity tugged on me. I felt myself begin to drop. "*Shinobu!* Help!"

Happy to oblige, the sword's metallic, inhuman voice whispered in my mind.

In my hand, the katana burst into vaporous, prismatic flames.

My muscles shuddered as the sword's power hit them and I let out a wild yip, not sure if it was pain or joy. Strength surged through me like a bomb detonating.

One of the Foul Women got over its shock and careened towards me. It slashed at me with one massive paw. I sliced its wrist open and kicked it straight in the gut. The momentum of the kick sent me flipping back – my body spun into a dizzy, cartwheel, three hundred and sixty degrees around the creature's body. I reached out wildly and grabbed a handful of hair. A second later I thudded to a stop against its back, between the stinking, chittering arches of its wings. The monster went mad, clawing at its own shoulders as it tried to reach me. I anchored my foot in the small of its back, dragged the head up, and cut its throat in one swift movement.

Isn't this fun? the sword murmured softly. You and me together?

I was laughing uncontrollably. "Yes! More!"

The monster thrashed, its gurgling sounds mixing with the hyena cackle of my laugher. It plummeted downward. I launched myself off the dying Foul Woman's shoulders, white flames still enveloping me and finally felt myself begin to drop, hurtling towards the concrete.

"Can I survive the fall?" I asked the katana.

You can survive anything, my lovely child, so long as you have me...

Shinobu's arms snatched me from the air, whirling me around. The white energy crackled around us both, exploring him eagerly. I pushed away without looking at him, skipping around the body of the fallen monster as I searched the sky for any sign of the remaining Shikome.

"Where are you? Come out, come o—out!" I sang. My voice was strangely distorted, silvery and metallic in my own ears. That only made me laugh more.

The second Foul Woman rose over the edge of the roof. It was the one Shinobu had wounded. Its vile smell slapped me in the face, and I grimaced, lifting the burning katana. "Come on, then! Let's see what you can do!" I waggled the blade enticingly. "Don't you want this? Here, birdie, birdie!"

The creature wheeled in the air, flapping away from me like its tail feathers were on fire.

"Aw…" I said. "So boooring."

Shinobu caught my free hand and began tugging at me, trying to get me to follow him. I yanked my hand away.

"Come on!" he said urgently.

"What's the hurry? We won!" I laughed again, prodding the giant clawed foot of the dead Shikome. It flopped sideways, which struck me as hilarious. I kicked it again, and again, making the stupid ugly monster dance there on the concrete. Something snapped loudly – a bone giving way under the force of my stamping boot. I let out a joyous cackle. God, it was so much *fun* to break things!

I wonder what they look like inside, the sword whispered. Want to cut it open and find out?

Yes. Yes, I did. Hack it up, pull it to pieces, shred it apart… I raised the sword. Shinobu swore under his breath. He grabbed my face and peered into my eyes. Then he reached over my shoulder with one hand and fumbled with the harness, pulling the gleaming black-and-gold saya out.

"Hey, what are you doing?" I jerked away hard enough to send me into a little spin. The world whirled around me and I felt a strange pang of alarm, as if something inside me was … afraid?

You never need fear anything, as long as you have me, the katana promised.

241

Yes, that was right. I stretched out my arms, almost purring under the loving stroke of the blade's energy. That was right. No fear. No worry. No past or future. Only the sword. Only my beautiful sword…

"Sheathe the blade," Shinobu commanded, his voice rudely breaking into my train of thought.

"What? Why?" I whined. "I don't want to."

"Just do it."

"No!" I danced back as he stepped purposefully towards me, the saya in his left hand. "Why are you ruining everything?"

He is jealous. He wants me for himself. He will take me away from you. The sword's warning sent a shiver of horror through me.

"Get back," I snapped, bringing the blade up. I pointed my weapon at the boy holding the saya, warding him off as the beautiful flames danced along the shining edge of the metal. *Mine, mine, all mine.* I would kill anyone who tried to take it away—

"Mio. Look at me. It is me."

Don't listen to him. Stand firm, my lovely one. I will protect you.

"I know who you are," I mumbled. "I know what you're after. Stop it. You – just get away from me—"

Shinobu stepped forward again. This time I refused to step back. Suddenly the very tip of the blade was dancing a hair's-breadth from his throat. Shinobu stood perfectly

242

still, his eyes riveted on my face, arms opened wide as if to embrace me.

"My love," he whispered. "Sheathe the blade. Please."

I could feel the katana pulling me forward, yearning for the sweet moment when it would meet flesh and pierce it—

Yes. Yes. We can be free, just you and me...

NO!

The internal voice was so loud that my whole body jerked. My arm was suddenly moving, whipping the blade away from Shinobu. My fingers flew open, letting the sword clatter to the ground. Shinobu dived after it and seized the hilt, slamming the flaring, sparking blade back into the saya.

The instant that the guard clicked against the koiguchi – the scabbard mouth – my body went cold. I staggered. Shinobu caught me before I went down, and I clung to him, burrowing into the warmth of him as he held me up. I let out a muffled sob.

"Shit," I whispered. "Shinobu, I – I didn't..."

"I know," he said, stroking my head with a hand that shook. "You didn't know me. I hardly knew you..."

"It was worse than last time. I didn't even realize what was happening. It – it unmade me."

It hadn't been like being drunk. Or even like the time I sat next to that guy at a party who turned out to be smoking a spliff, and I accidentally got high. No matter how trashed you got, and how stupid or dizzy or sick or angry it made you act, you were still *you*. The katana had literally made me into someone – something – else. It had tried to make me into what it was.

It was so inhuman. So cold. So utterly ruthless. The sword didn't want to heal or help anyone or any living thing. It would never do anything but destroy and ruin if it had the choice. That was why it had made me stronger and faster; not to protect me, but to make me a better tool. A better weapon for *it* to wield.

I shuddered against Shinobu and he squeezed me so tightly that for a second I couldn't breathe. Then he drew back, picking the sword up from where he had dropped it at our feet. The need to wrench the katana away from him flared inside me. I squashed it, even though the effort made me shake more than ever. He put the weapon back in its harness between my shoulders.

"We do not have much time," he said. "That thing will lead every Foul Woman it can find back here."

"It's all right. I can manage." My knees gave out as the last word left my mouth, and he caught me again.

"We will go carefully," he said.

I nodded. My head felt wobbly on my neck.

I did my best to keep up as Shinobu led me on a slower and more cautious scramble over the roofs, away from the site of the battle. He helped me to slide down a steep gable, lifted me over a bank of solar panels, and stopped me falling three times as we crossed what felt like acres of tiles, lead and asphalt.

"Sorry," I gasped.

I hate you, I told the sword silently. *I hate you. I hope you know how much I hate you.* The thoughts didn't stop me from checking to make sure it was secure in the shinai carrier as we went.

"Hush," Shinobu said, taking both my hands to pull me up over a section of fancy wooden balustrade. "No apologies from you. You saved us."

I slipped and landed hard on both knees with a noise like a ripe melon dropped on a rock. "Ouch," I whispered feebly.

I managed to get my eyes to focus on Shinobu's pale, anxious face. He crouched in front of me, his big hands the only warm spots on my shivering body as he carefully cupped the back of my head and the small of my back to keep me steady. It occurred to me that he was injured, that it ought to be impossible for him to bear my weight, to look after me like this. But somehow he did it anyway.

"This is not working," he said, casting a swift, worried look at the sky. "We are not moving fast enough."

I blinked tears out of my eyes and tried to take stock of where we were. Not a roof. A sort of roof-terrace garden that jutted out from the side of a taller building. A long bank of French windows ran alongside us, the rooms beyond – thankfully – shielded on the inside by white blinds. I was kneeling on wooden decking, and pots filled with miniature trees and shrubs crowded around us. Some metal patio furniture and a barbeque filled one corner. A little plastic shed sat in the other. My watery gaze zeroed in on it. It was roughly the size of two phone boxes shoved together. Its back wall was situated against the wood-clad building, and it was secured to the decking with metal loops. *Shelter.*

"Do you think we could both fit in that?" I asked Shinobu.

Shinobu turned to look at it, then cast another unhappy glance at the sky. "I think we will have to."

My knees twinged in protest, but I managed a heavy, stumbling walk towards the shed, with Shinobu's arm around my waist lending support. In its carrier on my back, the sword buzzed, agitated. It wanted out.

Not a chance, I told it fiercely.

The sword had done this to me. On purpose. I was sure of it. It had pushed my body so far and so hard that it had almost crippled me. If I was unable to run, I would have to fight. And in this state, the only way I could fight would be to call on the blade to help me again. When that happened, it would take hold of me – of my mind – exactly the way it just had. And take hold of me more firmly and more easily than before.

We had to get out of this ourselves.

The shed was closed with a plastic latch and a small

metal padlock. The flimsy plastic stood no chance against the hilt of Shinobu's sword. Within a second he had wrenched the door open, helped me inside, and wedged himself in after me.

The small space was lined with shelves of gardening tools and barbecue accessories. I folded up, my backside hitting the wooden deck with a bump, and squashed as far into the corner as possible to make room for Shinobu to sit next to me. He coiled himself up and wrapped his larger body around mine as if it were the most natural thing in the world. The steady rhythm of his breathing and heartbeat calmed my own, like a lullaby.

Shinobu was that kind of a person. The type you could rely on to calm you down, to help you, to do whatever was necessary to keep you safe. It was who he was. He'd sacrificed himself in his first life, back in ancient Japan. And then again, to save Rachel. He was determined to do the same thing now, blindly and unthinkingly, without even trying to look for a way out. He was so busy protecting everyone else that it never occurred to him to try to protect himself.

"I won't let you go."

I hadn't meant to say it. The words were hardly a whisper. But I could tell from the way he tensed that he had heard. His dark eyes met mine in the half-light. We both took a deep breath; it was a toss-up for who would start arguing first.

The shed went dark. Something had blocked out the sun.

The burning, rotten stench of the Shikome drifted in to us, faint but unmistakable, and enough to make me cover my nose with my hand. I could just make out that distinctive dry chittering noise somewhere overhead.

The shadow slipped away, and light trickled into the shed once more.

Another shadow darkened the shed ... and passed.

Another.

That wasn't one Foul Woman circling. It was lots of Foul Women.

I kept my palm clamped over my nose and mouth, trying to muffle the sounds of my breathing. Shinobu didn't seem to be breathing at all. We huddled together, motionless apart from my slight trembling. The Foul Women seemed like single-minded hunting dogs, relentless and faithful to their Mistress, but without any logic or common sense of their own. Even if they could smell the sword's power, the fact that they couldn't see it or us might be enough to throw them off. Just long enough for us to get out of here.

Maybe.

The shadows kept circling. I tried counting them, but it was impossible to tell how many there were. How many had Izanami managed to send into the mortal realm by this time? Too many. That was all I was sure of.

Go away. Go away. There's nothing here.
Fly away, you stinking freaks.

I froze in horror as the shrill, tinny notes of "Wind Beneath My Wings" filled the air inside the little shed. My hand shot down to my pocket, my finger stabbing the phone's power button. The music cut off.

Shinobu and I stared at each other in the stillness. Outside, even the faint chittering of dry feathers had gone quiet. Light shone through the vents in the walls. The moment seemed to stretch on for a breathless eternity.

Go away, go away, go away...

An eerie, triumphant shriek rang out above us. The walls of the shed rocked as shadows swarmed over it, wing-beats filling the air like thunder. We both flung ourselves flat. Something hit the shed. It rocked back, then tore away from around us. The metal rivets holding it to the deck pinged off the wall of the building. Chunks of wood and pieces of gardening equipment flew. There was a distant crash and then we were lying in the open, completely exposed.

Nowhere to run.

CHAPTER 15

HUMAN INTERVENTION

Five Shikome – including the one that Shinobu had wounded – raged above the terrace. The strength of their wing-beats swept plant pots up to smash into the walls, sent the patio furniture tumbling across the decking. Soil, ruined plants and shards of terracotta whirled across us. My nails dug into the smooth wooden planking. I hung on for dear life. Only Shinobu's weight, half on top of me, kept me from getting blown away.

The Foul Women's shrieks took on a tone of frustration as their claws skimmed inches above our heads again and again. The terrace was too small for them to land, and the balustrade kept them from coming in too low when they dived. The monsters seemed to realize it at the same moment that I did. One of them reared up, sculling so that it hovered jerkily above the balustrade. It fixed its huge back claws on the carved wood and heaved, pumping its wings frantically.

I screamed, "Shinobu—"

"Get ready!"

I could feel him gathering himself, his fingers curling into the back of my hoodie. I tried to get my legs under me. The deck shuddered beneath us as the wooden railing ripped loose with an agonizing noise of splintering wood.

The Foul Woman screeched in victory. She dragged her prize upwards with an almighty sweep of wings, and hurled the huge chunk of shredded wood directly at us.

"Now!"

We rolled out of the path of the missile, both of us grunting at the impact as we slammed against the wall. The balustrade smashed into the bank of windows next to us.

The glass shattered.

Shinobu didn't need to tell me to move this time. I scrambled to my feet and flung myself towards the gaping wreckage of the windows. He was right behind me. The Shikome swooped down on us.

The white blinds rippled and snapped in the vile-smelling wind of the Shikome's attack. The creatures screamed desperately. Wicked, yellowing talons slashed amid streaming flags of pale cloth. I felt something soft gently brush the back of my neck.

Fire seemed to brand the skin there. Then numbness

took its place. I jerked forward, out of range of whatever had touched me, and lost my balance.

I landed inside the ruined apartment. Trapped outside, the Shikome were ripping and rending the blinds and wrecking the terrace garden in their frenzy. Inside, books, pictures, ornaments and tides of broken glass flew everywhere, crashing and surging around us, caught in the crazy whirlwind of the Foul Women's wrath.

I tried to roll over. To get up. I couldn't. The numbness was spreading across my neck into my throat, into my skull, arrowing down my spine with terrifying speed. My limbs shook and flailed but wouldn't bend; shooting cramps ripped through me as I tried to force them to obey me. My teeth clamped together. I tasted blood. I had bitten my tongue or my cheek but couldn't tell which because there was no feeling there. No feeling anywhere. Nothing except the agonizing cramping sensation attacking every cell of my body. Words bubbled into my mouth with the blood and were trapped behind my teeth. All that I could squeeze free was an agonized moan.

Shinobu was shouting at me. He rolled me onto my back in the middle of the chaos. His hair brushed across my face. His hands cupped my cheeks and then grabbed my hands and tried to hold me still. I wanted to look at him, but I couldn't focus. My vision was shaking and shaking; my eyes rolled in my head. I caught a fleeting glimpse of my own shuddering hand clasped in Shinobu's. There was a dark purple rash spreading across the back of it.

They got me. The bitches got me.

It hurts.

Oh God, it hurts, oh God, oh God, it hurts so much…

The room tilted and wobbled crazily around me, then blurred. Shinobu was swinging me up in his arms, running for a white door. There was a jolt. Another. I heard a crash dimly through the roaring of the Shikome's wind in my ears. The white door disappeared from in front of my eyes. Shinobu had kicked it down.

Then we were in a corridor. The pale gold walls swam before my eyes. Shinobu's hands were fastened on me like steel vices – my seizure was getting more violent. He could barely hold me. The pain in my limbs and my head was increasing. A scream raged in my throat, but that same strangled moan was all that would come out.

I'm not getting better. It's getting worse. I'm not coming out of it like Jack did.

What does that mean?

What's happening to me?

Shinobu laid me gently down. A thick, soft carpet cushioned my body. Shinobu held my head.

"Please, please," he repeated, over and over. "I can't. Please, please, no. I can't lose you. Mio, *please*…"

"Oh my God!" a strange voice cried out. There was a

blur of movement from somewhere behind Shinobu, but I was trying, trying with everything I had, to focus on Shinobu's face. I wanted to see it. I had to.

"I'll call an ambulance," the strange voice said. "Hold her head like that. Hold her still. She's bitten her tongue, don't let her choke."

Shut up. Shut up. Let me listen to him. I want him to be the last thing I hear.

"Please, Mio," Shinobu whispered. The light glinted off his cheek as if it was wet. He was crying.

Don't cry. Don't cry…

The pain was unbearable, like hot metal stakes driving through every muscle. My heart was stuttering, skipping; its pace impossible. My body couldn't keep this up. It was too much strain for any human to bear. I tried again to say Shinobu's name. It came out as a thin whine that made him flinch.

I love you. I love you. I love you. I love—

The hammering inside my ribs stopped. My back arched up off the carpet. My spine let out a series of terrible cracks as my body contorted against the hard shape of the katana. My heels drummed on the floor. Shinobu's face disappeared from above me – everything disappeared from all around me – and for a moment everything was still and quiet and white and pain, pain, pain…

Very faintly, an inhuman, metallic voice seemed to

whisper in my head: *Oh no you don't. I still have plans for you.*

A stake of crackling energy speared through me and nailed me back to the earth, back into my body.

Thump.

My teeth popped apart and I gulped a cool, delicious mouthful of air.

Thump.

White ceiling. Yellow-gold walls. Pain gently draining out of my body as if each fiery cramp had been bathed in cool water.

Thump.

Shinobu's face, eyes huge and dark, lips parted in an expression of relief so extreme that it looked like agony.

Thump.

It was my heart. That was what I could hear. Slowly other noises began to seep in. Shinobu's deep, shuddering breaths, and my own fast, rasping ones. A woman's voice, high with anxiety.

"I've never seen anything like… It's coming off. The rash is disappearing. Just disappearing on her face. It's fading away like it was never there. No, no, she definitely still needs an ambulance. There's been some kind of accident here – they're covered in blood, both of them. I don't know what happened. We need the police—"

"You were too strong," Shinobu whispered, cupping

my face. He squeezed his eyes shut for a second, and another tear streaked down his face. "It could not take you from me. It could not take you where you did not want to go."

I drew in another shallow breath, the thick iron taste of blood making me grimace. "Police? Ambulance?"

"I was too busy to stop her," Shinobu admitted.

"Should..." I cleared my throat. "Should go?"

"What's that, sweetheart?" The woman peered over Shinobu's shoulder. She was quite young, with untidy blonde hair and bright green glasses askew on a button nose. She looked freaked out, and I couldn't exactly blame her. "Is she saying something?"

"Don't. Want. Ambulance," I said, as clearly as I could.

The young woman gaped at me. "W–what?" she squeaked.

I must look even worse than I feel. Shinobu shook his head, then slid his arms under my limp body and scooped me up from the floor in one fluid movement. "Thank you for your help. We will be leaving now."

"Wait! You can't – come back!"

Shinobu carried me swiftly away, and the woman's voice faded behind us. At least she wasn't trying to follow. Loopy and disoriented, I was tempted to smush my face into his shoulder and enjoy the princess moment, but I woke up enough to point out the lift when he would have marched right past it.

Inside the elevator, I made him put me down on my own two feet. If I had been wiped out after the katana's mood-altering stunt, I was wrecked now. My legs were like Super Noodles and my hands didn't even have enough strength to hang onto Shinobu's coat for balance. He had to wrap both arms around me to keep me upright. The mirror on the back wall of the lift showed a bruised, grubby, wild-eyed girl with hair that not even a mother could love. There were purple-grey bags under my eyes, deep hollows under my cheekbones, and...

"I grew again, didn't I?" I mumbled.

"A little, I think," Shinobu said, his lips pressing gently to my crazy hair. "Just a little."

"Easy for you to say. I'm the one that's going to end up as a giraffe if this keeps on."

The lift reached the ground floor with a cheery pinging noise. We stumbled out into a small lobby. There was a posh reception desk recessed into the back wall, and the front wall and door were made of glass. The receptionist – or security guard – that should have been sitting there was AWOL. Probably huddled at home with the doors and windows barricaded.

I wished I was too.

Shinobu peered out of the glass wall. No suspicious shadows flittered across the pavement outside.

"I know where we are," I mumbled, squinting. "This

place is, um, maybe five minutes from the house."

"Five minutes in the open is too long," Shinobu said flatly.

"The city's locked down; there won't be any taxis about. And even if the buses are running, we're not on a bus route. I can't think of any way to get home from here other than to run as fast as we can."

"You cannot run. You can barely walk," he pointed out.

"We can't hide here, Shinobu. It's not safe for us or anyone here – and that woman asked for the police, remember? They'll probably arrive any minute." I gestured to my dirty, ripped-up clothes and the splatters of blood, both human and Shikome, decorating them. "I'm pretty sure they will have some questions for me. We have to be gone before they get here."

"What if Foul Women attack us as soon as we get outside?"

I stared through the glass. Still nothing to see. The icy, prickling sensation down my back was absent too. The sword lay quietly between my shoulder blades. "We could prop the door open? The second you catch sight of a feather we can retreat."

He nodded reluctantly. I sat down on a leather chair by the reception area as he made a fat wedge out of some papers he had picked up from the desk, eased the door open, and shoved the papers under the edge so that it was stuck half-open. The movement made the torn arm of his coat gape open and I realized with a jolt that I'd completely forgotten about his injury.

"Jesus, Shinobu, your arm! How – you've been dragging and carrying me around like it was nothing!"

"It was nothing," he said, straightening up. He kept his back to me. "There is no need to worry."

"Is it still bleeding? We need to find another bandage—"

His shoulders jerked a little as if he was shrugging something off, then he turned back and walked towards me. He helped me up off the leather chair and held me against him so that I couldn't see his face. "It has already healed."

He said the words the way you would say, *It is incurable*.

I didn't need to see his face to realize that instead of being happy he wouldn't lose his arm or any more blood, he was miserably convinced this was more proof that he wasn't human. That he didn't belong here. Didn't deserve to stay.

I clenched my jaw. *Save it for later*.

"Are you ready?" he asked.

I nodded.

We slunk out like a pair of cat burglars caught in a floodlight. Both of us craned our necks, staring at every inch of sky visible between the buildings. I directed him to a narrow, shadowed alley. We scuttled down it as quickly as my stumbling footsteps would allow. Shinobu fixed one arm around my waist as I hung onto his side. His other hand sat on the hilt of one of his swords under his coat.

We crossed a road and ducked down a passageway behind a row of shops. My shaking was getting worse, and my breath came in short, shallow gasps. Surviving the Foul Women's taint had taken everything I had. The sword had only saved my life. It hadn't fixed my other injuries: the torn muscles and strained joints, the exhaustion. Of course it hadn't. That would be counter-productive. I had no reserves left to draw on now, and that was just how the blade wanted it.

Every time I tripped or lagged, Shinobu just tightened his grip and hauled me along with him. At last we turned the final corner, and there was my street. Quiet, wide, and completely open to the skies. To get to my house – to sanctuary – we had to walk right down it.

Without asking me, Shinobu stopped and stepped back into the shadowed gap between two buildings. I slumped down onto the cold pavement and put my head on my knees. My skull was throbbing so badly that I could actually hear it. If we didn't get to shelter quickly, I was going to pass out right here in the open.

The sword buzzed against my back, demanding my attention. *Me, me, me...*

No way, I snarled back mentally, shaking my head to try and clear it. It only made the throbbing worse.

"We have to go now," I said, my voice coming out like an echo from the bottom of a deep, dark hole. "I'm going to hang onto you and you're probably going to have to drag me. Just get us there."

I dug my house keys out and clenched them between finger and thumb, ready. Shinobu pulled me to my feet and put his arm back around my waist, while I fixed my other hand onto his coat with as much determination as I could. We both stared up at the sky for a long, tense moment.

Then we ran.

Or Shinobu did. Within two steps, I lost my balance and my grip on his coat. It didn't matter. Shinobu caught me, swept me up into his arms without breaking stride, and sprinted towards the house.

Ice spiked my spine. I didn't wait for the telltale sound and stink of wings. "Get down!"

Shinobu dropped. I hit the ground hard on my hip, grunting as I rolled away from him. He was already on his feet again, ripping out both blades in a blur of silver.

A Shikome swooped into the road. There was nothing here, in the centre of this broad, deserted street, to foil her attack. The chittering noise of feathers filled the air as two more Foul Women appeared over the rooftops. Too many. Could even Shinobu survive being torn to pieces by their claws? Would their supernatural disease have the power to kill him? I had no way of knowing.

Our choices had just narrowed down to zero.

I struggled up onto my knees and reached back for the katana. It buzzed and rattled eagerly against my back.

Shinobu slashed at the first creature. It whirled away into the air. Another – the one who had injured him before – dived down on top of him. He stabbed it in the gut. It shrieked with a sound like a huge, enraged seagull, its massive limbs tearing the air. Shinobu wrenched his sword back, but it was too fast for him again. The monster's talons raked his face. This time its shriek was one of triumph.

Shinobu dropped to his knees silently, blood streaming down his cheeks. I screamed. My hand closed over the sword grip, lips opening to say the sword's first name.

A man appeared in the road in front of Shinobu.

I had no idea where he had come from. One moment the road was empty except for us, the next he was there. He stood with his back to me, less than a pace from where Shinobu had fallen. A tall, motionless figure dressed all in black.

A katana glinted in his right hand.

The injured Foul Woman, Shinobu's blood still on its claws, turned on the new enemy fiercely. The man didn't raise his sword as the monster plummeted at him. His other hand came up and a missile flew, smashing into the centre of the monster's chest. Dark liquid splattered everywhere.

The man ducked fluidly into a crouch.

The dark liquid burst into flames.

Rearing up above the stranger, the Shikome was a black silhouette against the white sky, clawing at the fire as if it thought it could beat the flames out. With a dry whoosh, its wings caught fire too. The creature sailed over me in a cloud of sparks and half-burned feathers and ploughed straight into the tarmac in front of the house. Its massive body flopped and contorted on the ground as the fire consumed it. The agonized seagull cries deafened me.

The other two creatures hovered jerkily over the street, the yellow eyes on their wings staring down at their sister's agonizing death. The strange man had straightened up again. He made an inviting gesture with his sword. His relaxed posture telegraphed supreme confidence.

The Foul Women turned in the air and fled.

The burning Shikome fell silent at last – but the fire that had killed it raged on. The heat was overwhelming. Clouds of dense black smoke and glowing orange sparks billowed down the street. I pulled my hoodie up over my mouth and crawled slowly towards where Shinobu sat. As I reached him, he finally lifted his head. His face was streaked with drying blood. My stomach lurched. The creature's talons must have almost ripped out his eyes. But those eyes were fine now, and fixed on me.

He reached out his bloodstained hand. I grabbed it. Together, we looked at the man who had saved us. The orange light of the fire and the dancing sparks made weird patterns in the black smoke that swirled around him.

"Who—" I began, then choked on a mouthful of the vile-smelling smoke.

"Sir, where did you come from? Who are you?" Shinobu asked.

The stranger seemed to stiffen. He sheathed his blade with an abrupt movement, then slowly, as if forcing himself, turned to face us.

No. It's impossible. It can't be.

I whispered: "Dad?"

The front door slammed behind us with enough force to shake the house. My father released me, sliding my left arm off his shoulder and letting Shinobu take my weight. He stalked away from us down the hall, got to the kitchen door, then jerked round and marched back.

"What in all the gods' names is going on?" he demanded.

I blinked at him, dazed. "Dad – what are you doing here? Where's Mum?"

"She's in Paris. She's safe. Which is what you should

be. Why were you out there, Mio? Running around in the middle of this – this insanity – *fighting* – my God! What were you thinking?"

Shinobu's arm tightened protectively around me. "Yamato-san—"

"I don't even – who the hell *are* you? Are you the one that dragged her into a fight with Shikome? She could have been seriously hurt! She could have died out there!"

"Dad, don't," I began weakly. "It's not his—"

"No excuses, Mio," my father said, holding up a hand that shook with anger. "We left you alone for three days! *Three days* and London has literally gone to hell. And not a word from you! Why didn't you call us? Why didn't you answer your phone?"

Guilt clawed at me with ragged nails. I reacted the only way I knew how: defensively. "What was I supposed to say? How was I supposed to explain this? I didn't think you even knew what a Shikome was!" The last word cracked, turning into a semi-hysterical giggle.

"Do you think this is funny, young lady?" he fumed. "Typical! You live in your own little fantasy world where no one ever has to grow up or take responsibility for their actions and you expect everyone else to clean up after you when it all goes wrong!" He dragged his hands through his hair and yanked, as if he was tempted to rip it out.

I flinched. Shinobu felt it and wordlessly touched my

cheek, trying to comfort me. I turned my face away from the touch. *Dad's right. He's always right. I started this. It is all my fault.*

"Not a single word! Not a single call!" My father was still raging, pacing up and down the hall. "Do you have the faintest idea what I've been going through? How it felt to get that call from Rachel, and then nothing? Just silence! I have been completely in the dark. I can't believe how reckless – how utterly stupid – you have been!"

"Dad, I'm sorry, I—"

"I'm not interested in *I'm sorry*!" he yelled, ripping the katana out of his belt and flinging it down on the hall tiles with a crash of metal. I flinched again. "You're always *sorry* but it never, ever stops you! *You are exactly like my father!*"

SNAP.

I actually heard the crack inside me as all the fear and guilt of these terrible last days broke free – and caught flame. Rage engulfed me. I shoved away from Shinobu, ignoring the wobble in my legs and my aching head and the shake in my hands. I barely felt them.

"Screw you." My voice was low and wavering, venomous.

My father's face twisted with outrage. "What did you say?"

"You heard me," I spat. "You want to talk about *I can't believe*? I can't believe you have the nerve to bring

Ojiichan into this! Like it was all his fault? At least he made some effort to prepare me for this nightmare. At least he tried to warn me about the sword. If I'm like him, then I'm glad. At least I'm not like you!"

He made a slashing gesture with his hand. "You are completely out of line—"

"SHUT UP!" The scream tore itself out of my chest, ripping my heart with it as it went.

My father took a shocked step back. Then he squared his shoulders and moved towards me. In a reckless, light-ning-fast move, I drew the katana and pointed the shining tip at his face.

"Don't come near me. Don't you dare. You knew about the sword, didn't you? You knew about the monsters. I am your *daughter* and you left me completely alone in this. You – you left *me* completely in the dark. You bug-gered off on your holiday and *left us here with this thing in the house.*"

Fine wisps of white, vaporous fire were flickering down the sword's length, drifting around my hands like smoke. The caresses felt like the katana's version of comfort.

So much pain. So much sadness. Poor little mortal girl...

"Stop it now," my father said quietly. His face had gone ashen. "Put the sword down. You don't understand what's really going on."

"You're going to walk in here and say I've got no idea what you went through? Did you think for a second about what I've been through? The awful things I've seen? Did you spare one second to think about what I've had to do to stay alive? What I've had to become?"

"Mio-dono," Shinobu said softly. He placed his hand on my shoulder.

I shrugged it off without looking at him. "The only comfort I had in this – this *horror* was believing you and Mum were safe. You were far away, you had no idea about any of what was happening. And now I find out that you did know? That you knew everything all along?"

"I was trying to protect you—"

Don't believe him.

White sparks crackled down the shining curve of the blade. "Liar. You left me. I hate you for this. I swear to God I will hate you until the day I die."

Both Shinobu and my father recoiled. And I *didn't care*. This was too much. I just didn't care any more.

My father recovered first. "Mio—" he began weakly.

"Don't. Bother." I ground out. My voice was going raspy and rough, and I realized I must have been shouting at the top of my lungs. "I don't want to hear anything you have to say. All I want is for you to get away from me. Go back to Paris. Go to hell. Just leave me alone."

I rammed the smoking, flaming sword back into its saya, turned away from both speechless men, and marched up the stairs, adrenaline and rage carrying me up onto the second floor. I walked into the main bathroom, kicked the door shut, and bolted it behind me.

Then I burst into tears.

CHAPTER 16

WILL SET
YOU FREE

The tentative knock at the bathroom door came about ten minutes later.

"Go away, Shinobu." I tried to snarl the words but they came out as a wobbly whisper. *Pathetic.*

The knock came again, less tentatively this time.

"I said *go away!*"

Silence.

Lying there on the chilly tiled floor, aching, trembling and covered in three different kinds of blood, I couldn't stop thinking about the fact that both those men downstairs – both men that I had trusted, and loved, and who were supposed to love me back – had betrayed me. I clutched the katana convulsively to my chest.

Maybe I could forgive Shinobu for his lies. He'd been selfish, but at least I didn't doubt that he cared about me. He'd *died* for me, and he'd do it again if I let him.

But my father…

The man who had spent my whole life telling me the kendo I loved was a useless anachronism? Knew how to wield a katana. Had walked into this house wearing one like it was the most natural thing in the world.

The man who had hated my grandfather's stories about Japan and condemned them as gruesome nonsense that was only fit to give me nightmares? Knew what a Shikome was. And how to kill them.

He had looked at the sword, *my* sword – my fingers tightened around it even more, and it responded with a sharp buzz of energy – without the slightest bit of surprise. Even when it burst into flames at his throat.

He had known.

And he had hidden it all this time.

The scale of that betrayal made the foundations of my life shift and crumble away to dust beneath me. The man I thought was my father, the rigid, uptight dentist who disapproved of fantasy and fairy tales on principle and believed in order and logic and common sense – the man that I had grown up with, fought with, fought so hard to please and then fought even harder to piss off?

That man didn't exist.

He had never existed.

And the man who should have prepared me for all this – could have warned me – the man who could have *prevented* this whole disaster? Had hopped on the

Eurostar and left without a backward glance. Had left me to make the biggest mistake of my life, or anyone's life, without the faintest attempt to stop it.

There was a quiet scratching noise at the door, like an animal begging to be let in. With an effort, I lifted my head off the tiles and squinted blearily at it.

It swung open.

My father stood on the other side, tucking a credit card back into his wallet.

"Seriously?" I rasped out, letting my head drop to the tiles again. "What part of eff off and die is so hard to understand?"

There was a long pause.

"Oh, Midget ... what have we done to you?"

I'd never heard that tone of voice from him before. Guilt, regret, sadness; they were all there. Maybe he'd been too caught up in his self-righteous shit before to notice the state I was in. Well, if he felt bad now – good. He deserved to. My bitterness was strengthened by the knowledge that a few days ago I would have reacted to that evidence of concern like a neglected puppy to a kind word. But it was too late for a soft voice to melt my anger at this stage. Light years too late.

I heard a familiar long-suffering sigh, and stiffened, curling up tighter around the katana. It felt like my only anchor to reality right now. The irony was toxic.

Then suddenly I wasn't on the bathroom floor any

more, but in my father's arms.

"What are you doing? Put me down – leave me alone!" Treacherously familiar dad-smell enveloped me, but I refused to be comforted. I squirmed weakly.

"I've tried that already," he said matter-of-factly, hefting me across the hallway and kicking open the door to my room with no visible signs of effort. I'd had no idea he could lift a dumbbell, let alone a nearly grown woman. "It didn't work. It's time to try something different. The truth."

He put me down carefully on the bed and straightened up. I scrambled back until I was sitting against the headboard, trying to get as far away from him as possible. My strained muscles and bruises protested against the movement. I couldn't hold in a tiny whimper of pain. He frowned.

"I'll get you some painkillers—"

"Stop it!" I burst out. The words were raw and thick with tears, and I hated that he'd made me break. Now he could see how much he'd got to me. "Stop pretending to care! Just stop it! *Get out!*"

I turned away, burying my face in my forearm. The tip of the saya jabbed into my ribs but that was just another tiny thread in my blanket of misery right now. I couldn't bring myself to care.

After a moment, I heard my father's footsteps retreating, and the sound of the door swinging to. I stayed where I was, gritting my teeth to keep the sobs inside.

The rattle of china made me look up again. I hadn't even heard the door open.

My father set a TV tray down on my bedside table and one of his first-aid kits on the edge of the bed. The tray held a mug of tea, a plate of buttered toast, and a bowl of soup.

"You can hit out at me all you want, Mio," he said, folding his arms. "This time I'm not going to fight back, or walk away. I'm your father."

"Congratulations," I sneered. "It only took you fifteen years to figure that one out."

I closed my eyes again, huddling against the bed-head. I didn't know why he was suddenly acting all nice, or what he wanted, but I wasn't playing along.

Dad settled the tray on the bed in front of me. Then, moving faster than I would have thought possible, he somehow got me propped up against the pillows – and the next thing I knew, the tray was over my knees, and a mug of tea was in my left hand.

"Stop doing that! Stop – stop *arranging* me like a child!" I shrieked, banging the tea back down onto the tray. "Where's Shinobu?"

"Downstairs waiting for you and me to finish talk-ing," he said. "Don't worry, I haven't tried to chase him off. I doubt if I could. He read me the riot act after you ran up here. He told me a little bit about what you've been through. You need to refuel before I patch you up."

I knew I was gaping at him again, but I couldn't help it. Who was this calm, imperturbable, care-taking person, and what had he done with my father?

"It's getting cold," he said, seating himself in the creaky old chair that went with my desk/dressing table. "You hate cold toast."

I felt slow and bewildered, as if I was trying to make sense of a dream. Nothing was unfolding the right way, the way I would have expected it to. The smell of the food was making my stomach do crazy leaps inside me, but I wasn't sure if it was hunger or nausea. I probably did need to eat. I clearly wasn't getting rid of my dad until I had at least made an effort.

I tucked the katana in tightly next to my leg and picked up a piece of toast.

My father smiled. It was infuriating.

"What do you want?" I snapped.

"I want to tell you the truth. Keep eating."

I munched on the toast and washed it down with some tea, then picked up the soup spoon. "There. I'm eating. Satisfied?"

He shook his head. "You are so angry. So like me."

I dropped the spoon. *"What?"*

"I'm not trying to insult you. It's the truth."

"You're out of your mind. In what bizarre universe are you and I anything alike? You've spent my whole life trying to change me and fix me and make me over into something else! Why would you do that if I'm so like you?"

"Because you're my little girl and I just – I wanted you to be *happy*. I wanted you to be ... safe."

The words *Safe from what?* formed in my mouth. They died unspoken as I looked down at the katana, and my bruised, bloody fingers wound around the saya like a knot of skin and bone.

My father nodded. "Exactly."

I picked up the tea again with my free hand. "All right. Start talking."

"You must have figured some of this out already, I think. Our family has dedicated itself to protecting that sword for the last five hundred years—"

"I know that. No thanks to you, since you've lied to me my whole life."

"And I would do it again, if I thought it would work."

I gaped at him, stunned that he had the front to admit it. *"Why?"*

"I never, ever wanted you to be involved with the katana. I never wanted you to know about any of it. Understand, Mio – growing up a Yamato was like growing up in a cult. And the cult had one belief, one principle, one rule that was to be followed no matter what. That the sword was more important than any of us."

I frowned. "Ojiichan wasn't like that."

"Oh yes he was." My father stared down at his boots, face hidden from me. "He didn't know why the katana was so incredibly important, or why it had been entrusted to us, or even what it really was. But as far as he was concerned, that was just the way things had always been. The way things were. The sword was everything. The reason for our existence. The reason for my existence."

He looked up, and my mouth went dry, despite the tea I had just drunk. There was something in his eyes. Something terrible. A kind of dull suffering, worn-out and weary, and yet still overwhelmingly hurtful. The kind of suffering that might be carried for a whole life-time without someone ever getting resigned to it...

"Ojiichan couldn't have believed that," I said, suddenly moved to try and comfort. "You don't – I mean, he loved you. He did love you, Dad. He loved both of us."

"Of course he did," my father said wearily. "But you're old enough by now to know that there is no universal definition of love. To my father, 'love' didn't mean giving the people he cared for choices and freedom and letting them be happy. It meant moulding them into what he thought they should be. There were no other options.

"Do you know why he brought me to this country? It wasn't because my mother died, Mio. It was because she wanted to leave him, and she wanted to take me with her. But his family had dwindled until he was the only one left, and he couldn't risk having the line of Yamato sword-bearers broken. So he stole me in the middle of the night and fled here. He gave her no warning, no trail to follow. He just told me my mother was dead, and he took me away. I was too young to realize what had really happened."

One of my hands crept up to my mouth. "He wouldn't – he couldn't have – that can't be right."

My father ignored my feeble interruption. "From the moment that I was old enough to walk, he trained me. Sword work, fighting skills, concealment, endurance, the names and weaknesses of every monster in every myth, and most of all, he trained me to revere the sword. The sword was everything."

Ojiichan's voice echoed in my mind, passionate and persuasive. *Swear on your life. Promise me, Mio.*

"But you *don't* believe that," I said slowly. "Do you? So what happened?"

"My mother died. For real. Father had kept track of her, so he knew when she got sick, and when the cancer finally… Well, I believe he loved her too, in a sense, even though he left her behind in that brutal way. I suppose the shock of knowing that she was gone made him – vulnerable. Opened a chink in his armour. And because the burden of his lie had always troubled him, and he wanted absolution, he confessed to me. That my mother had been alive all those years. That she had searched for me until the day she died."

His voice choked off, and he grimaced, clearing his throat. "I gave him what he wanted – because I always did. I told him what he wanted to hear. That I understood. Forgave. But it wasn't true. I didn't understand. And I don't think I've ever forgiven him. Not even now. I don't think … I don't think I ever will. Because she never knew what happened to me, or where I was, or if I was dead or alive. I'll never know… Anyway, a year later, the day he had been waiting for all my life came around. I was finally sixteen and he ceremoniously took the blade from the box to hand it – and the title of sword-bearer – over to me… I looked at it, and him. And I asked: Why?"

"Why what?" I breathed.

"Why *any of it*," he said, eyes flaring with sudden intensity. "Why we followed the rules, believed in monsters and magic, and trained until we bled. Why we dedicated our lives to an item which had never benefited our family in any way, or lead to anything except sacrifice and loss. Why things had to be the way they had always been."

There was a pause as my father stared at the sun shining in through the window. Eventually I spoke. "How did he take it?"

"About how you would expect," he said dryly, turning his eyes back to me. "I ran away for a while. Over a year, actually. All his training had taught me how to take care of myself, at least. I lived rough."

Ran away? Lived rough? *Dad?* He threw a fit if I hung the dishtowel up the wrong way!

Maybe … maybe that's why he throws a fit if I hang the dishtowel the wrong way…

"When I eventually came back, my father had changed. He looked years older. He'd had a taste of what he put my mother through. Searching for me everywhere, not knowing if I was alive or dead – he thought I was gone for good, that he'd lost the only person he had left. So, even though he still thought I was wrong, he told me he would accept my decision. He promised he would respect my right to choose my own path. To prove it, he took the katana and locked it in the travelling chest with a brand-new, shiny lock, and gave the key to me to keep. It was a symbol that I could trust him."

My father's eyes focused on me again. "I still have that key. I've carried it with me every day for over two decades. So what happened, Mio? What changed my father's stories from myths to reality? How did you end up with the katana?"

I heard Ojiichan's voice in my head again, as clear as it had ever been.

Promise me on my life, on your mother's life, on your own life.

You will keep the sword hidden, no matter what.

And I remembered exactly what had started all of this. That day six years ago. Grandfather coming in the night before to tuck me in and tell me one of his stories about Japan, setting my little Mickey Mouse alarm clock to get me up early so we could "practise". The way he had challenged my father that morning. Started a fight that would send Dad storming off. The way Ojiichan had sprung into action the moment my parents left us alone in the house. The crowbar from the garage – he had known just where to find it – and how skilfully he had used it to bust the padlock on the katana's metal box.

The padlock he had promised never to open again.

I met my dad's eyes for a long, tense moment as memories reordered themselves in my head, old events suddenly lighting up with new significance or fading away into the background. I had grown up in the middle of a battle between my father and my grandfather, and like most kids, I had chosen a side. I had chosen my grandfather, chosen to believe everything he did was right and everything my father did was wrong. But I was just a *kid*. I didn't know what was really going on between them. I had made my decision based on who laid down the law and who sneaked me treats, who made me feel important and who made me feel like a baby.

Ojiichan had loved me. I was sure of that. But … I had carried the sword myself now. I knew what it could do, how it could *push* at you, even when it was sheathed, how it could get inside your head. My grandfather had been its guardian for *years*. What if Ojiichan had loved the sword more than he loved me? More than he loved my dad? More than anything, even his family's safety and what was right?

What if I'd picked the wrong side?

Promise me. You will never speak of this to your father.

I'm sorry, Ojiichan. But you broke your promise first.

Haltingly at first, then faster, the words tumbling over each other in my eagerness to confess it all, I told my father how the sword had come to be mine. I told him about that day all those years ago, and the dreams, and the fancy-dress party. About Jack and Rachel, the Kitsune, the Nekomata, and the Foul Women. I told him about Shinobu. I told him everything.

Except the solution that Mr Leech had proposed to us. I couldn't bring myself to think of that, let alone explain it to my father.

When I'd finished, Dad was silently scrubbing at his face with both hands. It took him a little while to speak. Then he said, "Do you know the worst part? I mean really, the most horrible thing of all?"

I shook my head.

"When I opened that bathroom door, I was sick with anxiety for you. Guilty. Desperate to make things better. But when I saw that you were holding the katana? For a heartbeat all of that was wiped out. All I could feel was jealousy. Jealousy that you had my sword."

"It's my—!" I bit the indignant exclamation in half

282

and swallowed it, nearly choking on the surge of possessiveness. Involuntarily my fingers tightened into a fist around the saya.

He stared at my red-and-yellow knuckles and made a sort of chuckling noise that broke halfway through and became something else. Something low and hurt-sounding. "I never even took the sword from him, but it didn't matter. It was in my blood. Every day, every single day, the compulsion has hounded me. Pulling at me. Calling me. Every day of my life since I turned sixteen and your grandfather held the katana out to me and told me it was mine.

"My hands were shaking with the need to reach out that day. My heart was thundering. I actually thought that I might die if I didn't take the katana from him. But I also realized that if I laid my hand on the sword there in that moment, it would all happen again. I would become what he was. In twenty or thirty years I would look into my child's eyes and sacrifice him or her to the katana, just as he was doing. I would take away my own son or daughter's choices in life, rob them of their free will. I couldn't do that. So I found the strength to say no." He lifted his head to look at me again. "And in the end, it didn't matter. None of it mattered. In the end, the katana won. You ended up as its servant anyway."

"I'm not its servant," I said. The denial sounded weak even to my own ears. *Aren't I?* No. Not now. But how much longer was I going to be able to hold out?

My father reached into his pocket and pulled out a yellowing, crumpled piece of paper. "This arrived for me at the beginning of last week. It's from your grandfather. He left it with his solicitors along with his will. It was to be delivered to me just before your sixteenth birthday."

"What does it say?" I asked, fascinated and unnerved.

"He asks for my forgiveness – again. And he says that you are special, Mio. As soon as you were born, he began to have dreams in which the spirits of the old country talked to him. They told him you were the key to everything. When you became the sword-bearer, everything would change. He says he thinks the sword will call to you more strongly than it has ever called anyone, and I will not be able to resist giving it to you. That trying would drive me insane."

"The beginning of last week…" I repeated slowly.

"As soon as I got this, I arranged the trip to Paris," my father said. "The compulsion – the overwhelming *need* to pass on the sword – had been growing stronger and stronger for months leading up to that point. Maybe years. Your grandfather was right. It was driving me mad. I knew if it got any worse, I would be in danger of giving in without even realizing what I was doing. Being away from you when you turned sixteen seemed like the only way to avoid it. That first night, in France, the feelings that had been plaguing me suddenly eased. The calling, the yearning, the sense of being half-empty … it all faded, and I realized that it was the first time for years that I'd felt fully at peace. I was sure I had done the right thing. But I was wrong. The sensation of relief was because you had taken the sword, wasn't it? It let go of me – at least partially – because it finally had you."

He heaved a deep sigh. It was the same, long-suffering sigh I had hated and dreaded for as long as I could remember. But all of a sudden it seemed obvious that it wasn't aimed at me. It never had been. My dad sighed in regret over a life of constant stress and struggle and resistance. In weariness at this silent, bitter battle that he had fought day after day, every day. For me.

All for my sake.

"I'm sorry."

We both spoke at the same time, then stopped awkwardly.

"Don't apologize," he said. "You haven't done anything wrong."

"I'm the one that took the sword. I'm the one that unleashed Yomi on London. I'm the one that made your nightmare come true. *And* I was a huge bitch to you just now."

He winced again. "Don't call yourself that."

"But—"

"I mean it, Mio. Look me in the eye here – I need to know that you really get this. These events were set in train before you were even born. What's happening here, what's happened to you, is not your fault. And I was a bitch to you first."

"*Euw!* Don't call yourself that."

"What? You're allowed to say it but I'm not?"

"Yes. No. I don't know."

"Well, that was clear," he said in his driest voice. "Why don't you think it over and let me know when you've worked it out?"

"*Dad!*"

"And she's back," he said, aiming a grin at the ceiling.

"Dad," I repeated, and he looked at me again, suddenly serious. "I am sorry."

"So am I, Midget Gem. So am I."

Rachel burst out of the hospital doors and onto the street. Her head turned frantically. She couldn't be here. There were parked cars and people, people everywhere. She had to get away from them all before she hurt someone else.

Hunt. Hunt! BITE.

No, she had to remember… She had to remember Jack.

Jack, oh God.

Oh Jack. What happened to you?

What did I do to you?

She sprinted through the car park, around the side of the building, and found herself in a deserted area filled with rubbish bins. Safe. Her knees buckled and she dropped down next to a massive blue skip. She was shaking convulsively. Her cheeks were sticky with layers of tears, dried and fresh. The itching in her face and hands made her want to claw at her flesh, claw it right off, just to make it stop.

Claw ... tear ... drink. Drink sweet, rich blood...

No. That's not me. It's not me!

I'm Rachel. I'm me. How did I get here? What did I do?

The last thing she remembered before Jack was that boy – that stupid, stupid boy who just had to play the tough guy with his stupid little knife. Why hadn't he left when she told him to? Why had he provoked her? Something had broken lose. He had run and she ... she had chased. After that it was a blur of exhilaration and motion, instinct and reaction, the intoxicating smell of fear leading her on. She had played with him – played cat and mouse – hunted him through the debris and towering weeds of the scrubland, now letting him think he would get away, now pouncing just to hear him scream. She had backed him into a corner, savouring his panic and desperation, and lunged, intending to bite...

Then nothing.

She couldn't remember anything else. She didn't remember what she had done. It was complete blackness, as if she had fallen asleep in the middle of the attack. She had woken up in the hospital. Standing over Jack.

And Jack had been convulsing. Fitting ten times worse than she had when the Shikome first infected her. The rash had been black against her bloodless skin. Rachel had screamed for help. Once help had come, she had run.

She had left her little sister alone. All alone. She ran away. She couldn't even trust herself not to hurt someone in the hospital. She couldn't trust herself not to hurt Jack.

Please be OK, Jack, please be OK. Please, please, please...

What had she done? Had she already hurt someone? The boy? What had happened to him while she'd been blacked out? Had she...?

Frantically she began to pat at her clothes. She couldn't find any wet, sticky patches. She held her hands out in front of her. No blood.

Blood...

She let out a choked moan of horror as the ends of her fingers burst open again. The terrible black claws slid out, curving and sharp.

"No, no, no, no more. Go away. Stop."

The burning itch in her skin was getting worse. Especially in her hands ... *her hands...* They were stretching, wrists lengthening, fingers twisting, distorting. Veins of blackness darkened beneath the skin like bruises writhing up to the surface. She cried out as a fiery cramp ripped through her core, doubling her over. Her hair fell around her face. From the corners of her eyes she could see it moving, wriggling like worms. Like the Nekomata's tentacles had wriggled over her, wrapped around her, dragged her into the darkness of its lair...

This is it. Despair made the next cramp even more agonizing. *I'm changing for good. I can't turn back. I'm really a monster now.*

Hunt soon. Hunt now. Claw. Tear. Bite. Drink.

She squeezed her eyes shut in agony. When she opened them again, her gaze glanced over something on the tarmac and then snapped back. A manhole cover.

The sewers.

That was where monsters belonged. Deep down in the darkness, where no one would ever find them. Where they could hurt no one.

Alien growling noises welled up in her throat as she crawled towards the cover, arching and shaking with the pain of the change. She dug the hated black claws into the metal lid, twisted it, and heaved, dragging the cover sideways until there was a gap. A gap big enough for her.

Part of her wanted to lift her head and look at the sky one more time. Part of her wanted to wait, and pray and hope. Part of her wanted to pretend that she didn't have to do this, that everything would still, somehow, be all right.

The rest of her knew that it was too late.

Without hesitation, she swung her legs down into the hole and let herself fall.

CHAPTER 17

PANIC STATIONS

Dad turned out to be a lot better at cleaning and bandaging wounds than I was. Thinking back to when I was a little girl – back when I'd still run to him whenever I fell and grazed my knee – I realized that he had always been good at taking care of people, really. I'd just forgotten.

After I'd taken the painkillers he insisted on, I combed my hair and washed my hands and face while he ventured upstairs into Jack's room again and borrowed more clothes. I was praying I didn't wreck these ones; if I carried on this way she was going to come home to an empty wardrobe.

"You're going to have to shell out for some new stuff for me to wear," I told him, slightly on the defensive, as I emerged from my room. I was relatively clean and dressed in a pair of skinny jeans – a lot less skinny on me than they were on Jack – and a black jumper, with my sword harness on top. "Everything I own is headed for Oxfam."

Dad gave me a calculating look. "Why don't you use your savings account?"

"Because when I wanted to buy that leather jacket, you said my savings account was for university, not 'expensive rags'." I folded my arms smugly.

He pretended to scowl, but his eyes were smiling, amused. My breath caught. God, how long had it been since I saw that? An honest-to-God smile in my dad's eyes? It made him look years younger. Had the strain of resisting the sword and its compulsion – the strain of trying to keep me out of his fight – taken that much of a toll on him? Looking back, I could see the change happening in my memories. The laughter and lightness had slowly stripped away from him, day after day, year after year. I hadn't understood. He was my dad, but I hadn't ever really understood him. Not until now.

Shinobu was waiting for us at the bottom of the stairs. As I rounded the landing, he was staring into space, eyes distant. He looked like his thoughts were a thousand miles away, somewhere dark and cold. When he heard my footsteps his face changed, lighting with concern and then relief. Any remaining anger I felt towards him dissolved painlessly. His love for me *was* flawed – because he was flawed, just like all human beings. I was capable of being every bit as selfish and short-sighted. If I didn't want other people holding my mistakes against me, then I couldn't keep hanging onto theirs. I had to learn to let things go.

I had to learn to be less like Ojiichan.

I limped stiffly down the staircase and into Shinobu's arms. The long, silent hug unknotted muscles and eased tensions I hadn't even realized were hurting me. We might have stayed like that for an hour if my dad hadn't cleared his throat behind us.

"Much longer," he said sardonically as I turned to look at him, "and I'll start to wish I'd stayed in Paris."

I swallowed my automatic retort of *We already wish that* – being mean to him was another thing I needed to learn to stop doing – and got off the bottom step, pulling Shinobu aside with me so that my father could get past.

My dad stepped down into the hall, his eyes fixed on Shinobu. Wordlessly, he held out his hand. Shinobu stared down at it. I bit my lip. What had gone on between these two while I was hiding upstairs? And was the manly handshake a ritual Shinobu would have absorbed while following me around in spirit? I needn't have worried. Shinobu reached out and they clasped hands, exchanging one of those long, steady, *mano a mano* looks.

"Thanks for taking care of my little girl," my dad said.

Shinobu smiled his quick, sweet smile. "It is the other way around."

And a bromance is born...

Standing next to each other in the hall, the extra inches of height that Shinobu had on my father, and his powerful, muscular build, were very obvious. But somehow despite being shorter and more slight, my father didn't appear overwhelmed by Shinobu's physical stature. Smiling, like he was now, Shinobu looked like a big, sweet, slightly shy guy. It was only when he had a sword in his hand that his deadly skill became obvious. Dad, even empty-handed, had an atmosphere. He looked like someone you should think twice about messing with – and who would make you regret it if you didn't. I remembered the confidence in his stance when he had confronted the Shikome, and the easy way he had handled his katana. Had he always exuded menace that way? Was this yet another thing I just hadn't noticed about him before?

Then again, I had been a completely different person the last time I saw him...

"Dad, where did you get that sword?" I asked suddenly. "The one you had in the street? And how did you get your hands on a firebomb?"

"You can make a reactive Molotov cocktail from everyday household items," he said. "If you remind me I'll show you one day. And I had the katana under my bed."

"Under your bed? Didn't Mum notice?"

"I hid it. It was in the case that was supposed to hold my snooker cues."

I frowned as I worked this out. "Then where are – wait a minute, did you ever actually play snooker?"

"Not if I could help it." He smirked. "Most boring game in the world."

"So when you were supposed to be out with your friends, playing…"

"I was in a dojo across town," he confessed. "I've always kept up with my training. I might not have bought into my father's beliefs about the sword, but I wasn't stupid enough to deny that the thing was powerful and probably dangerous. I had to know that I could protect you and your mother if anything ever happened."

My eyes prickled. I stepped forward to give him a quick, hard hug. One of his hands hovered above my back, then patted me awkwardly. Some things hadn't changed. Dad might be a different person than I had believed, but he still wasn't the huggy type. Oddly, this was the most comforting thought of all.

"Let's go into the kitchen," he said, as I stepped back. "Obviously we have a lot of talking to do, and I haven't had a decent cup of tea in three days."

"Um … are you sure you want to go back in there?" I asked.

"I can handle it." As he turned away, he muttered

under his breath, "as long as I remember that it was either you or the table..."

In the kitchen, I sat down on one of the stools, glad to get the weight off aching legs. The food and the pain-killers had helped a bit, but my entire body was still painfully stiff, and my muscles felt like Play-Doh. I was weak. Dangerously weak. I couldn't let either of them realize that.

The sword sent a beguiling vibration of energy snaking down my back. I could practically hear its voice whispering: *Free me. Give into me. I can make it all better...*

Shinobu leaned against the end of the breakfast bar next to me, while my dad filled the kettle and put it on the boil, then started washing the things from my meal earlier. Shinobu spoke up over the sound of splashing water. "Mr Yamato, I am more than thankful that you arrived when you did, but I cannot understand how you were aware that Mio-dono was in trouble."

My dad glanced back at us over his shoulder. "Rachel didn't tell you that she got through to me, then."

I gasped with outrage as I suddenly remembered what he had said earlier. "That sneaky— I *told* her not to!"

"Yes, she made it clear you didn't want me coming back," my father said, skewering me with a look. "It's a good job she ignored you, or you might be dead. We both owe her some thanks for that."

"But – I – oh, fine," I grumbled, knowing he was

right. The moment my annoyance disappeared, guilt and anxiety rushed in to fill the gap. *Oh, Rach, where did you go? Where are you?*

"She was understandably a bit leery of telling me all the details. In fact, she promised me three times that she wasn't drunk or doing drugs. But as soon as she mentioned the katana, I knew I had to get back here. I was packing while she was still on the phone."

"And ... Mrs Yamato?" Shinobu asked delicately. "I'm surprised she agreed to stay behind without you. From what Mio has told me, she is a strong-willed lady."

"Hmm. Yes. Well." Dad fixed his eyes on the plate he was polishing dry. "I tried to convince her to stay. I wasted an hour arguing. But she was having none of it. So I waited until she went to the bathroom and I ... stole her passport. And her wallet, and her return ticket for the train. Then I ran for it."

My jaw dropped. I stared at him, speechless.

"I left her some money," he said, a hint of defensiveness in his tone. "And I paid for the room and full-board at the hotel for another week."

"She is going to *kill* you."

"I couldn't risk her putting herself in danger. Until she can get the British Embassy to sort out replacement ID, she's safely out of this." He sighed. "But yes. Yes, she is."

Shinobu turned away, putting his hand over his face to hide an amused smile.

My dad lifted the teabag out of his mug, put it in the bin, and then added milk. "From what Mio tells me, most people can't even see you, Shinobu, is that correct? But I spotted you in the road without any difficulty."

Shinobu nodded slowly. "You also saw the Shikome. My guess is that contact with the energy of the katana alters—"

I shifted in my seat to reach into the pocket of the jeans for my phone. It had been switched off since our disastrous attempt to hide from the Shikome, and now I was worried that my mum might have called me, freaking out. I should at least text her and let her know we were OK…

Five missed calls stared at me from the screen. They had all come in the last hour, from a number that I didn't recognize. *Rachel? Or … the hospital?* We'd given them my mobile as an alternative contact number. For emergencies. Frost breathed down my spine. I pressed call back.

The phone rang. And rang. And rang.

"Can I help you?" The woman's voice was stressed and her uneven breaths made rough, gasping sounds into the receiver.

"Um, I'm returning a call from this number. Five calls, actually. My name is…" I thought for a second. "Rachel Luci. My sister, Jack, is there in your ward."

My dad and Shinobu had stopped talking and were looking at me.

"Oh, Miss Luci, of course." The woman was making an obvious effort to calm down, but there was a strange note in her voice as she went on. "You're your sister's guardian, aren't you? We'd – we'd like you to come down here as soon as possible. I know the advice is for everyone to stay in their homes, but—"

Her voice was cut off by an alarm sounding in the background. Someone shouted, and I could just make out the words: *Another one's in arrest. Where's Doctor Singh? Someone help me, for Christ's sake!*

I got to my feet, my fingers clenching around the phone's case. "What is wrong with Jack?"

"I have to inform you that your sister's condition is giving us cause for serious concern. She's slipped into an unresponsive state. We can tell you more when you—"

Another alarm went off. A new voice yelled: *What's happening to them all? What is this? I can't—*

"Oh God!" The nurse's voice cracked. "I'm so sorry, I have to go. Just get here as quickly as you can. If you can. You – you might not have much time."

There was a clatter and the phone went dead.

The deserted Tube carriage rattled around us. Our three faces, reflected in the darkness of the window opposite, were pale and dark-eyed, like ghosts'. I huddled into the faded grey sweatshirt that my dad had loaned me to go over my jumper and the katana.

"A non-responsive state isn't the same thing as a coma," my father said from the seat on my left. His fingers were clenched around a fold of his long, black overcoat, which concealed the hilt of the sword attached to his belt. "It could mean any number of things. You mustn't panic yet."

Shinobu's large hand clasped my right one, but I felt no warmth from the contact, no comfort. All I could feel was scared. "What if we don't make it in time? What if she— God, we shouldn't have left her there by herself. We should have gone back for her. Done more. Done something."

"It was the only way to keep her safe," Shinobu told me firmly. "We had no choice."

"There's always a choice."

"Perhaps." Shinobu met my eyes. "But there is not always a good one."

I looked away first.

Keep fighting, Jack. Hold on. Just keep fighting it. Don't let go.

I had to be able to work something out – find some way to do what needed to be done without losing anyone. The blade had *so much power*. It had eradicated the taint from my body without even being unsheathed. What if I called its second true name while it was in the saya? Would that muffle its energy enough to make it controllable? Maybe then I would be able to channel it, the way that Mr Leech had said and use it to heal Jack – heal everyone – the way it had healed me.

But what if it didn't work? Mr Leech had definitely implied that the explosion of power the first time one of the sword's names was called – when the seal was broken – was a one-shot deal. I had to get it right because there wouldn't be another chance.

The blade … it wanted me. It wanted the chance to control me, and it wanted that badly. So maybe I could bargain with it. I could talk to it – promise it … whatever I had to. Make some kind of deal. Anything, so long as it would fix this. So long as it would just fix Jack.

If I can't do anything else, at least let me save Jack…

The Tube pulled into a station and the doors opened. A single passenger shuffled on-board. I had a vague impression of a sort of human mushroom, greyish brown all over, with a straggling beard and ragged clothes. He was muttering to himself, snorting and grumbling as he – inevitably – took the seat opposite me.

I fixed my eyes on the floor in front of his ratty trainers.

"See 'em everywhere!" he said as the train pulled away. "Try to tell 'em, but no, no one listens. Laughing and chattering like nothing's wrong. Never listen. Chattering away. All mad as hatters!"

The next stop was ours. I closed my eyes and counted the seconds.

"See 'em everywhere. Flapping over the roofs like pigeons!" The old man's voice rose. "Monsters! Monsters in the air!"

Monsters in the air? My eyes snapped open.

A bright, sharp grey gaze met mine, young eyes that were out of place in that wrinkled, dirty face. The man winked at me. "That's right, lovey. I can always tell, me. You's one of 'em as knows. You just watch yourself, lovey. You stay out of sight till theys gone!"

I nodded at the homeless man. "I'll try."

"Mio," my father said sharply. "Don't—"

"It's all right, Dad," I interrupted. "He's all right."

The man grinned at my father, revealing a mouthful of empty gums and a single brilliant white tooth. "She's a knowing one!"

The Tube lurched. A metallic squeal rang out. The lights flickered off, on again, off, on, and then died, leaving us in pitch-darkness. I grabbed at the armrest as the carriage shuddered violently, nearly flinging me out of my seat. Shinobu's arm shot across my body, holding me in place.

The Tannoy came on, its recorded words slurring oddly as it announced our stop. The lighted platform jerked into view outside the windows; the carriage jumped, shuddered again, then slammed to a halt, nearly sending the homeless man flying this time. "Whoops-a-daisy!"

The doors groaned, squeaking only partly open.

As I dragged myself to my feet, my dad ran to the exit, braced himself against one side of the doors, and pushed. Shinobu joined him. Working together, they forced the doors open just wide enough for the three of us to squeeze through. At the last second, the homeless man slipped out too and joined us on the empty platform.

The train let out an echoing shriek and lurched away. It disappeared into the tunnel, rails rattling, almost … chittering. Icy forewarning stabbed my spine. I whipped round to stare into the tunnel we had just emerged from. Something flashed in its black, gaping mouth.

I shouted, "Shikome!"

Two Foul Women hurtled out of the darkness.

The homeless man stood on the edge of the platform, his face frozen into a rictus of terror. I lunged at him clumsily, tripping over my own feet. We hit the floor together with mutual sounds of pain. The first Shikome sailed over our heads, towards Shinobu and my dad. I heard glass breaking, then the hungry gasp of fire.

The Shikome burst into flames. Shrieking, it shot straight up and crashed into the ceiling. Tiles fell from the walls, shattering like gunfire. The burning monster plummeted onto the platform with an impact that shook the ground. Its thrashing body was a wall of deadly fire between me and where Shinobu and my father stood.

The second Foul Woman gave a piercing cry and dropped down directly at me where I knelt. Its landing shook the platform a second time. I just had time to shove the homeless man aside. Then the monster attacked.

Natural as breathing, the katana was unsheathed and in my hand. I slashed wildly at the leathery grey paws that reached out to grab the blade. My stiff muscles screamed in protest. I couldn't move fast enough. It was like being in a nightmare, weighed down, my arms and legs made of lead. Black hair and dead feathers boiled around me. Yellow eyes glared like spotlights. I rolled and heaved upright and found my back against the tiled wall. Nowhere to go. I blocked a swipe of the monster's left paw – amber blood splattered across my face – too slow, too slow – jerked the blade free – and saw the right paw coming at me, vicious, yellowing claws aimed at my gut.

With a hoarse yell, the homeless man jumped into the way.

The Shikome's talons hit his chest with a heavy, wet thud.

The green blade flashes down in the red light—

The old man gasped and staggered back against me. The smell of unwashed hair and skin filled my nostrils as he slid down my body to crumple at my feet. Blood bubbled out of the frayed folds of his clothes.

The Foul Woman's wings spread in a rattling stretch of triumph, teeth bared in its monstrous, eyeless face. In the tunnel there was the sound of another train approaching.

The echoing clatter of wheels drowned out the creature's cry as it lunged at me.

A furious howl ripped out of my throat. I struck with everything I had.

The monster's head and the top half of its left wing fell away in a crisp, diagonal line.

The massive body toppled backwards. It rolled, twitching, off the edge of the platform, right under the wheels of the train as it shot out of the tunnel. Amber blood fountained upwards, splashing across the train windows and showering the platform like rain.

I slid down the wall, my fingers clenched and shaking around the katana's hilt. I stared at the shining silver blade, drenched in blood. *Too slow.*

I could make you faster, the sword murmured sibilantly in the back of my mind.

"Be. Quiet."

Jerkily, I wiped the blade on the front of my sweatshirt, and rammed the katana back into its saya in the harness. I squeezed my eyes shut for a moment. But he was waiting.

His grey eyes were blank and staring. There was no fear in his face. He'd acted too fast for fear.

"Thank you," I whispered. "I'm so sorry."

"Mio!" My father's voice made my head jerk up.

The train had passed by. Dad and Shinobu had climbed down onto the track – the only way to get past the smouldering bonfire of the Shikome that was belching black smoke on the middle of the platform. They clambered back up to where I knelt.

"Are you all right?" my father demanded as he approached. He caught sight of the old man and blanched. "What happened?"

"I'm OK," I said, dully. "He tried to help me. He threw himself between me and the Shikome."

Shinobu knelt next to me and gently slid the old man's eyes shut, laying his palm on the wrinkled forehead in a gesture that might have been blessing, or thanks.

"Poor old man. He never stood a chance," my father said sadly. "What happened to the Foul Woman?"

I gestured to where the remains of the Foul Woman – the part not liquefied by the train – had fallen. My dad's face went slack with shock. "You did this?"

I didn't answer. I didn't think he really wanted me to.

"I wonder who he was…" I said, touching one of the man's dirty hands. His skin still felt warm.

"We know who he was not. He was not a coward. He was not a poor old man," Shinobu said sternly. "He was a warrior. A hero in waiting."

Shinobu helped me to my feet. I stumbled against him, the surge of battle adrenaline wearing off to leave me stiffer and shakier than before. It was a miracle I wasn't dead.

I looked down at the homeless man again. Already he

was less like a person and more like a jumbled old pile of rags. Whatever bright, sharp spirit had lit those eyes, had driven him to act with such amazing, irrational courage to save a girl he didn't even know, had fled now. There was nothing left but skin and bones.

"He made his own choice, and died well," Shinobu said. "That is all any of us can hope for."

The green blade flashes down in the red light—

I shuddered, clutching Shinobu's coat for balance as the memory flashed into my head, stronger than ever before. And as clearly if he was whispering in my ear, I heard Mr Leech's words:

What are you prepared to sacrifice?

CHAPTER 18

THE SWARM

My fingers tightened into fists in Shinobu's coat. I forced the memories and the choking sense of panic down, deep down inside. *I won't let go.*

My father reached out tentatively and touched my hand. "You're like ice. Are you really OK?"

I drew in a slow, deep breath. "I am. I have to be."

I opened my eyes again and uncurled my fingers from the coat fabric, straightening my shoulders with an effort. "Anyway, we can't go back. What if there are more Shikome in the tunnels?"

My father muttered a swear word.

"How many of those firebombs do you have left?" Shinobu asked him.

"Not enough." Dad's hand moved to my shoulder. His eyes searched my face. Finally, he nodded. "OK. Let's go."

I tried not to let them see how much worse the

desperate fight with the Shikome had made me, but it was hard. My body still wouldn't *move* the way I needed it to. The sensation of being in a nightmare was growing. But there were no nightmares for me any more. The things I dreamed were all real now.

Shinobu put his arm around my shoulders, taking some of my weight. "You are not all right," he said softly.

"It doesn't matter," I said, just as softly. "She doesn't have time for it to matter. We have to get there. I can't leave her there alone to..." I cut myself off before I could say the next word. I didn't even want to think it.

His worried frown deepened, but he didn't argue. He knew the truth as well as I did. Yes, in any ordinary situation I'd be a liability. But I was the sword-bearer. The not-so-secret weapon. Without me, there was no point in going anywhere. In its saya on my back the katana was throbbing gently, content to wait. It knew soon I would be down to zero choices again. Soon I would be faced with my dying friend, and I would have to decide...

Would the seal break if I called the sword's second true name while it was sheathed?

Could I possibly control its power, command it to do my bidding, if I unsheathed it?

Did I have the strength to resist it long enough to save at least Jack before it took control of me?

Would Shinobu be able to stop me before the blade used me to kill someone – maybe even someone I loved?

My footsteps echoed mockingly through the deserted station, making a drumbeat for the questions that taunted me. *What am I going to do? What am I going to do? What am I going to do...?*

My eyes were drawn to a tall, slender figure lurking near the entrance of the station. He leaned casually against the central pillar that separated the two wide exits, a grey hoodie pulled up to hide his face. There was no particular reason why he made my spider-senses tingle – but he did. I was sure there was something supernatural about him.

Not another monster in disguise, please...

I grabbed my dad's arm, giving him a warning look as he tried to move past me.

"What's the matter?" His voice rang out, puzzled and loud. "Why are you pulling faces?"

"Oh, for f—" I muttered.

The figure had heard us. He straightened up, and as he moved I glimpsed a very familiar tail poking out of the seat of his jeans. "Hikaru? Hikaru!"

"Finally!" He trotted towards us, shoving back his hood to reveal vivid green eyes, exactly like his grandmother's, and his long burnished copper hair. "I've been waiting for you for twenty minutes!"

"What are you *doing* in the mortal world?"

"The king sent me to warn you—"

"Of what?" my father asked silkily, gliding forward to put himself between me and the Kitsune. His hand strayed to that telltale fold of his coat again.

"Um … who's this guy?" Hikaru asked, eyebrows arching.

"This is Mio-dono's father," Shinobu said.

"You brought your dad with you?" Hikaru asked me. "What – you need a permission slip signed or something?"

"Shut up," I said to Hikaru. "He's a badass and he knows all about the katana." I whacked my dad lightly on the arm. "And you – stop it. This is the Kitsune friend I told you about. We owe him big-time." I turned back to Hikaru. "I can't believe the king let you come here."

"There was no other way to contact you. Look, my grandmother's been scrying – watching London magically to try and keep an eye on you – and it's not really an exact science, but she knew you were going to be here, out in the open. Bad idea."

"Why?" my father asked, his eyes still riveted unlovingly on Hikaru's tail.

"The levels of spirit energy in this realm are peaking. We think a portal is going to open. The Foul Women will swarm through it. Swarm for real. You have to go back to the house; it's the only place that will be safe for you when they come."

"We can't," I said. "We can't go back."

"Look, I get it. Jack is at the hospital and you want to be with her. But both you and she will be safer if you're miles away from her when the swarm comes for you.

They can batter our protections for a year and they'll never get in."

"No, Hikaru, you don't... Jack's worse. It's bad. Really bad. It doesn't matter what's happening out there. We have to get to the hospital."

Hikaru rocked back on his heels as if I had punched him. "Is she ... dying?"

"We don't know." It sounded bald and heartless – but I just didn't have any words to comfort him with.

He looked away, his body tensing up, and I thought for a second that it was all going to be too much, that he might take off. Instead he swallowed audibly. "OK. All right. I'm in. All for one, one for all. That's what we said back in the spirit realm, right? I'm your friendly neighbourhood fox spirit. Just point me in the right direction."

"Hikaru, no," Shinobu protested. "It is too dangerous in London for a Kitsune."

I backed him up. "The king told me what happens to foxes who get infected, remember? I saw it myself. I can't let you come with us."

"Well, I can't go back," he said flatly. "I lied. Her Majesty didn't send me."

"*What?!*" The word burst out of me like a hiccup.

Shinobu interrupted. "Then how did you get here?"

"I snuck out. It was chancy and I almost didn't make it, but I had to warn you about what she'd seen. I knew I was going to be stuck here for a while – the plan was to drag you back to your house and hide out there until we could work out how to banish those bitches. But if you're not hiding out, neither am I."

"You couldn't anyway," my father said. His hand had fallen away from his sword at last. "The Shikome are in the Tube tunnels now. There's only one way out of here." He nodded to the entrance.

"Then we're all in the same boat." Hikaru flashed his sharp, reckless smile. "Cosy."

As if to underline his words, there was a harsh, seagull cry from the stairs leading down to the Underground. The hiss of dry feathers drifted up to us like the warning noise of a rattlesnake's tail. I didn't think they'd be able to squeeze themselves up the stairs very quickly, but I did know that they would die trying.

Shinobu clasped Hikaru's arm. "It will be an honour to fight by your side again."

Hikaru nodded, then turned away. As he did I saw the grin drop from his face, leaving it pale and set.

My father unsheathed his blade on my right, and Shinobu did the same on my left. The need for secrecy wasn't exactly gone, but it was a lesser concern now. I was betting anyone out on the streets of London in the next few minutes would have far scarier things to worry about than us anyway. By unspoken agreement, we moved towards the exit.

I drew the katana, feeling its sudden excitement

buzz against my palm. The energy travelled through my body, loosening my tight muscles a little. Flames flickered, ghostlike, down the sharp silver smile of the blade's edge – tempting me, reminding me of the power and strength I had tasted before, the power it could still offer me, if only I—

No. Shut up. Just shut up. I haven't called your name. I haven't invited you in. I don't want to hear a word single word out of you. You are not in control of me.

Not yet, the blade whispered.

I averted my eyes quickly from the mesmerizing flames and forced my legs to move.

"Do you have a weapon?" my father asked Hikaru.

Hikaru laughed. It wasn't a happy laugh. "You'll see it soon enough."

He had said once that he was too young to control his lightning like the other Kitsune did. Hikaru was a single-tailed spirit fox, only twenty years old and born here in the UK. But he had managed to open the gate of the Nekomata's lair for us when Hiro and Araki – both hundreds of years old, with multiple tails to prove it – had been unable to. So I let myself hope he had something good hidden in that tail of his.

The moment we cleared the exit and stepped outside, it was obvious we were going to need whatever help we could get.

An icy wind wailed around the station's rain shelter.

It tore at our clothes and hair with sharp fingers. I could feel the spirit energy buzzing in it, stinging like paper cuts on my skin. In the time we'd been underground the sky had been swallowed up by a thick canopy of low-hanging clouds that seemed to slither over the rooftops. It was almost dark. Even in December, it shouldn't be as dark as this, this early. The unnatural dusk had caused the streetlights to spark to life up and down the street and on the traffic island in the middle of the wide dual carriageway. The orange glare of sodium lights did battle with the creeping shadows, and lost.

Around us, the broad sweep of pavement was nearly deserted, the stalls of the famous street market empty and hidden under stripy waterproof coverings. All the shops and cafes had closed. A middle-aged lady scurried by, clutching a shopping bag to her like a shield as the gale buffeted her. Her wide, anxious eyes passed straight over Hikaru and Shinobu as if they weren't there, then skittered anxiously from me and my father. She walked faster, ducking her head.

"Where do we need to go?" Hikaru asked. "I've never been to the human hospital."

I pointed across the road with my free hand. The Underground station was directly opposite a pelican crossing. Right now the thoroughfare was quiet by city standards – though not quiet enough to make a straight run across both lanes of traffic possible.

"Once we're on the other side," I said, "we'll follow the main street for about a hundred yards, then turn that corner, past that cafe that's painted orange. There's a narrow-ish pedestrian-only road that'll take us to the hospital entrance."

"Easy-peasy, right?" Hikaru jerked his shoulders. "Five minutes, tops."

"Oh yeah," I muttered. "It'll be a doddle."

I met Shinobu's eyes for a moment. In the strange light they looked opaque, almost black. He raised an eyebrow. I tried to squeeze out a smile for him.

"I don't like the look of that," my dad muttered, craning his neck back to stare at the clouds.

Understatement of the century. "Then let's go before it gets any worse," I said. The words came out like an order.

I stepped forward and the others came with me, naturally forming a triangle with my father and Shinobu on either side of me and Hikaru one step ahead.

"Shikome are attracted to bright colours, loud noises, and anything that runs away from them or moves quickly," my father said, voice low. "Walk slowly. Keep your head down. There are thousands of humans in this city. Maybe they won't realize who we are."

It seemed pointless to remind him that the sword – and I – stank of an energy that the Yomi creatures could sniff out from miles away. So I said nothing. We headed straight for the crossing. I pressed the WALK button for form's sake as I reached the kerb, but kept my eye open for a break in the traffic. Now was not the time for respecting traffic laws.

The wind whistled between the buildings, making the bare branches of the trees lining the street opposite moan and creak. Hikaru and Shinobu's hair whipped around their faces. My father's black coat billowed out behind him.

I had a sudden vision of a massive tide of energy breaking through the city streets. A rising maelstrom of power, inimical to human cells. To human life. I grabbed the metal pole of the pelican light to keep my balance as that power washed over me. My other hand tightened around the silk wrappings of the katana's grip. It pulsed fiercely in response.

A black cab whizzed past us, exceeding the speed limit by at least ten miles an hour. A heartbeat later, there was a horrific squeal of tyres. I turned in time to see the taxi swerve to the left and mount the pavement about five metres away. It ploughed straight into the abandoned stalls of the market, sending metal trolleys and chunks of plywood flying. The cars behind the taxi careered across the road as they tried to avoid its rear end and the debris of the crash. Bumpers crunched and metal shrieked. But my attention wasn't on the effects of the accident. I was staring at the cause.

A Shikome was crouched on the taxi's roof.

The monster's cry rippled through the wind as it straightened, spreading its wings out to their full, rattling span.

The car door popped open and the taxi driver staggered out, clutching his bleeding head. The Shikome's front paw swiped at him—

And the man was down on his knees, unharmed apart from the cut on his forehead. Silent as a shadow, Shinobu leapt onto the boot of the taxi, his swords flashing. The monster roared as two long gashes opened on its chest and abdomen, gushing amber. Shinobu ducked its talons and thrust his blade out again. His sword hilt thudded home in the centre of the Foul Woman's chest.

He was leaping off the car before the creature had even begun to fall and sprinting back towards us. He was shouting; the wind ripped his words away, but his sword tip pointed over our heads. We turned.

The clouds were boiling, dilating around a black hole in the sky, a gaping maw of absolute darkness. There were no stars in that dark, nothing except a pure white full moon. A moon where no moon should be. The black hole was an entrance to Yomi – and it vomited Foul Women.

Dozens of them swept down towards us in a wave, chittering and screaming as they came.

"Run!"

We scattered into the road, dodging around the slowed traffic. Car drivers honked and flipped us off. A motorcyclist zoomed around me, nearly hit my dad, and ditched his bike, skidding over the tarmac. He rolled to a halt in the gutter.

A Foul Woman swooped on me, talons outstretched. I dodged a car and ducked, but the claws grazed my head. Blood spilled down my neck, burning hot on my chilled skin.

Shinobu's wakizashi caught my attacker a glancing blow to the side. It shrieked, wings pumping as it skewed in the air. I forced my shaking legs to propel me upwards, thrusting the katana up into the Foul Woman and dragging the blade through its flesh as it passed. The monster shot up out of reach of our swords, injured but not incapacitated.

The sword throbbed with frustration at being deprived of its kill. I can help you. Let me in...

"No! Shut up!"

Another Shikome dived. Shinobu dipped under its back talons, the deadly claws missing him by a millimetre. A third Foul Woman stooped to join the battle.

Fire flared directly overhead as one of Dad's bombs caught the first monster right in the wing. It lurched sideways, struggling to stay in the air, then dropped – and hit the two creatures below. The unnatural wind screamed around the burning Foul Women, whipping the blaze up. I grabbed the back of Shinobu's coat and hauled him out from beneath the firestorm—

Directly into the path of a lorry. The driver honked desperately, unable to avoid us.

Hikaru was suddenly there, yanking us forward. We all staggered onto the traffic island together. The lorry shot past.

"Idiot!" the driver screamed out of the window.

I caught sight of my dad, a slim silhouette outlined against the fire in the sky. He whirled out of the lorry's way, vaulted the metal safety barrier on the traffic island, and sprinted down the length of it towards us.

The burning monsters plummeted into the road like meteorites.

The lorry rammed straight into them.

The car following the lorry rear-ended it and juddered under the impact of the car behind. More and more vehicles skidded and crashed to a halt. The air was filled with the crunch of metal and the shrill drone of car horns. The lorry that had hit the burning Foul Woman had already caught fire. The driver was limping away from the vehicle with his arms over his head.

Hikaru shouted: "It's going up!"

We didn't question him. I hit the ground, new bruises throbbing to life on my knees and elbows.

With a hollow *whoomph*, a fireball enveloped the lorry. The explosion lit the underside of the low black clouds with vivid, dancing orange. Chunks of flaming debris spewed across the road and into the air. Another Shikome fell from the sky, with fire streaming from its wings. The creature crashed into one of the bare trees on the other side of the road, sending jagged branches, some of them alight, cascading down into the next lane of traffic.

"Oh my God..." I wasn't sure which of us said it. We were all thinking it.

The traffic on both lanes lurched to a halt, people flinging open their doors and fleeing onto the street. Their abandoned cars made a higgledy-piggledy maze on the tarmac.

"Is anybody hurt?" my dad yelled over the wind. "Mio?" A long, shallow cut bisected his eyebrow, trickling blood down his cheek. The left shoulder of his coat was singed.

"I'm all right!" I looked at the other two, who both nodded. I tried to clear a space in the throbbing of my heart, the pounding of my head, to think. "We have to go!"

"Stay low and use the vehicles for shelter!" Shinobu shouted. "There are too many of them to fight."

"And don't let the feathers touch you!" my father added.

Crouched low over our bent legs, we scurried through the abandoned cars. My back and thigh muscles trembled, and the rough road surface grazed my knees and free hand every time the wind gusted at me and knocked me off balance. Overhead the sky was full of Shikome. They rioted, ripping the roofs off the stationary vehicles, smashing car windows, screaming. The wind stank of burning monster flesh and the sickening decayed stench of the living creatures themselves.

In my hand, the sword was pulsing steadily now, calling to me, begging me inside my mind. *Let me help you. Let me make you strong. Let me take your pain...*

No!

As a group we reached the kerb and came to a halt, crouching in the shelter of a battered Land Rover and a florist's van that had skidded up onto the kerb. Before us was the broad, bare pavement that we needed to travel down to get to the pedestrianized road. Right now it looked like a barren wasteland. There was no cover there, no shelter. Once we stepped out, we'd be completely unprotected.

Hikaru cast a glance up. "I think they've lost track of us."

"They'll soon see us when we leave the cars," my dad said grimly. "I've only got one Molotov cocktail left. Bright ideas?"

Hikaru bared his teeth as if he was nerving himself up. "I think I've got something. But it's a little ... risky."

"What are you going to do?" I asked. "Listen, Hikaru, don't be reckless—"

"Sez you," he shot back with a ghost of his usual grin. A pang went through my heart. That was Jack's line.

Shinobu said, "Once they realize where we are, it will

be impossible for us to escape. We must have the element of surprise."

"He's right," my father said.

"Then let's go now," Hikaru said. "You're just going to have to trust me."

I grabbed his knee and gave it a squeeze. "I do. But be careful. I don't want to lose you out there."

"Right you are, cupcake," he said, his grin a little stronger. He squeezed past me, turned his head left and right as if measuring distances, then nodded decisively. "OK, I've got this. When I say run, you run. Go on three. One, two…"

Crouched in filthy, icy cold water below the surface of the city, Rachel could feel the storm breaking somewhere above. A low, ululating croon vibrated in her mouth – a mouth filled with blood and razor-sharp fangs. The unrelieved blackness of the storm drain was bright as day to her now, but her eyes didn't see the tunnel. They were focused somewhere far away, somewhere deep within.

"She is coming…" Rachel moaned, not even aware that she spoke. "So close. So close…"

She felt her spine stretch and ripple, bending in half like a snake's. The words rose to a high-pitched cat scream as the worst pain yet ripped through her body.

"My Mistress!"

CHAPTER 19

DARKNESS
HIDDEN

"Three!"

Hikaru darted out from between the cars.

I slapped one palm onto the road and heaved myself up, flying onto the pavement with my dad ahead of me and Shinobu right behind.

There was a shriek of recognition above us. The cry was taken up by a hundred other voices, the shrill, seagull calls making the fine hairs on the back of my neck struggle to rise under their coat of blood. My father glanced back, whipped his head forward again and shouted, "Don't look!"

My legs shook. Hot wires of pain shot up my thighs and calves as I tried to keep up with my father and Hikaru. The breath tasted bloody on my numb lips, and in my hand, the sword's energy was scorching the skin, its frustration burning through my tissues like radiation. Me, me, me!

Shut up!

Shinobu was a shadow at my side. He was holding back for my sake; he would've passed me in a second otherwise. I dug the balls of my feet into the pavement, vainly trying to squeeze out some extra speed. Above us, like a towering tsunami gathering to destroy all in its path, the dry rattle and chitter of Foul Women's wings swept down out of the black sky.

Suddenly Hikaru wheeled round, dodged out of my father's path, and lifted his hands above his head. As his palms clapped together, I saw his tale whip out behind him. A slender branch of lightning formed over his head, hit his joined hands and ... *bloomed.*

Each of his fingers sprouted a tendril, and each tendril sprouted three more. The lightning multiplied silently through the air above Hikaru like an electrical forest growing up out of nowhere in less than the blink of an eye. I ignored my father's order and looked back, blinking against the silvery after-images the lightning left on my vision.

Hikaru's single bolt of energy had become an immense net of light hanging beneath the clouds. The unstoppable tsunami of Shikome flew straight into it. Pierced by delicate branches of lightning, the monsters shuddered and convulsed in midair. Their wings still flapped helplessly, like puppets dancing on Hikaru's string.

Hikaru's face was dead white, and in the eerie neon

flicker of his lightning there was a sheen of sweat standing out on his skin. A pinprick of white light glowed in the pupil of each bright green eye. His teeth clenched in agony. With a snarl, the fox spirit ripped his hands apart.

The web of lightning winked out.

Thunder boomed through the city like an earthquake. The air vibrated – or the ground did – but either way we all staggered. Hikaru fell to his knees as Shinobu and I grabbed at each other for balance. My dad extended his arms like a sailor on the deck of a storm-ridden ship.

Then it stopped.

The stillness was almost frightening. Even the wind had dropped. The katana's grip trembled in my hand. I thought I could feel its disappointment.

A hundred Shikome lay dead or dying around us, their bodies smoking. On the pavement, on the road, lying on the cars and draped over the rooftops. Their blasted corpses had blanketed the ground around them in drifts of grey feathers, like snow. Shinobu and I exchanged a long, awed look.

When Araki-san said that Hikaru was special, she hadn't been kidding.

"Are you OK?" I asked him breathlessly. "What – what was that?"

"Ouch," he groaned, clutching his skull. "Oh great and little gods, this must be what a hangover feels like. It was the heavenly net of a thousand stars. One of my grandmother's favourites. I … can't believe it worked. I didn't know I had that much juice."

"What would have happened if you did not have the 'juice'?" Shinobu asked.

"You'd be talking to a pile of ashes." Hikaru grinned at us weakly through his fingers.

"Hikaru," I began, and even I could hear that I sounded exactly like my dad.

"You can shout at him later," my father said. He caught Hikaru's hand and pulled the Kitsune to his feet. "Let's get moving again before—"

As he spoke, a chill breeze sprang up around us. It fluttered around our feet, growing as it rushed between our bodies, moaning angrily. My head snapped back. The clouds over our heads were boiling again, slowly bulging open to reveal a darkness that I knew all too well.

"It's not over," I cried. The wind shredded the words. "Come on!"

We fled towards the cafe on the corner of the street, skidding around the hospital signs and onto the narrow pedestrian way. Tall buildings rose on each side of us. On the left side parked cars lined the road. Ahead of us was open space – a line of bollards, ambulances and doctors' cars – and the entrance to the hospital building.

The first Shikome dived into the street directly on top of me. I ducked down to one knee, slashing the katana above my head. The blade sparked with white flames, slicing through the monster's hind leg like a paper knife through an envelope. The birdlike creature shot up with a squawk. Its massive paw dangled on a thread of skin.

Another monster took its place, swooping at Hikaru.

"Down!" my father shouted.

Another firebomb – his last – left his hand and smashed into the Foul Woman's wing. Hikaru ducked under the monster's legs as it whirled in the air. It crashed into the tarmac, shrieking, wings thrashing wildly. My father leapt back – but he didn't move quite fast enough.

The tip of a wing brushed his face.

He frowned, confusion in his eyes as his left hand lifted to his face. Then he collapsed on the tarmac like a marionette with cut strings.

"Dad!"

I ran to his side and knelt in the road beside him. He was already fitting. The purple marks darkened on his face as I watched, turning almost black. His eyes were half-closed, their whites gleaming at me through the gap under his eyelashes. His mouth yawned open in a sound-less scream. I could hear a voice echoing in the distance, crying the same word over and over and over. The word was "No". The voice was mine.

We were almost there.

The green blade flashes down in the red light—

A Shikome stooped over me. I threw myself forward, shielding my father from its attack. Shinobu flashed past;

his blades crossed in the air, and the creature reared back, its huge front paws scrabbling at its abdomen where Shinobu had almost disembowelled it. It smashed into the wall, bounced off, and somersaulted over the rooftop out of sight.

Dad's back was arching up off the pavement, his head thudding against the ground. The seizure was bad, really bad, worse than Jack's. He was reacting to the taint the same way I had, like both of us were more allergic to the monsters than regular people.

"Help!" I screamed, struggling to hold him.

Shinobu thrust his blades back into their sayas, bent down, and scooped my father up in his arms. I ran after him and Hikaru ran after me as Shinobu carried Dad to a line of parked cars and laid him down on the thin strip of pavement next to the wall of the cafe. I ripped my stained sweatshirt over my head and wadded it up to cushion the back of Dad's skull as Shinobu held down his flailing hands. I was crying. Harsh, painful sobs that barely let me breathe. I couldn't stop, couldn't push it back.

Why isn't he coming out of it? Come on, please, please come out of it. This can't be happening!

Hikaru had squashed himself into the gap between the two parked cars next to us. He was staring at my father in horror. "Is he – will he—?"

A Foul Woman skidded over the car roofs, claws raking the metal with a long *screeeeeee*. I flung my body over my dad again as the other two ducked.

"Hikaru, do you have any juice left?" Shinobu demanded.

The fear on Hikaru's face hardened into determination. "I have enough."

"Try to hold them off," Shinobu said.

Hikaru nodded sharply. He turned away, getting up onto his knees and lifting his hands again. A fine whip of lightning crackled through the air and slapped the Shikome above us out of the sky.

I stared down at my father. He had gone still, his head falling to the side, mouth slack.

"Dad, come on! Wake up."

I picked up one of his hands and pressed it to my cheek, squeezing my eyes shut. I barely knew him. I had lived with him all my life, and I'd just begun to figure out who he was. And he didn't really know me either. He had no idea, under all my snark and defensiveness and anger, how much I loved him. I'd never told him.

Why hadn't I told him?

"Daddy. Please. Please wake up…"

"Mio."

Shinobu's voice forced my eyes open, choking off the sobs in my throat.

"We are trapped. There is no hope of reaching shelter now." His face was set, and his golden skin was pale. The beautiful dark eyes were fathomless with sorrow.

"Whatever solution you were going to find, whatever miracle you were waiting for, it is too late. There is no more time and there are no more choices. You have to do it."

Lightning cracked through the sky again – weaker this time. No matter how brave he was, Hikaru wouldn't be able to keep his defence up long.

"You know that I can't."

"No." His gaze bored into mine. "You know what to do. You have the sword's second name. You would not have fought me so hard, been so hurt and angry, if you were not convinced, deep down, that you could make this work."

The green blade flashes down in the red light—

I won't let go.

I shook my head frantically. "There has to be another way, something else – I can call the sword's second name without… I'm strong enough. I can find a way to control it—" I made as if to lift the sword, scrabbling to my knees. Shinobu's hand found mine on the hilt and held it down.

"It will overcome you. If you try to do this alone, it will take your mind, and its power will go into more destruction, more death. Not healing. You know this."

"You can't ask me to sacrifice you!"

"You would sacrifice yourself," he said. He leaned forward, clutching my hand on the katana's grip. His hand was too tight, painful. "But it would all be for nothing. It would be wasted. Mio, I know you. I know that if you could take my place, you would give your life in a heartbeat to save Jack, your father, everyone. But that is not your task. You must survive. You are the sword-bearer. You are the key to this battle – the one who will end this war. Let me play my part. Let *me* save *you* this time."

The green blade flashes down in the red light—

In my mind I saw the man from my dream. The man who had come to bring the girl the katana as she waited in vain for Shinobu to return. He bent over Shinobu as Shinobu lay in the red leaves, dying. The man's long face was gloating and pleased. His eyes shone pure white in his face.

Izanagi.

In his hand he held a sword, the blade curved like a leaf, carved from some mottled green stone. He raised the sword above Shinobu, then plunged it down into Shinobu's chest.

What are you prepared to sacrifice…?

Of course I knew what to do. I'd known almost before the old man opened his mouth; I had seen it in my dreams and visions so often. Shinobu's spirit had been bound into the blade when Izanagi murdered him. To return his spirit to its prison, I would have to murder him again in the same way.

But how could I? How could I kill the one I loved the most, even if the world was at stake?

"Shinobu—"

"My love." His voice was calm again. Something had changed; he had seen the knowledge in my face, and surety replaced anguish in his eyes. "I never had a choice before. But I can choose my fate this time, and that is all I ask. I want to leave you knowing that I have done all I could to keep you and your loved ones safe. I want my passing to be worth something more than a lonely death on a bleak battlefield. If you love me, do not take that choice from me."

How could anyone refuse the one they loved the most when the world was at stake?

My dad was horribly still now. I looked down at the tiny fine lines around his mouth and eyes, lines of strain and struggle. The icy wind of Yomi wailed around us, ruffling his short black hair, and for the first time I noticed a few silver threads at his temple. *There is no universal definition of love...*

Shinobu whispered, "You have to let me go."

I reached across my father's body and grabbed the back of Shinobu's neck, burying my fingers in his soft hair. I kissed him.

It was a moment that lasted a thousand moments, a breath that stretched on for a thousand breaths, a heart-beat that stood still in time. I clutched at it, at him, drawing every tiny detail into my heart forever. The slide of his hair against my palm. The taste of his breath. The moth's-wing flutter of his eyelash against my cheek. The warmth, the glorious living warmth, of his skin touching mine.

Hold on tight.

Don't let go.

Don't ever let go.

The katana's power blazed against my palm, fighting me, blistering me with its fury. No, no, no, no! I ignored it.

Our lips parted.

Our eyes locked.

My vision turned black at the edges, the intensity of my focus setting light to his face until he seemed to shine as painfully bright as the sun. Shinobu's hand tightened even more over mine on the hilt of the katana. Both of us were shuddering with fear and misery.

Together we drew the sword back.

Together we plunged the blade into his heart.

The green blade flashes down in the red light—

The guard thudded home against his breastbone. I heard his agonized gasp of pain and cried out in horror. Despair squeezed my eyes tight shut. I forced them open a second later, but it was too late. The boy I loved was already disappearing, fading away like dark ink swirling in a flood of clean water.

And then, in Shinobu's place, there was light. It

coalesced around the blade, pulsing softly – pulsing in time with my own heartbeat – a blazing starburst of shimmering prismatic colours that the unnatural twilight couldn't dim. I realized that I was looking at Shinobu's soul. Who he was, what he was, inside.

It was the most beautiful thing I had ever seen.

As I watched, the light slowly sank into the blade, passing into the flame-shaped ripples that marked the metal and melding with them until all the light was gone.

The hilt of the sword was cool in my hand again. Its furious buzzing had stopped. It lay quiescent, inert. The wind whistled around me mournfully.

I knew then the shape of the darkness hidden inside me. It was the same darkness that had lurked in Ojiichan, and maybe even my father. They had each loved me so much, they had tried to mould me, make me over. Make me better.

Ojiichan wanted the perfect guardian for the sword. A warrior who followed orders unquestioningly. Who loved the blade as much as he did. He had trained me to fulfil this destiny from the moment I could walk and talk.

My father? He wanted a blank slate. A chance to undo the wrongs that had been done to him by his father. He needed me to be some ideal average British teenager, only caring about homework and curfews, with no thought for my heritage or the past.

They had held their love and approval in front of me

like a carrot, trying to get me to grow into the shape they desired. They had made me powerless in their struggle with each other, and kept the knowledge that I needed to make my own choices from me. Between them, they had harmed me more than either of them could ever know.

And yet, even knowing how it felt, I had still tried to do the same to Shinobu, the one I loved.

Of course I had. I knew if I let him make his own choice, he would leave me.

Now it had happened, just as I had always feared. Just like I'd always known, down deep, that it would. I hadn't held on tight enough, and he had slipped through my fingers.

I had let him go.

Hikaru fell between the cars on his hands and knees, gasping. "I'm empty. Sorry. That's it." He stopped short and stared. "Where's—?"

A pair of Shikome shot directly down over the roof of the cafe towards where we sat.

"Protect my dad," I told Hikaru, ignoring his exclamation of shock as I got to my feet.

I lifted the sword above my head to point at the monsters. And then I said the name Mr Leech had whispered in my ear just before the window slammed down between us.

"Kusanagi-no-Tsurugi."

The sword burst into flames. Pearly and glittering with barely seen colours, warm as summer rain, they cascaded down over me, cloaking my whole body in a mantle of light. I felt strong, gentle arms wrap around me.

"*Shinobu.*"

The streetlights around me flared like Roman candles, sparks fountaining everywhere. A lance of white light broke from the point of the katana's blade and rose up, passing through the attacking Foul Women and turning them to ash in an instant. The light shot further upwards, piercing the black clouds above the rooftops and reaching past them too, past the blue bowl of our atmosphere, into the heavens themselves.

"*Watch...*" Shinobu's voice breathed in my ear.

The glorious white flames rippled out around me in concentric circles like waves in a still pond, travelling fast, fast, faster than anything but light itself could move, carrying my mind's eye with them as they went through the bricks and the concrete and the glass.

Through the whole city.

Through all the people in London who were smeared by a dark sickness – the taint – which dimmed the vital glow of their souls. The flames washed over them, and that darkness dissolved in the brilliance of the light, nothing more than nightmares disappearing with the dawn.

At my feet, my father's eyes snapped open, the rash

rapidly fading from his skin.

In a hospital room near by Jack sucked in a deep breath and shot upright in her bed.

In the darkness of a drain far below, Rachel's poor contorted body gently untwisted, her pain and anguish lifted from her along with the black stain, tarry and vile, that had been the legacy of the Nekomata's bite.

The light found everything. Malignant cells that had turned people's own bodies against them, awful injuries that had lost too much blood, dangerous swellings that pressed against the wall of the skull, irreparable wounds to the tissue of the spine, broken bones, infections, cuts and bruises. Lifted away, dissolved, healed. All over London, people who had been thought past hope suddenly opened their eyes.

The black clouds of the Underworld swirled around the katana's column of light, spinning faster and faster, shredding and dissipating under the force of the power that drew them down. The Shikome – dead and alive – came with the clouds. They were sucked, shrieking and flapping, into the vortex, and then disintegrated. They blew away on the wind as harmless powder.

A colossal black mushroom-shaped cloud gathered over my head, over the rooftops of London. At the heart of the cloud was the dead black eye of Yomi with its savage white moon. Far away there was a crazed screaming, a wail of denial. Izanami was fighting the katana, fighting to keep the rupture she had made in the veil between the realms open.

Then, as the white column of light broke from the sword's tip and fell, Izanami's gateway to hell snapped shut.

The white column scattered into millions of star fragments and tumbled down over me and my father and Hikaru, protecting us from the blizzard of glass that blasted through the air. The windows – every window for miles – had shattered under the immense pressure of the katana's power. The waves of white fire were returning to the sword now, flowing back and folding into the blade. Last of all they drew all my hurts and injuries away, healing me where I stood.

For a moment I was whole, and Shinobu was holding me, and everything in the world was right.

I felt a ghostly kiss brush over my lips and invisible fingers tuck the tangled hair back behind my ear.

Then the light winked out, and I was alone again. All that was left was a drifting blanket of pale grey clouds and piles and piles of glittering glass fragments everywhere.

"Shinobu?" I whispered. "Shinobu?"

There was no reply.

Slowly, moving like an automaton, I lowered the blade again. It lay quiescent in my grasp, its energy nothing more than a faint hum against my skin. Finally silenced. I eased it back into the saya on my back, and sank down onto the pavement, among the broken glass.

I was vaguely aware of my father and Hikaru stirring, getting up. They came to kneel beside me.

"Midget Gem," my father whispered. "Mio. Are you OK? Are you hurt?"

"What happened?" Hikaru asked. "Where's Shinobu?"

I didn't respond. There were no words in the icy black hollow inside me. My dad put his arms around me, urging me to lean against his shoulder, but my body was stiff and unco-operative. There was nothing left. It was all gone. Shinobu had taken it all with him, and I didn't think anything could ever fill me up again.

Time passed. Overhead, the late afternoon sun, golden red as it began to set, broke through what was left of the Yomi clouds. Emergency vehicles arrived at the site of the freak, "localized storm". People came and went. Eventually my father and an EMT urged me to my feet and made me sit inside an ambulance. The EMT fussed over me, trying to get me to talk and searching for injuries. There were none. None that anyone could see anyway. The wound inside me was one that no one would ever reach.

More time passed. The EMT left me alone after a while, and drew my father off to one side of the vehicle while they had a heated, anxious conversation. I picked up words like "traumatized" and "non-responsive", followed by "admit for observation" and "psychiatric evaluation".

For the first time I felt a flicker of something – rejection, refusal – in the emptiness. My muscles twitched and tensed, tingling with pins and needles as I quietly got off the trolley and stepped down, slipping around the side of the ambulance and blending into the crowds of survivors and bystanders that had gathered around the edges of the spectacular car pile-up.

Instinct drew me forward, past the flashing lights of police cars parked on the pavement, past the orange painted cafe, past the place where my father had fallen, past the place where I had plunged the blade in...

I found myself standing at the line of bollards that separated the no-parking zone from the car park, a little way from the hospital entrance. Others milled around me. I ignored them.

I waited.

A few minutes later the automatic doors opened and people – dozens upon dozens of people – began to spill out.

They walked or ran or skipped, and the ones waiting outside surged forward and greeted them there in the car park of the hospital in a euphoric explosion of happiness and hope and joy. Behind the escaping patients, through the hospital doors, I saw lines of medical staff, white-coated doctors and nurses and health-workers in blue uniforms. They looked exhausted, dishevelled and disbelieving. But more than any of that, they looked happy.

It's not every day that all your patients get up and walk out of hospital on their own two feet.

The car park frothed around me like a stormy, laughing human sea.

Like a spire of rock in the sea, I waited.

At long last, she came.

Hikaru walked beside her. She was dressed in the wrinkled clothes she'd been wearing the day before – was it only the day before? – when she arrived here in an ambulance. Her hair, obviously in need of a good wash, stood up around her head in untidy tufts that made her dark roots even more obvious.

There was no sign of a rash on her face.

She was OK.

She was alive.

The moment she caught sight of me, her face lit up with a massive grin. She broke into a sprint, streaking away from Hikaru and through the crowds straight towards me.

She smacked into me so hard that we both nearly fell to the ground. Then I was enveloped in a crushing bear hug. I felt her breathing hitch as she grabbed handfuls of the back of my top.

"You did it. You did it again. You saved us all."

Not all.

I was taller than her now. But nothing in the whole world could have stopped me from burying my face in her shoulder right then and crying.

We stood there like that for a long time. The other patients and their friends and relatives ebbed and drifted away. The medical staff trailed out of the hospital lobby. Jack never let go. Even though I was gasping and shaking and wailing, sobbing like a baby, soaking the arm of her pullover with tears, she never let me go.

After a while, Hikaru patted me sorrowfully on the back and disappeared. He came back a few minutes later with my dad.

"Mio! There you are. My God, where did you—!" His voice cut off as he did a double-take at the sight of me weeping on Jack's arm, and sighed, his shoulders slumping. "Never mind."

I blinked my tear-swollen eyes at him. The rash that had marked his cheek was gone, just like Jack's. And the nasty gash over his eyebrow had healed up without even a scar. Hikaru – brave, reckless Hikaru – who had nearly turned himself into a pile of ash trying to help us, was staring at me with a mixture of concern and eagerness. And I knew that somewhere in a horrible, dank sewer tunnel not too far away from where we stood, Rachel was lying, cold and uncomfortable and dazed with shock – but human again – waiting for us to find her.

The cold emptiness inside me was still there. It might always be there. I had lost something so precious, so irreplaceable to me, that I knew I could never be quite the same. A part of me had gone with Shinobu into the dark, and I would never get it back.

But I hadn't lost everything. I still had all of this.

I had all of them.

Something new stirred in the hollowness, gradually taking shape, taking form, hardening until it was as tough and heavy as steel. Determination. Implacable, unbreakable and cold.

I wouldn't lose anyone ever again. I wouldn't need someone to sacrifice themselves for me ever again.

I would never let go again.

"Mimi, what happened to you? What happened to Shinobu?" Jack's voice was hushed. She reached up to push the tangled hair out of my eyes. I flinched from the touch and gently disentangled myself from her hug, putting some distance between us.

I'd had my moment of weakness. Now the time for weakness was done.

"Please tell us what's going on," my father said, a note of pleading in his usually dry tones. "Just talk to us. Tell me that you're all right. Tell me you're OK."

Hikaru nodded. "Come on, kiddo. Give us something."

"I'm fine," I said flatly. "I'll tell you everything, but not now. We need to go and find Rachel."

"Rachel?" Jack breathed. "Oh my God, is she—"

"She's been through a lot. She needs us to take her home. I know where she is – it's not far away. Come on."

I moved past Jack, starting towards the back of the hospital, but before I could go anywhere, my father nipped nimbly in front of me, blocking my path. He placed a gentle hand on my shoulder. His gaze searched my face. "Mio, after we've found Rachel and after we're home safe … what are you going to do? Are you going to be all right? Do you have a … a plan?"

"Plan?" I looked at him steadily for a moment. Then I reached back and drew the katana from its saya in a single, smooth motion. A soft, pearly gleam of flame rippled along the cutting edge; the sword's energy seemed to quiver under my touch, almost as if it was afraid. "My plan is to make the gods wish they'd never been born."

I turned from him and walked into the gathering darkness.

ACKNOWLEDGEMENTS

So much has changed in my life between beginning work on this book and writing these acknowledgements that I'm not really sure whether I should be thanking those who've helped me to write or those who've helped me to survive. But either way, there are many who deserve to be thanked.

Firstly, my family – my mother, Elaine; my sister, Victoria; her husband, Robert; and their three delightful daughters, Esme, Alexandra and Clemence. I love each of you very much.

Next, with respect and gratitude, to my editor, Annalie Grainger. And to Gill Evans, Maria Soler Canton, Hannah Love, Jo Humpheys-Davies, Victoria Philpott, Paul Black, Sean Moss and all those I've worked with over the past year at Walker Books. Thanks are also due to the marvellous team at Candlewick Press, including

Hilary Van Dusen and her assistant, Miriam; and to Ann Angel, editor of the *Things I'll Never Say* anthology.

My incomparable agent, Nancy Miles, for her endless compassion and support with all aspects of my life and career.

The funny, sweet, kind people of Twitter and Facebook, most especially the YA Thinkers, for always being ready with a virtual hug.

My life-saving, life-changing friends the Furtive Scribblers, who are too numerous to name but too precious ever to be forgotten. I would be a sight less sane than I am right now without all of you.

The Society of Authors, for the timely grant which made vital, practical research for this and the final book of the trilogy possible.

Finally, and most importantly, to my father. You slew dragons every day and made me believe I could do the same. You are at the heart of every story I've ever written, and every story I ever will. You were proud to be my father. I will always be proud to be your daughter.

See you, Dad.

Love The Name of the Blade series?
Love Zoë Marriott's other books!

 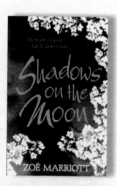

 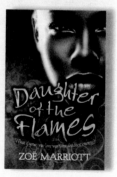